A Heartbeat Away

$\mathcal{A}$ Heartbeat $\mathcal{A}way$

Rachel Ann Nunes

BONNEVILLE BOOKS™

Springville, Utah

ISBN: 1-55517-688-7
e.1

Published by Bonneville Books
Imprint of Cedar Fort Inc.
www.cedarfort.com

Distributed by:

Typeset by Kristin Nelson
Cover design by Nicole Cunningham
Cover design © 2003 by Lyle Mortimer

Printed in the United States of America
10 9 8 7 6 5 4 3 2 1

Printed on acid-free paper

Library of Congress Cataloging-in-Publication Data

Nunes, Rachel Ann, 1966-
A heartbeat away / Rachel Ann Nunes.
   p. cm.
ISBN 1-55517-688-7 (acid-free paper)
1. Teenage girls--Crimes against--Fiction. 2. Murder victims'
families--Fiction. 3. Kidnapping victims--Fiction. 4. Future
life--Fiction. I. Title.

PS3564.U468H43 2003
813'.54--dc21
                          2003002633

Dedication

*To all those who have lost a loved
one under tragic circumstances.
May hope fill your hearts.
May you know that your Father in Heaven
loves you and is keeping your loved one
safe in His arms—only a heartbeat away.*

Author's Note

Recent events here in Utah and in the United States have left us all in shock and in mourning. I'm sure that like me you have spent many hours thinking about the children we've lost to very evil people, and the suffering of not only the children but of their families. How many prayers have you offered in their behalf? How many of you parents have spent sleepless nights checking on your children to assure yourselves of their safety? How many of you grew more distrustful of strangers, or even your own neighbors? The heartache seems without end—especially for those kidnapping victims whose families do not understand the great Plan of Happiness and thus have no hope of being with their child for eternity.

For months thoughts of kidnapping victims have burdened my heart. Along with many of you, I longed for relief and for justice. I felt many things I did not know how to understand. I wished there was some way I could help. I wanted to change things with my words—yet how?

When Lyle Mortimer first invited me to his office to talk about writing this book, I have to admit I was skeptical. I believed a book about kidnapping might not be successful in this market. Yet the more I considered his suggestion and bounced plot ideas around in my head, the more I knew that this story could be done well and what's more, that it *should* be done. I felt confident that with inspiration and deep thought, I could create something my readers would appreciate—perhaps even something they *needed* to read.

So I began.

The first several chapters had me in tears. As a writer, I must enter the heads of my characters to experience their inner feelings; in a way I become the characters for a short time—and often that is not an easy task. My heart and soul cried out for relief. And then a miracle occurred. While writing this story my aching heart was healed! I felt an urgency to share that healing, to reach out to my readers and to my community.

I offer this story to you with the spirit of hope. Keep in mind that this book is completely fictional, from the prologue to the epilogue, which are important excerpts from the diary of one of my characters. In researching this novel, I have studied various kidnapping cases, but a resemblance to any specific case is unintentional.

For plot purposes I have shown several scenes in the immediate Hereafter. Though many people have had experiences beyond the veil, and prophets such as Joseph Smith and Brigham Young have written about it, I didn't feel it necessary to my story to cover the Hereafter in detail. Rather, I was content to give readers a feeling of the happiness that awaits: "The spirits of those who are righteous are received into a state of happiness, which is called paradise, a state of rest, a state of peace, where they shall rest from all their troubles and from all care, and sorrow" (Alma 40:12). I also wanted to reaffirm that the "same spirit which doth possess your bodies at the time that ye go out of this life, that same spirit will have power to possess your body in that eternal world" (Alma 34:34).

For what details I did need to include for plot purposes, I accept full responsibility, while at the same time urging you to remember that this is a novel and *not* a true story. I think you will enjoy the portrayal and more particularly the hope it brings. I've written this novel with the same attention to relationships and love that marks my other novels because I believe that it is love that makes everything possible.

As always, thank you for your support. I couldn't do it without you!

Rachel Ann Nunes

Prologue

From the Diary of Meghan Marshall Burke

Sometimes you don't know when you will be called upon to endure something you thought would be impossible to endure, and then there is a surprise: you can endure. Not only endure, but excel and be happy. The Lord truly is our strength and our salvation. I believe that now as I never did before. I didn't know enough sorrow in the beginning to experience true and lasting joy. All that has changed now.

I must share my story. Writing it has helped me heal, and I believe it will help you as well. The story begins with Kristin, my sister. But I'll let you read it—or at least some of it—through her eyes . . .

Chapter One

You think it's never going to happen to you. I know because that's how I was—untouchable. Bad things only happen to someone else, usually to someone you don't know very well. Take a really sick child in your neighborhood. Their family has to deal with problems every day, but you just catch a glimpse of the wheelchair at church, or see the parents' reddened eyes as you meet them in the grocery store. The only thing you're required to do is to ask how they're doing, not really looking at them, but staring in the direction of their right ear so you won't make them feel worse.

If anything remotely bad ever did happen to you or your family, it was always something the doctor could fix with fiberglass or a pill. My little sister broke her arm twice and both times chose a fluorescent pink fiberglass cast. Besides my mom's occasional bout of sinusitis, that's about the worst thing that ever happened to my family.

At least until the year I turned thirteen.

I had my whole life before me then. I dreamed of going to college and becoming a heart surgeon. Of marrying and having a half-dozen children. I wanted a nice house with a swimming pool and someone to do the cooking. (Hey, I could afford that if I became a heart surgeon.)

All those dreams ended in a blinding flash. Well, the dreams didn't exactly end, rather they changed. But I'm getting ahead of myself.

My name is Kristin Marshall, and it was the September after the summer that a bunch of kidnappings were in the news. I'm sure you remember the one. I used to jerk awake in the middle of the night and see my mom tip-toeing into my room to make sure I was okay. I never told her that sometimes she nearly scared me to death because I thought someone *had* come to take me away. I knew seeing me there in bed gave her peace of mind, so I kept quiet.

Dad said there really weren't more kidnappings, only a lot more awareness from the media because of the way two girls in two different towns had been stolen right from their bedrooms. Mom said we needed an alarm just in case someone tried to get into our house.

"Oh, Mom, nothing's gonna happen," I once told her. "We're too old. Even Jacky's too old. She'd kick a kidnapper right between the legs. Don't worry so much."

My mother heaved a great sigh, the irritating kind of sigh that said I knew as much as a newborn baby did, or even less. "Oh, Kristin. You think it's so easy, but it's not. Jacky's only eight, and a kidnapper would be much stronger. Take that little girl in the paper last month. She kicked and screamed and it did her no good. He still got her into the car."

I didn't listen. It wasn't my job to worry—they could do that. I knew nothing would happen to us. Parents can be worrywarts, if you know what I mean, and my mom was the queen of worrywarts.

On a Friday after school in mid-September my older sister, Meghan, and I asked our mom to take us to the Rec to swim. Rec means the Orem Recreational Center, but we just call it the Rec, like it was a train accident or something: the Wreck. Mom said she had to take our van to the shop to see why the engine light was on, and if we didn't mind going with her there first, Dad would pick us all up and drop us off at the pool. We were lucky because eight-year-old Jacky and Benjamin, who's ten, had gone home with our cousins after school. Mom never let the little kids go without her to the pool, even if we were with them. That's kind of funny because we all swim real well, with all the lessons we've had—even Jacky. She swims like a dolphin. But like I said, Mom's a worrywart. She says someone has to be.

Meghan was excited because some of our neighborhood friends would be at the pool. Especially a boy named Wade Burke, who was a senior in high school. When he moved in last year he wasn't much to look at, but this year he suddenly shot up and filled out. He was tall, dark, and handsome, according to Meghan.

I guess she was right, but I didn't like the jock type. All they cared about was sports and nothing about science or books. I loved books. It didn't matter what they were about. Though science texts and adventure romances were my favorite, I read all kinds of literature. Meghan loved only the romances. In fact, she read them so fast that she was always books ahead of me on any series we were reading together.

"Do I look all right in this new swimming suit?" Meghan asked from our bathroom. She had bought it on sale at Wal-Mart at the first of the summer, but it had been a little too big then. "It doesn't make me look fat, does it?"

Meghan would have to gain twenty pounds to be anywhere near fat. She's even skinnier than I am. Despite her being two years older than me, we're basically the same size except she's an inch taller. "You look fine," I told her, trying not to roll my eyes.

"You'll be nice to Wade, won't you?" she asked me as she spread blemish cream over an almost invisible pimple.

"I don't mind Wade. It's that weird friend he hangs out with. What's his name? Jaybird?"

"Just Jay. And he's nice." Meghan patted her blonde hair that reached almost down to her waist.

"What a dumb name."

"Maybe, but I think he likes you."

"Oh, where can I throw up!" But her words gave me a warm feeling inside. Much as I would never admit it to Meghan, Jay was my make-believe hero in the adventure romance novel I was reading. He was a junior, though, and way old too for me, only an eighth-grader. Then again, there were only three years separating us, and I liked to remind myself that my dad was four years older than my mom.

"Oh, I wish I had more up here," Meghan tugged at the top of her suit. "You're almost as big as me and I'm older."

"Hardly." I rolled my eyes before escaping from the bathroom. If I didn't leave she'd be on about how she wished her eyes were as dark blue as mine and that her hair was lighter. My little sister Jacky and I have hair the color of sunshine, as my dad always said, and blue eyes as deep as the night sky. We liked to joke that we were twins born five years apart. To Meghan's disgust, her hair was darker, like the color of gold. I thought it was beautiful—and a darn sight better than Benjamin's dirty-looking blonde. Meghan didn't agree. As soon as she got a job, I bet she'd get color contacts and dye her hair.

When we arrived at the shop, Mom opened the van door. "Good afternoon, Big Ned," she said to Mr. Lyman, our mechanic. She tucked her short, golden hair behind her ear and smiled like she was really happy to see him.

He reached out his large hand. "Hello, Angie. It's good to see you."

What a name—Big Ned. Sounded like the mafia guy in my adventure romance book. But he didn't look like one. He had a grizzled beard and was as tall and strong-looking as a bear. He reminded me of a mountain man, not a guy in a suit with body-guards. I asked Mom once why they called him Big Ned and she said he had a son named Ned. I wondered if they called his son Little Ned. I didn't think he'd like that much. I wouldn't.

Just then Dad came in and they began to talk about when the van might be ready. Meghan jumped out of the van and grabbed her swim bag, filled to the brim with her curling iron, hairspray, and who knew what other junk. I didn't budge. Mom and Dad knew Big Ned from the old neighborhood when I was a baby. After discussing the van, they would move on to other things.

My eyes returned to my book. The heroine was posing as a maid to try to free the hero, who in my mind resembled Jay. Even though it was just a book, my heart pounded in fear for them both. I read as fast as I could to see what would happen.

At last Mom called me out of the van. "You want to get to the pool, don't you?"

Shoving my book into my bag, I climbed from the van. As I approached my parents I heard Big Ned saying, "I'll have my nephew get right to it as soon as possible. Give you a call a bit later. Let you know. But it's likely it won't be done till late tomorrow." He reeked of cigarette smoke, and I wondered how Mom and Dad could stand being so close to him. They must really like him. They told me once that he was the most honest mechanic they'd ever met in all of Utah Valley.

"Meghan, come on," Dad called. My sister was in the back of

the garage, talking to some guy. I was surprised. At home she's all talk, but around strangers she's very shy. I don't understand it because what one person has to say is just as important as what any one else might say.

"I know that in my heart," Meghan told me once. "It's like I have a whole bunch of good ideas, but when I go to say them aloud, they don't come out quite right. They come out in my diary just fine. In fact, I think maybe I should be a romance writer."

"I'd read all your books," I had answered. "In between heart surgeries, that is. Just don't make them too sappy."

Now Meghan came running over to us, looking flushed and rather pleased with herself.

"What took you so long?" I asked Meghan as we got into Dad's car.

"Mr. Lyman's nephew." Her voice lowered and her blue eyes became dreamy. "He's really cute. He has kind of messed up brown hair and his face is very tan. He said he's from Florida. And he's got these big brown eyes that seem to look right into you. Anyway, I saw him here last time, but I've never talked to him. Today he approached me! He said he thought I looked seventeen, can you believe that?"

I couldn't. My sister was fifteen and looked maybe fourteen. "How old is he?"

She shrugged a shoulder, bare except for the strap of her swimsuit. "Don't know. It's not like I'm serious about him—you know I like Wade. But he's nice to talk to. I tried to get you to come over. We were waving at you."

"It's okay. I was reading that book you gave me."

In the front seat Mom was pointing the way to the pool, though Dad already knew where to go. "You'll have to pick up the girls, Gary," she said. "On your way home from work, I mean."

Dad nodded. "I need to make up this little bit I've taken off to drive you home, but I can be there by seven-thirty. Okay girls?"

"Seven-thirty?" groaned Meghan. "Dad, it's almost five now."

"Two and a half hours is plenty of time to be in the pool," he said in his do-not-argue-with-me-young-lady voice.

"Your dad's right. It gets dark by seven. And besides, we're going to a party tonight and we'll already be a bit late. We'll need you two to baby-sit." Mom dug in her purse and came up with a few dollars. "Here, you can each buy something from the vending machine. But remember not to keep your father waiting."

"We won't," we mumbled.

Outside the Rec Mom said as she always did, "Now remember, stay together and don't go anywhere with strangers."

"Yeah, yeah. Of course not." We scrambled out of the car. "Bye," I shouted. Without a backwards glance, we ran down the sidewalk to the entrance.

We left our towels and clothes in a locker and hurried to the indoor pool. The warm air was thick with chlorine, and the sound in the huge room was odd, giving everything an echo. The water shimmered under the lights, moving randomly until it slapped against the sides of the tiled pool. There was a shout from the far side where some kids were playing with a ball.

"There they are," Meghan said, turning to me. "You go first, okay? I don't want to seem too anxious."

I started over while Meghan followed uncertainly. I began to wish she weren't so shy. At home, she was normal, but she suddenly changed when she walked out our door. Sometimes it was hard seeing my big sister act like a little kid. Then again, I was probably so outgoing because she's the way she is; someone had to speak up, and since Meghan never did, I learned to.

"Hey," I greeted our friends as I sat on the edge of the pool. The water felt cool to my bare feet, not nearly as warm as I'd hoped.

Wade looked up at us and smiled very brightly. His sister Tamara did, too. She was a year older than me and a year younger than Meghan. We both really liked her.

Jay threw the ball at me. "So, you made it." He looked kind of funny with his blonde hair plastered down with water, but I didn't mention it like I would have normally; they never mention that kind of thing in my novels, and for the moment at least, he was my hero.

"Why not?" I shrugged. I threw the ball back, hard enough to hurt if he didn't catch it. He did.

Wade swam to the side of the pool and was talking to Meghan, his dark eyes never leaving her face. I wondered if he could see how awkward she felt. He was so close to her that the ends of her long hair brushed his face as she slid forward into the water.

Some other kids arrived and we played tag for a long time. I was the fastest and only Jay could catch me. Then we had a water fight. Jay and Wade dunked me after I splashed them good. It was a lot of fun.

After a while the boys climbed out of the pool. "We have to get going," Wade said. "We're going to a movie later. You guys want to come?"

Meghan looked at me, obviously embarrassed to remind them that we were too young to date. Even if going with them wasn't exactly a date, just a bunch of kids going to the movies, Mom and Dad would never see it that way. The prophet of our church, The Church of Jesus Christ of Latter-day Saints, says no dating until sixteen; and then in our family we were allowed only to group date until we turned eighteen. I knew Wade and Tamara's parents were a little more lenient, but they should know better than to ask us.

"Can't," I said. "Our parents are making us baby-sit." I'm never one to beat around the bush, as my dad would say, but I said this for Meghan. In a few months she would be sixteen and could go with them as much as she wanted.

"Yeah, our dad'll be here soon anyway," Meghan said. "But thanks."

We got out of the pool and dressed. While Meghan dried and curled her bangs, I rubbed my hair with my towel until it hung in loose waves to my shoulders—all one length.

"Got an elastic?" I asked Meghan. She did and I put my hair in a ponytail so it wouldn't make my neck cold.

When we got outside it was pretty dark, though not quite seven-thirty. I shivered since my suit was still wet under my T-shirt and jeans. I began to wish I'd changed out of it like Meghan. A brown-haired man with a hat pulled low over his head came from behind us, followed by an older couple. They got into separate cars and drove away. Then we were alone.

"Look, it's Wade!" Meghan pointed to a rather battered dark car that pulled up beside us. Jay was driving.

I leaned my arms on the window opening of the back door where Tamara was sitting, while Meghan stood by the front passenger side facing Wade.

I bent to whisper in Tamara's ear. "I think they're hitting it off."

Tamara nodded and gave me a wide smile. I could tell she approved.

"Want a ride home?" Wade asked Meghan.

She looked indecisive so I popped my head out of the car, nearly pulling out my ponytail on the hook above the window. "Our dad's on his way," I assured Wade as I rubbed my sore head.

He smiled. "Oh, that's right. You told us already."

"I have my cell here," Jay said from the driver's seat. "We could call to make sure."

I shook my head. "Thanks, but it won't do any good. Our parents are always on time."

"Okay, then. See you around."

We stepped back from the car and watched Jay take off. Meghan sighed heavily. I ignored her and started down the sidewalk to pace, hoping it would warm me up a little. The dark sky was cloudless and the stars seemed so close, though I could only begin to understand how far away they really were. I remembered my science teacher at school saying that if you were lucky enough to live to seventy-seven and a half years old, you could look up at the star Regulus in the heart of the constellation Leo and you would be seeing the light that star emitted on the day you were born. Pretty interesting stuff.

Sometimes when I stared up at the sky, I thought I might become an astronomer instead of a heart surgeon. I wondered what it would be like to visit a star.

I laughed aloud at myself. "You've been watching way too much *Star Trek*."

I walked almost to the end of the sidewalk. Glancing behind me, I saw Meghan sitting on the steps that led to the upper entrance of the Rec. She was staring in the direction Jay's car had gone, as though hoping he and Wade would return.

I decided to walk the remaining few steps and go back. The

large lawns of the Rec gave me a feeling of eerie calmness in the dark, but I liked the solitude of it. Sometimes with all the noise at home, it's hard to think.

My thoughts scattered at the sound of an engine. Twirling my dark blue CTR ring on my middle finger, I looked up to see a car coming toward me, headlights blazing like twin suns. I blinked, trying to see past the light. Probably it was Dad, and he'd already picked up Meghan on the stairs. I couldn't see where she had been because of the light in my eyes, but I was sure he would have spotted her first. Stepping to the curb, I reached for the door and opened it.

It wasn't my father's car.

As I registered that fact, a hand whipped out and pulled me inside. It all happened so fast I didn't have time to scream. Or to kick or yell. The driver peeled off in a squeal of tires.

As he turned the car around a corner, I collected myself enough to began to fight back. I clawed at the hand grabbing me, but it held like iron. His other hand left the wheel for a moment and slammed into my head. Stars burst into bright flame all around me and then I was falling backward into a dark hole.

Chapter Two

The next thing I knew I was lying on the floor in the car with my hands tied behind my back. Darkness filled the space around me and except for the sound of the engine and the passing cars, there was silence.

"Ah, so you're awake."

I jerked at the voice. I guess I should have pretended to be asleep. My eyes went to his face, but it was so dark, so I couldn't make out any features.

Then the headlights of a passing car illuminated his face with amber. I knew him.

Despite my situation, I felt a little relief. This was all some kind of bad joke. A mistake. Then again, he'd hit me. No one I knew would play a joke like that.

Another car's light illuminated his face. His hair looked strange, as if messed up during our struggle.

"Let me go," I said. Or at least I tried to say. Though he hadn't gagged me, my mouth felt stuffed with cotton, and my throat was so dry, all I could do was let out a little croak.

"Don't worry," said my kidnapper. "Everything's going to be all right. I work for the FBI, you know. And I had to take you into custody because of an investigation."

I didn't believe him. Yet the complete sincerity of his words made me more frightened than ever.

"Come on. Sit up here. It's a long way to the rendezvous site."

I didn't move.

"Get up here now!"

His voice was harsh. Terror rippled through my body. I struggled onto the seat and sat uncomfortably with my hands pressing into the stiff black leather behind me.

We drove on the freeway for what seemed like a long time. The only thing I could think about was how I wasn't wearing a safety belt and how upset my mother would be if she knew.

The night grew deeper. What little I could see of the land stretched out flat or peaked gently in small hills. I began to think of Meghan back at the pool. Had she seen something? Was my dad looking for me?

I had to get out of here! I had to do something. But I was so frightened.

"I have to go to the bathroom," I finally managed to say through a sob. Then I added, "Please."

He hit the steering wheel with the heel of his hand. "This will make us late," he growled.

But after a few more minutes, he pulled off the freeway and drove to a gas station. I felt a sliver of hope prick the numbness in my heart. Surely I could call someone's attention to me when I went inside to use the restroom.

Something about the gas station didn't meet his approval. With a grunt, he turned the car out of the parking lot. "You can go along the side of the road," he muttered.

"No," I said, my voice rising to a squeak. "I have my swimming suit on. I'd have to take it off. People will see." I hoped he'd buy that.

"Would that be so bad?" He reached out and slid his fingers up and down my arm. I shivered and pulled away. He laughed. The hard pit that had appeared in my stomach grew heavier.

We drove to another gas station. This one pleased him, and I could see why. The bathroom was located on the far side, out of view of the attendant. He tied me to the seat and made me wait on the floor under a blanket he fished from the back seat, while he went inside the station and got the bathroom key. Then he released my hands from the rope and took me to the bathroom, practically dragging me since my legs were so weak from fear.

I staggered inside and he followed, folding his arms over his chest. "Go ahead," he said.

I shook my head. I didn't want to go with him watching.

The muscles in his jaw clenched and for a moment I thought he was going to rip off my clothes and make me go, but he stepped back. My plan to lock the door was ruined when he kept his foot inside. "FBI training," he said, seeing my disappointment. He smiled but it seemed more like a sneer. "No funny business, Kristin. I'll be right here." My name sounded funny coming from his lips.

I stared at the toilet, gleaming softly in the dim light. Thoughts of Meghan and of my family overwhelmed me and the tears began to fall. I just wanted to go home. I wanted to feel my mother's arms around me.

The bathroom wasn't very clean. The acid stench of urine assailed my nose, and there were paper towels and toilet paper all over the floor. Suddenly I bent and gathered up the papers, sticking them in the toilet to wet them, not daring to use the sink by the door. *Hurry*, I told myself. I arranged the word *HELP* on the floor by the toilet. For good measure, I tore out some of my hair and put it under the word.

Afterward, I quickly used the bathroom. Then I washed my hands. My heart pounded as he pushed the partially opened door a little wider and motioned me to him.

For a moment I thought I had gotten away with it. But he grabbed my arm so hard it hurt and pulled me back inside. First he checked the mirror; then he saw the word by the toilet. Growling, he kicked at the wet paper. His hand squeezed tighter on my arm until I nearly fainted from the pain. He dragged me to the car, looking around to make sure no one was watching.

I wished instead of holding me he had a gun in my back. I would have run. My mom had told me a dozen times it was better to die running or struggling than to suffer whatever a kidnapper would do to you. Running away might give you a chance. Even if you were shot, the sound would bring someone. My kidnapper didn't have a gun that I'd seen, only a fist seemingly made of iron.

He retied my hands, this time in front of me, and knotted the other end around his own leg. We drove for some time before he turned off the freeway again. Now there were no other cars at all.

"This isn't my first job for the FBI." He glanced over at me. I didn't like how intense his eyes were, how they seemed to pierce right through me.

I guess I was supposed to say something, but I couldn't speak past the fear.

"I've had other jobs. I have pictures. Funny. They all look like you. But you're the prettiest. You really are. I should know."

A tear dropped from my right eye, making a cold line down my cheek. I was shaking.

"Cold? I'll turn on the heater. Don't worry, we're almost there."

He stopped the car after another few minutes. I was still shaking badly. He was breathing funny now, and talking in short bursts as he rattled stuff around in the back seat. "We've already got the blanket. And we'll need this." He set a small duffle bag on the dashboard. "Here, put this on." He threw a long white nightgown at me. "Oh, I forgot your hands are tied. I'll undo them."

He watched me while I undressed. I was crying now, with shame and with helplessness. I'd never been naked in front of a man before. Even my doctor was a woman. Wasn't there anything I could do? No, nothing but obey.

When I had the white gown on, he tore the elastic from my still-damp hair and fluffed it up. Then he took a camera from the duffle bag on the dashboard and snapped a photo of me. As he replaced the camera, I lunged for the door and managed to get it open. Then I ran as fast as I could. There were no trees—nothing but flat land and a few scrubby little bushes. I spied a little hill and ran toward it, but he caught up quickly, jumping on me and knocking me to the ground.

"Don't run from me," he said, slapping my face hard. "Now you won't get to use the blanket."

He pushed me back into the rough, sandy dirt. I fought him with all my might, careless of the pain, but that only seemed to urge him on. I was so scared and mad and sad all at once. And also glad that Meghan wasn't here. This would have destroyed her. But I was strong. I would fight. In determination, I scratched at his neck. He answered with a fist to my jaw that made bright pinpoints of light echo in my skull.

When I couldn't fight anymore, he began to do things to me. I was ashamed and glad for the darkness, even though I knew none of it was my fault. There was a lot of pain, but that was just the beginning.

Months before when I heard on the news about a child dying from a beating given by his own parents, I had said to my mom,

"Don't you think God took away his pain so he didn't feel them hurting him?"

I'll always remember the look on my mother's face as she sat very still, pondering my question. Her blue eyes seemed bluer and turned inward, as though searching deeply. "I think," she began after a very long while, "that we don't really understand a lot of things. This life is so short. The pain that baby felt, while very terrible—unacceptable—was also very short. And it is that pain and suffering that will stand as a testimony against those people on Judgment Day." She sighed. "I really don't know the answer, honey, but I do know that whatever that baby felt, or what any innocent person feels when they suffer, will eventually be swallowed by the love of Christ in the life to come."

Well, I can tell you that I felt what my kidnapper did to me. Every sickening little bit. I thought at any minute I would die from the pain that seemed to go on and on in wave after wave of agony.

Then all at once the pain ceased as though it had never been. Just quit. I figured I must have lost consciousness, though I could vaguely feel him on me, and knew that he was still hurting me. There was a lot of blood. I wasn't dead, at least I didn't think so, but the pain had simply stopped. After so much torture, the nothingness was the most wonderful feeling I had ever known. *Thank you, God,* I prayed.

I closed my eyes, feeling weightless from my head to my toes, as though I were encased in warm clouds. All the horror in these past hours slid away, belonging now only to the past. The lightness in my body increased until it seemed I was floating.

"Kristin."

I opened my eyes and saw a woman about my mother's age. She had golden hair swept into a loose bun. Her perfect skin glowed and her lithe body fairly burst with energy. She seemed familiar somehow, and I didn't feel a bit afraid.

"Are you my guardian angel?" I asked. Though I was a Mormon and all my life I'd heard about angels visiting Earth, I was not really convinced such a thing existed.

Her smile was gentle as she regarded me with her lovely hazel eyes. "You could call me that."

I heaved a sigh of relief. "Good. That means I'm not dead yet, if you're still guarding me, that is."

"You don't want to be dead?"

I thought that was an odd question. I mean, of course I didn't want to die. I wanted to get away from my kidnapper. I wanted to be in my mother's arms. I wanted to forget all of the things he had done to me. "I'm not afraid of dying," I said. "At least I don't think I am. But my whole life's ahead of me. There's a lot I want to do. I'm going to be a heart surgeon, you know. And my mom—she'd miss me. And Meghan's birthday's coming up. She'll be sixteen and get to date. I can't miss that. I think Wade might ask her out."

She nodded, and I felt she was telling me that I would do all I had planned someday. I started feeling more relaxed. Looking around, I saw that I was still in the desert where my kidnapper had taken me. His dark car reflected the light of the moon. I realized I was looking at it from up in the air.

I looked again and saw my kidnapper kneeling near a bush. Something bright glistened in his hands. I couldn't see beyond him. Had I somehow gotten away?

"Come," the lady said to me, holding out a hand. When I hesitated, she put her arms around me and I felt a happiness effuse me that was more than double the pain I'd so recently experienced. The love emanating from her spread around me until it found every last little bit of hurt and fear and uncertainty and banished it to some place far away.

I went with her willingly. A part of my mind knew my earthly body was down there somewhere on the ground, but I wasn't so anxious to feel that pain again. None of it really seemed to have a connection with me anymore. My grandfather had once told me about a near-death experience he'd had during gall bladder surgery, and how he'd seen Grandma, who had died the month before. The visit had helped him want to live again.

Yes, an out-of-body experience must be what I was having. And I can tell you—I sure was hoping I would get to see Heaven.

Chapter Three

A bright light gathered around us. We were walking, but I didn't feel anything under my feet. The light shone, pointing like fingers from somewhere in front of us, as though we were walking in a tunnel toward a source of great light. With each step the way became even brighter, though my eyes felt no sensitivity. The ever-increasing light carried on its golden wings the unmistakable touch of love.

Faint singing began, growing louder as we walked. Like the Mormon Tabernacle Choir that my dad loved so much, only better. The words had the power of physical touch and could wrap about me like a warm quilt, while at the same time being smaller than an atom so they could seep into my body and warm up my insides too. I laughed, and my laughter added to the music, making it more wonderful—glorious even.

Without warning we came into a large, bright garden area. I couldn't see where the choir was, but its music still filled every single part of me. I stepped forward onto the greenest grass I had ever seen.

"It's so beautiful," I breathed. I knew a lot about Heaven from church, of course, but it's quite another thing to actually see it for yourself. The colors were so much more vivid than I remembered on Earth, and there were more of them. When I looked at each plant or flower, I could see into its very heart—how it was made and what sort of thing it was. I saw one big yellow daisy with welcoming petals and knew at once how it had brightened the life of a woman on Earth. Now it was here, forever in bloom, and praising God.

Everything was like that. I felt as though a dark veil had been taken from my eyes and mind and heart; for the first time in my life I could see and feel. Experience. Overhead the sky was bright blue, like on a perfect summer day, and a few marshmallow clouds inched their way across it. I saw no sun, though everything was alight and glowing.

My guardian saw me looking and said, "You'll see the source of the light soon enough. Come, let's walk."

I put my hand in hers and she squeezed it firmly, just as my mom had done so often before. Stumbling, I looked back, but all I could see was garden, stretching far behind us.

The woman gave me a little tug. "Your mother will be fine for now. She is strong—like you."

Feeling more than a little guilty, I matched her forward pace up the walk which was made from small stones pressed tightly together—cobblestones, like in many of the novels Meghan and I had devoured. I really didn't want to go back to Earth, but thoughts of my family and the way I had left worried me. I wondered how long I would get to stay here and how long it would be before someone found me in the desert.

We began to pass people dressed in white clothing like my guide. I looked down and saw I was wearing my jeans and shirt with my swimming suit still underneath. I'd rather have a white robe, and even as I thought about it, my clothes changed. I smiled.

Some of the people I thought I almost recognized, but I couldn't exactly remember where I'd seen them. The memories tugged on my mind, but I was still thinking of my family too much to concentrate on them.

To my left, I saw a huge outstretch of buildings. Though they were very far away, I could see them clearly, as though standing next to them. In one building with glass walls, I saw many people at desks, looking very busy.

"What are they doing?" I asked. At once we were closer to the buildings, though I didn't see how we crossed the distance so quickly.

"Those are people who are studying the gospel while they wait for someone on Earth to do their temple work. They'll stay in this area until that happens."

I stopped walking. "Wait a minute. Does that mean they're in Spirit Prison?" In church I had learned that Spirit Prison was a place in the Afterlife where people went when they didn't accept the gospel or had never heard of it.

"Well, sort of, in that they can't progress until they are baptized.

But all of the spirits you see here have accepted the gospel of the Lord and will eventually leave this place. Unfortunately, there are those who don't desire to follow the Father and the Son. Their conditions are much different. Bleak, in our view. Theirs is truly a prison of the soul. For some—those who followed Satan—their torment is unspeakable."

"I see." I was glad those who had accepted Jesus had a good place to wait for their baptisms to be done on Earth. Outside the building, I saw some men talking to a group of other spirits, and I knew they were preaching the gospel of Jesus Christ.

"They're missionaries," I said.

My guide nodded.

"But it's like I can almost hear them."

"It's the Spirit. When you learn with the Spirit, information can be transmitted so much more quickly than on Earth. It's a very pure form of communication—spirit to spirit. It happens here all the time if the parties desire it." She smiled at me. "Sometimes we do it without meaning to. Like you did a while ago when you were thinking about your mother."

So that was how she knew so much about me. "Too bad I didn't have that ability for history and geography," I said. "I still don't know the capitals of all the fifty states."

"Fifty?" she asked.

I looked at her quickly and she laughed. "Oh, you're joking," I said. "I didn't know angels could joke."

"We're exactly like we were before—only better. A little more pure. Nicer. You'll like it here."

We turned in the direction we had come and walked to a tall, magnificent gate that seemed to be made of pure gold. There were two sentinels dressed in brilliant white robes, holding flaming swords vertically before their faces as though ready for action. My angel exchanged some words with them and they appeared satisfied with her answers because they let us through. On the other side of the gate was another garden, more beautiful than any I had seen thus far. Nearby, a herd of horses galloped freely, and birds flew through the trees.

"Is this Heaven?" I asked. "Or maybe I mean Paradise."

"Yes, this is Paradise, where we'll stay until we're resurrected and stand judgment."

I hadn't really needed to ask. The music in the air was even sweeter, and the colors brighter. There were scents, too, that I seemed to experience with all my spirit, just as I did the music. A few tall buildings in the distance glistened like diamonds, and we slowly made our way toward them.

"Of course, we all have jobs to do while we wait," she said. "Is there something you would like to do?"

"Well, I guess you don't need heart surgeons here, even if I stayed."

A frown creased her face so fleetingly I wasn't sure it had been there at all. But then her smile was back as warm as ever. I could feel her sympathy for me and her great love, and I wondered why she cared so much. I guess she liked her job as a Heaven tour guide.

We had reached a place near a building where a few glistening diamond benches sat empty under beautiful emerald trees. "Kristin, someone's here to see you." My guide lifted her arm and pointed behind me toward a man who was so bright and perfect-looking, I can't even describe how He looked. Mere mortals do not have the words, so even if I could tell you, you wouldn't understand. I knew immediately that He was Jesus, my older Brother, the source of the Light. He held out His arms, and I ran to them. I know He had a resurrected body and that I was just a spirit, but He held me tightly all the same. I could feel Him holding me, and I knew He was the one making the contact happen. He really is all-powerful.

My heart was full to bursting as He looked down into my face. We communicated without words, spirit to spirit, a pure flow of knowledge. In my mind I saw everything I'd ever experienced in my life and knew He loved me in spite of it all. He understood that I hadn't meant to hurt Meghan the last time I teased her, or tell that partial truth to my parents. Every little misdeed I'd ever committed came to my mind, making me feel horribly guilty and unworthy. Embarrassed.

Then He showed me all the good things I'd done, some of which I'd never seen as doing good—like helping Jacky read, or playing cars with Benjamin while my mom took a nap, or smiling at a new girl at school. He helped me see that I had honestly done my best, that the good in me was far more than the bad, and that because of His Atonement I really was worthy to be there with Him.

I realized that in the Garden of Gethsemane, He had willingly experienced the pain I had gone through in the desert. In fact, He had been with me somehow the entire time, though I hadn't known it. And with this perfect knowledge, He knew precisely how to comfort me, how to help me understand why He allowed things like my kidnapping to happen. I can't adequately describe the understanding I gained from Him. The best I can say is that everything—even really awful things—happen for reasons we can't begin to comprehend on Earth; but because of His endless, all-encompassing sacrifice, every experience can be a beginning of something better; every horror or sadness can be swallowed completely in His love until it is as though it never happened. That is, if we allow Him into our hearts.

My mom was right.

I felt tears on my face, and I wiped them away in amazement. I had never before cried because I was happy.

"Please let me stay," I begged as He released me. But even as I spoke, longing thoughts of my parents arose in my mind.

Jesus looked at my guide. "Catherine?" He didn't exactly say Catherine, but spoke in a beautiful language that was strange and familiar to me all at once. Catherine is the best translation I can give. It was the first time I'd even thought of my guide having a name. As Jesus spoke, images of my thoughts and longing for my parents appeared in my mind. I knew Catherine was receiving the images, too.

"You were right," Catherine said to Jesus with a little sigh.

I started laughing. *Of course Jesus would be right. Like, duh!*

He looked at me, brow furrowed slightly, although His deep blue eyes seemed to share my amusement. "Sorry," I said, choking back my laughter. But inside I was still laughing.

He raised His head toward Catherine. "She needs to go back."

I felt a sudden panic. "I don't want to!"

He took my hands and looked into my eyes. I could see how

much He loved me, more even than my parents had, if you can believe that.

"I mean, do I have to?" I amended. "I know my body is a wonderful gift, and I know how important it was for me to be born and to have a physical body. I'm so grateful for that chance. Honest! And I have always treated my body like a temple. I'll gladly go back, but I only just got here. Can't I stay awhile?"

"You want to be a heart surgeon, don't you?" Jesus said. "Well, there's a family on Earth whose hearts are broken. The Father has heard their prayers and is sending you to help."

"You mean I'm going to be an angel?" I had watched the angel shows on TV long enough to be familiar with that sort of thing and the idea appealed to me. "Cool." I leaned forward eagerly, my hands still in His. "What's my first assignment? Has the family been in a feud for generations? Has their son decided not to live the gospel? Is their daughter hanging out with the wrong crowd?"

He shook his head and smiled at me. There was love in that smile and complete understanding. "They've lost their daughter to a kidnapper and her body hasn't yet been found."

I swallowed hard and blinked back new tears. "I—I died." It wasn't a question. I think I'd known from the start—you don't experience that kind of pain and not die—but I'd been fooling myself into thinking that life would go on as before after my wonderful experience here in Heaven.

"Not really dead, as you can see." He motioned to my spirit body. "Just beginning a new phase of life, that's all. One that will never end. A rebirth of sorts."

Hearing it from Him this way, and seeing the love and acceptance in His eyes, I have to admit I was kind of glad it had worked out the way it did. I mean, now they *couldn't* send me back to Earth, at least not permanently.

Except why did I keep worrying about my parents? Everyone else I'd seen here was happily involved in whatever they were doing—why did I seem stuck in this mode of regret?

"Because they can't let you go yet," Jesus told me with a deep emotion I could clearly see in His face—as though my parents' pain and loss was His own. "It is a terrible thing to be ripped from your mortal body the way that you were, but still more terrible for those left behind. We can help them. There are many prayers being offered in their behalf . . . and in yours."

"They don't need to pray for me," I said. "I'm fine."

"Then that's what we need to let them know."

I wondered silently how I would do that.

"You will know when the time comes, and Catherine will help you," my Brother said. "They will not be able to see you, but at certain moments, they will feel your presence. You will not be able to read their thoughts, as the reading of mortal thoughts is given only to Me and to the Father, but as a spirit you will be very attuned to their emotions, even ones they do not voice."

"Thank you," I whispered.

He kissed my forehead and gave me another hug. Love enveloped me. I wished His hug would never end. "Come and see Me whenever you want. The Father will visit you soon. Good luck on your assignment. I know you'll do great." He walked away and the brightest of the light went with Him.

I expected Catherine to take me immediately to Earth, but instead we went to a rather large two-story house flanked on one side by a sea of bright green grass and on the other by groves of tall trees. The house was a bright, happy color I had never seen before, an involved mixture of clear grays, glowing reds, and sunny yellows. A lovely wrap-around porch made a nice frame for the huge windows. "Welcome to your home," she said, motioning me inside. "This is where you'll be staying for as long as you like. Probably at least until after your assignment is finished. Then you will be deciding what you will study first and where you'll work."

"Study?"

"Yes. We all have much to learn about the building of worlds—creation. And a million other subjects."

"Then it is true—that the more we learn on Earth the farther along we are in Heaven."

"Certainly, it's true. And even in our spirits, without the barrier of our imperfect bodies, it takes time to learn, though it's much easier than on Earth. Believe me, there is still so much we can—and should—do while we wait for the resurrection."

I knew the resurrection meant that our spirits would be reunited with our perfected bodies. "So will learning be slower again after the resurrection?" I asked. "I mean if spirits learn so fast."

She shook her head. "It's as Brigham Young once said: 'When I again receive my body, I shall learn a thousand times more in a thousand times less time; and then I do not mean to cease learning, but shall still continue my researches.' "

That was impressive, but all that work seemed a little daunting to someone who had spent a good deal of time reading and daydreaming. "So is that all we do—work and study?" I asked. Maybe I wouldn't like it here after all.

Catherine laughed. "Goodness, no. Many people take a nice long rest to do whatever it is they've always wanted to do—read, swim, lie down, climb trees." She grinned and added, "Sit on a cloud and play a harp. But all that gets boring after a while. Especially when there are so many wonderful things here to learn and to do."

As she finished speaking, we stepped inside the large entry hall. She led me past a beautiful sitting room and up the stairs to a bedroom. Inside was a single bed covered by a quilt I recognized from my own house.

"Hey, my grandmother made this." I picked it up and rubbed it against my cheek.

"Yes, I know. I thought you might like to have it here. It's not the real one from your bed at home, but a spiritual copy. We don't need sleep in the way you know it, but having familiar things makes the transition easier."

"But all this does seem familiar somehow." I sat on the bed. "Not this house. I mean the gardens. And Jesus—the language He spoke. Even you. Like I've known it all before."

She didn't seem surprised. "When we're born on Earth, a veil is drawn over our eyes. The things you're remembering came from before. Don't worry, it will all come back to you quickly. You were only on Earth a short breath of time compared to the time you spent in the Premortal Life. I'm surprised you do not remember more already."

"He and I were good friends—I remember that." My eyes watered and I brushed a happy tear away with my finger.

"Yes, you were. Our Brother loves all the Father's children. And you will soon be seeing more family and friends—ones you knew both before and on Earth. Some live here when they're not working or exploring. Others are only a thought away."

"You mean, like spiritual e-mail?"

She laughed. "Much better than e-mail. But speaking of computers, come look at this." Crossing the room, she paused at a small cherry desk that had a large slab of clear stone jutting out at an angle. For some reason I thought of the Urim and Thummim I'd learned about in church, though it didn't seem to match the description I was familiar with. Could it be something similar?

"What is it?" I asked.

"We call it a Translator, but it is so much more. For instance, you can call up any subject you want to study, and it will direct you to top people in each field. It can also tell you just about anything else you want to know."

"Can it show me my family?" I settled in the matching cherry wood chair.

"Yes." She ran her fingers over the smooth edge of the desk. "Mothers who leave young children behind find that particularly comforting." She spoke like she knew this from experience, and I wondered about her family and where they were. "But why don't we try something else first? Think about what you'd like to learn."

I was going to do as she requested, when I realized that I could see a reflected outline of myself on the stone, and that I looked very different than I remembered. My hand went to my cheek. Immediately, the stone's surface became a mirror.

Sure enough, I wasn't myself anymore. I mean, I was still me, but a grown-up me. At least twenty or twenty-five. I looked at Catherine for an explanation.

"Your spirit is mature," she said. "Only your earthly body was still a child."

I didn't think thirteen was much of a child. Hey, my great-grandmother had been married at fourteen, but I didn't say any of that aloud. "You mean this is what I look like when I'm an adult?"

She nodded. "Yes, you're beautiful. You look a lot like your mother."

I did. My hair had darkened to a bright gold color, and my cheek bones were more prominent, my mouth a touch wider. My figure had matured. My skin was unblemished by pimples or even by the scar on my chin where I'd had stitches once. Only my eyes were the same deep blue they had always been. I was very pleased.

"So I actually am older, aren't I?"

"Yes. You'll find your thoughts will be more mature now as well. You'll see things you didn't see as a little girl."

I believed that already. Take Jesus' Atonement for instance. I hadn't really understood the concept on Earth, but I did now. Perhaps that's why I kept worrying about my mom and could understand how much she was suffering with my disappearance.

While Catherine watched, I experimented with the Translator. A mere thought on a subject would bring up information on the clear stone, which would then project it through the entire room. I was actually inside the images, experiencing them instead of watching from a distance. I saw a heart surgery and could almost understand what the surgeon was doing and why. After a short time, I began to anticipate his moves, because I could feel what was wrong. I couldn't yet do any part of the operation myself, or retain all the information, but it was an exceptional beginning. I knew with further study I'd understand more and more until my knowledge in that one area would be perfect. "This is incredible," I murmured. "It would have taken me months to learn all this on Earth."

Next, I called up geography, and everything my eighth grade teacher had been trying unsuccessfully to teach me fell into place and made perfect sense. I saw each state and knew it intimately. Each had its own personality, which I could identify. But even then I saw there was so much more to learn, and I was eager for it. The world—no, the Universe—was mine!

Just so you get an idea of what I was experiencing, comparing the Translator to a computer would be like comparing Earth's fastest computer to a manual typewriter. Or more aptly, to a pencil with dull lead, and then times that by a million. I could have stayed at the desk for days—or maybe an eternity—without a care in the world.

I'd once known a guy who said there couldn't really be a God because not even an all-powerful Being could hear all the prayers of so many people, much less take care of their needs. When he heard that in my church we believed in numberless inhabited worlds in the Universe, he just shook his head. "That only makes more people praying to a God who can't possibly know their individual names or circumstances," he told me.

Now seeing the Translator, I knew the Father who had created such an incredible device could easily take care of all His children. To Him time didn't even mean the same thing it does on Earth. Thought in the mortal realm is so linear. (As you can see, my spirit really is grown up; on Earth I didn't even know what linear meant!)

There was a touch on my shoulder. I looked up to see Catherine standing there. She was wearing a different white dress, and her hair was flowing loosely around her shoulders. "You changed," I said.

She smiled. "You've been here quite some time. But now you need to visit your family." She looked down at the clear stone, which now showed my church house. People dressed in somber clothes were moving slowly up the walks, full of shadows that marked the coming of night. "Normally, Translators are not used to visit Earth, mind you, but we have permission."

"Okay," I said. "I'm ready." But I wasn't really sure if I was.

Catherine took my hand as the church house grew up around us. We took a step forward.

Chapter Four

Angie Marshall had never felt such pain. The agony went on and on inside, filling up all the spaces, like a sickness that had no cure. She didn't want a cure. She wanted her daughter back. She wanted to know that Kristin was safe and sound. She stayed awake every night wondering if her baby was crying for her mother, if she was hungry or cold.

Kristin had been missing one week—one torturous week that seemed to last an eternity. Her relatives and the community had rallied together to form search parties, bring food, and donate money. Yet even in the midst of so many helpful and supportive people, Angie felt alone. Every part of her being ached for Kristin, and nothing but the return of her daughter could make her whole again.

An arm tightened around her shoulders. Gary. He sat next to her on the church bench listening to the bishop greet people who had come to hold a candlelight vigil in the parking lot, an evening of prayer for Kristin's safe return. Angie knew Gary was doing his best to comfort her, though she found little hope in his arms. Part of her was so angry at him. If only he had been a little earlier picking up the girls that night. If only he had taken care of her van repairs weeks ago when the engine warning lights first went on so she could have picked them up. If only . . .

Her life was now an endless gray stream of if onlys.

Gary suffered as she did; there was no mistaking that fact. His tall frame had lost needed weight, and the bags under his pale blue eyes told of many sleepless nights. His skin was rough and rugged from being out in the sun searching for Kristin.

He'd installed a burglar alarm in the house yesterday at her insistence, but she still didn't feel safe. She made Benjamin and Jacky take Gary's place next to her in their queen-sized bed, while Meghan slept on a mattress nearby. Angie just couldn't bear to be apart from any of her children. She was so frightened of losing one more.

Evening had settled over the city. It was time to go outside for the vigil. Angie arose, stepping away from her husband's arm. His reddened eyes met hers, begging for forgiveness. But how could Angie forgive him when all logic said the kidnapping hadn't been his fault?

Outside, the people began forming a large circle and lighting their candles. There were so many people from their church and the community that the circle extended around the entire parking lot. An inner circle was also formed, facing the outer circle. In the deepening night, the flickering lights were beautiful—like magical fairies dancing in the moonlight.

Someone brought out a microphone and offered a prayer. The microphone passed to someone else, a school friend of Kristin's who tearfully said how much she missed her. The microphone passed again, this time to a neighbor.

The torture in Angie's soul was lightened by their words. Not that seeing others' pain made hers any less, but rather their suffering gave her permission to mourn her daughter, to let a little of her torture escape the ever-growing tempest inside her soul.

She's not dead, Angie told herself. *She can't be dead! I don't know how I can live if my baby girl is dead.*

She lifted her head to the heavens, a dark blue color like her Kristin's eyes. *Please dear Father. Please bring my baby home.* She tried to pray with faith, though the police had warned them that most kidnapping victims were killed within forty-eight hours of being abducted.

Angie felt something brush her arm. Looking down, she saw it was just the three-quarter sleeve of her dress rustling in the light wind. Then all at once a warm, tingling feeling came to her heart. *My baby's alive. She's fine. I know she is. Please Father, make it so!*

★ ★ ★

I couldn't take my eyes off my mom as she held the candle and prayed to God for me. She looked exhausted. Her brow was drawn tight with pain, and her red eyes peered out from dark circles. Her normally golden hair hung limply to her jawline, with no shine, curl, or style, and she was wearing a wrinkled dress. I couldn't hear her thoughts, but I knew what she was thinking by her expression—that through her pain, she still held a bright hope for me to come home.

"Oh, Mom," I said, touching her arm, though I knew she couldn't feel my hand, nor I her skin. "I'm fine. I really am. It was awful for a while, and I wish I could have stayed, but I'm okay now. I'm in Paradise. Heaven's just like you and Dad taught me it would be. It's wonderful. I'll be meeting all our relatives soon, and I'll be there to meet you when you come."

My mother couldn't hear me, of course. I'd hoped her spirit could a little, but she didn't look any happier.

"Mom, I'm learning so much. Mom, can you hear me? Listen—I saw Jesus! You can't imagine how He made me feel." I was crying now.

My mother turned to my father. "She's alive. I feel it. We must find her." She looked at him as though she expected him to jump into his car and drive right to me. I knew he couldn't do that. Even if he could, it wouldn't make any difference.

"Oh honey, I think she's okay, too," he replied, his voice low and tense. "We won't give up hope. Not ever."

I turned to my guide, Catherine, whose normally bright face was somber. "Poor Angie," she said. I could see this was difficult for Catherine and wondered if this was the first time she'd played guide to a murder victim.

"Come." She pulled me down the line of people. I tore my gaze away from my parents and let her lead me away. My tears soon dried as I searched the surrounding faces. I was surprised at how many people had come to light a candle for me. There were kids from school I didn't know well, all my neighbors, and relatives I hadn't seen in years. Of all my friends, only Wade's sister Tamara was absent, and I wondered about that until I heard she was home sick with her mother.

"Your grandfather has aged well," Catherine said.

I looked in his direction.

"I always wondered if he'd go pure white like that," Catherine continued. "I thought he would. He's a little stooped, though."

"He's like ninety or something," I said.

"Eight-one," she corrected. "I'm glad he hasn't gained too much weight. He had that tendency."

"You knew my grandfather?"

A smile curved her lip. "Oh yeah, I knew him."

"Well, he never did eat much after my grandmother died. At least that's what my mom said. I don't remember him then. My grandmother died when I was four or five. Like Grandpa, she was kind of old. She had my mom when she was forty." Then something dawned on me, something I knew should have been obvious to me all along. "Hey, I know who you are. You're . . ." I let the sentence dangle.

"Yes, I'm your grandmother. I thought you might recognize me sooner, though you were too young to remember me from Earth Life, and I've changed my looks since you saw me in the Premortal Existence."

"But of course you're my grandmother! It's so obvious!" I hugged her. "I can't believe I didn't see it! It's so nice to meet you— I mean to see you again! Why didn't you tell me?"

My grandmother smiled. "Well, you were a little concerned with whether or not you were dead, and pretty wrapped up in worry about your mom and Meghan. So I decided to wait until you were ready. I knew you would make the connection."

She was right. I had been rather caught up with the everything that had happened. To tell the truth, I had even been afraid of dying. Not anymore. I tightened my hold around her waist. "I wish I could tell Mom I was with you."

"So do I. But she'll realize it soon enough, if only she thinks about it."

"Not if they don't find my body." I frowned. "I knew a boy from my school who drowned in the ocean on vacation two years ago. They had a funeral and everything, but his parents never gave up hope that he was still alive somewhere."

Grandmother Catherine sighed. "Unfortunately, many lost loved ones' remains are never found. This is our job, to heal your family's hearts, regardless of what they do or do not find."

"Can she ever see me? Could any of them?"

She started to shake her head, but then slowly nodded. "Permission is given occasionally for people to see beyond the veil, as I was once permitted to appear briefly to your grandfather during his surgery—he had given up and needed a little talking to. But I don't know if that will be the case here. I know appearing to your parents might seem like a fix-all, but it's not. They have to be ready for it. Their hearts must be ready."

"Oh." I didn't really understand, but then my grandmother's spirit thoughts touched mine and I saw what she meant. Something along the lines of how we must have faith without seeing a sign. A person who asks for a sign often lacks the faith required to be given one, and those who have worked to have such faith, don't need a sign. That's the best I can put it in mortal language.

"There's your sister," my grandmother said.

We had walked all around the outer circle and were nearly back to Mom and Dad. Meghan was standing next to our cousins, the ones who lived a couple streets over, and whose dad was our father's older brother. Amy, Scotty, and Garen were nine, eleven, and seventeen respectively. Meghan stood next to Garen, holding hands with our little sister, Jacky. Both my sisters had silent tears rolling down their faces.

I bit my lip hard to stop from crying myself. Meghan looked completely lost, and even when people spoke to her, she didn't say a thing. She just stared at her candle as though willing herself to disappear into the flame.

"I'm sorry, Meghan," I whispered, trying to touch her hand. "I would have stayed near you if I'd known. I would give anything to let you know that I'm okay."

Of course she didn't see or hear me. I moved my hand from hers to rest on Jacky's sun-bright hair. She looked up suddenly. "Did you feel that? It was Kristin! I felt her! Just like she always touched me." She rubbed her tears into her face as she looked around, as if expecting to see me standing there.

I glanced at Grandma Catherine in surprise. She shrugged, unable to tell me what had happened.

"Shush," Meghan whispered. "Stop that. Kristin's not here. She's missing!"

"But I felt her!" Jacky's bottom lip quivered.

"That would mean she's dead, and she's not! The police are going to find her, you'll see. There'll be a ransom note soon."

I blinked at Meghan, more than a little puzzled. My parents didn't have any money to speak of; there was no way she could believe I'd been kidnapped for money. Whatever comfort it might give her to think of me as being alive, this wasn't one of her novels.

Jacky twisted her hand from Meghan's grasp. "I *did* feel her," she muttered. I was still touching Jacky, my little look-alike, and now I pulled my hand from her head. She didn't react. Had she felt anything in the first place? Or had it only been wishing?

"Maybe the Lord gave her what she needed," Grandma Catherine said. "Little children are pure. They often see and feel things beyond the veil."

Whatever had happened, at least Jacky's tears had stopped. I didn't like the way she was glaring at Meghan, though. I remembered how Mom had told Meghan and me so many, many times that we would be best friends all our lives after we finally grew up and stopped fighting. Even though I couldn't be a part of that earthly relationship now, I wished it for my sisters.

"Where's Benjamin?" came a frantic voice. My mom stood on the other side of Aunt Lesa, scanning the crowd. "I can't find Benjamin! Benjamin!" Panic burst from her, threatening to flatten everyone in voice range with the force of her fear.

"He's right there—look." Aunt Lesa's large hand motioned to the inner circle where Benjamin was holding two candles high in the air above his head, oblivious to everyone around him.

He was holding one of the candles for me. I don't know how I knew it—maybe because he was only ten, still a child, and his spirit called to mine; or maybe being in my spirit body I could just read him better, as Jesus had promised.

Months ago, when Benjamin had been down in bed all day with a bad cold, I had played cars with him. Since he'd been too tired to move his little Jeep, I had moved it for him. Up and down around the couches. I had invented a story about them to entertain him. "Hey, I know you'd do the same for me," I'd told him when he'd thanked me. "I will someday," he promised.

Tonight he was holding a candle for me because I couldn't do it myself. I laughed, though I choked a little at the end. I wished he could feel it if I hugged him.

Grandma Catherine took my hand. "He's a special kid, that Benjamin."

I nodded, blinking back tears.

My mother rushed over and hugged Benjamin for me, spilling hot wax on herself in the process. Her breathing was still fast and her expression lost, even though she had found him safe.

As the vigil ended, my family thanked everyone who had come. Some people stayed, talking with my family. When I saw my kidnapper talking to my mom, I felt sick to my stomach. I hadn't noticed him before, though I should have known he would be there. Helpless rage bubbled up inside me. I ran over to him and punched at him. My hand went right through his somber face. "Big hypocrite," I muttered. "If only they knew, they'd fix you good." More than anything, I worried for my family and what he might do to them.

Grandma Catherine pulled me away. "He will be punished," she said calmly. "One way or the other. There is nothing you can do now." Knowing she was right, I stomped away. My feet penetrated the blacktop and disappeared, but I hardly noticed until my grandmother gave me a little tug up, making me glide over the surface instead.

I found Meghan on the outskirts of the group, kneading a small ball of warm wax in her fingers and staring at the ground.

"Meghan," Wade said. We both started suddenly, not having noticed his approach.

My sister looked up, but didn't speak.

"I'm really sorry. Really sorry. Is there anything I can do?"

She shook her head.

"I . . . uh . . . you're going to have a birthday soon, aren't you?"

She stared at him. I had the feeling she was ready to burst out screaming at him about what difference could it possibly make. But she would never do that to anyone.

"He's trying to ask you out," I said. "Tell him to get lost. The nerve of him. My corpse is hardly cold! You need time." To Wade I said, "Leave her alone!"

He didn't. "I know you're worried about your sister, but . . . well, I hope you know that I'm here for you."

"Thank you," Meghan whispered.

Just then a police car drove into the church parking lot. The two officers sauntered over to the small group of remaining people in big, confident strides. "Anyone seen a Wade Burke?" one of them asked.

I felt Meghan stiffen.

"Right there," someone said, pointing to where Wade and Meghan stood, a short distance from the others.

Wade's father left off talking to my dad and came over. "Is something wrong? Wade's my son." Wade's father was a tall, impressive-looking man, and in his suit, he resembled a high-paid lawyer, though I knew he sold insurance.

The policemen took a few steps back so they were out of earshot of the rest of the group. Meghan stumbled after them, and so did I.

The taller policeman spoke. "Due to some information we received about the car that took Kristin Marshall, we searched your house. Your wife let us in voluntarily."

Wade's father nodded impatiently. "Of course she did. We have nothing to hide."

The tall policeman's eye slid to Wade, who was staring at the ground. "We understand. But we do need to talk to your son. Would you mind coming down to the station to answer a few questions?"

"We don't mind," said Wade's father. "But I would like to know what this is all about first."

The officers didn't reply, and Wade's eyes were still glued to the ground. Behind him a few feet, Meghan's mouth gaped in horror.

"Wade?" his father asked in a tone I recognized all too well. It was the tone my father used when he would not accept silence.

The tone worked on Wade. "They're not mine," he said, glancing up at his father. They were nearly the same height, though

Wade was a lot thinner. "Jay came over with them last night. I told him to take them back, that I didn't want them in my room, but he said his mom was cleaning and would find them. He was coming back for them tomorrow." He held up his hands in a helpless gesture. "I didn't look at them, I promise. I only saw one picture that Jay was looking at before I made him stuff them under the mattress. Ask him. He'll tell you. He was here a minute ago."

Wade's father shook his head, obviously not understanding. "What are you saying?"

Wade glanced at the policemen helplessly. I'd never seen him in this light before. He looked like a little boy caught doing something he knew he shouldn't be doing.

The shorter policeman cleared his throat. "We found some magazines in your son's room," he explained. "Pornography. Since Wade was one of the last people to see Kristin Marshall, we need to check out every possible lead."

I half expected Mr. Burke to get upset, to demand what connection this had to my case, but he merely looked at Wade with a sad expression. "Okay, officers. Let's go. But I hope we can make this quick. My wife will be worried, and she has enough on her hands right now with our daughter being sick."

"But Dad, they're not mine," Wade said. His face, his eyes, his very posture pleaded with his father. "Really. It happened just like I said." He sounded so embarrassed and mortified, I almost felt sorry for him. "And I don't know anything about Kristin."

His father nodded shortly, mouth clenched. He put a firm hand on Wade's shoulder. "We'll work this out."

"Give me just a minute. I'll be right there." Wade gestured toward Meghan. His father gave a sharp nod and followed the policemen.

"The magazines aren't mine," Wade told Meghan. "I didn't even know Jay looked at stuff like that. I didn't know what to do when he brought them over."

Meghan lift her chin slightly. "I didn't see what kind of car took my sister," she said softly, "but it was dark like the car you and Jay were in." Tears gathered in her eyes. "Do you know where my sister is, Wade?"

He stared at her, his deep brown eyes wide with disbelief. "No. I don't. I promise. I liked Kristin. I would never hurt her." His brow creased with his torment. "But I can't vouch for Jay. Like I told the police last week, he didn't come with us to the movie that night. The one he'd wanted to see had already started and he'd seen the one we ended up going to. He dropped us off, and Mom came later to pick us up. Please, believe me."

Without saying anything Meghan turned away. Wade watched her for a moment and then walked toward the police car, his shoulders hunched in defeat.

After they drove away, my parents and my aunt and uncle crowded around Meghan, asking questions. She shrugged them all aside and buried her face in my dad's chest.

There was a lump in my throat, one I couldn't seem to swallow. In that instant, I would give up all the joy I'd experienced in Heaven to take away my family's pain.

★ ★ ★

I know you want me to tell you if Wade did it or had any part of my abduction. But I can't. You need to see how it all came about, the way it appeared to my family. Besides, right then even I didn't know how everything would turn out.

Chapter Five

"You're awfully quiet," Grandma Catherine said to me. We were back in Paradise, walking among the trees outside her house.

"It's just that I don't know how I can help them." I sighed and pulled a leaf off a tree. It felt real under my fingertips, though it was in spiritual form just like me. To spirits, spirit things are real, and earthly things have no substance. "I know it might sound a little selfish, Grandma, but part of me doesn't even want to go back and try. I mean, it's so wonderful here. So many things to learn and do. I want to explore every part of Paradise and the Universe. I want to go and teach the gospel to those who've never heard it. I want to meet all the ancient prophets." I took a deep breath and stared through the trees at the slice of perfect blue sky overhead, where I caught just a glimpse of an eagle sailing by. "When I go back to Earth I see my family's pain, but I can't give them any of my joy. I feel so helpless, and I have to wonder, what's the point?"

"Even if you can't see it, you are helping them," she said quietly. "And their spirits will be comforted; I have no doubt of that. But a little time needs to pass for them to heal completely. Don't worry, it won't all be horrible. There'll be good things to experience there as well." A wide smile filled her face. "Like Benjamin and his candles."

I smiled despite myself. "I guess I won't have to go back every day."

"No. And in between your visits there, we can explore Paradise together. There is much that I haven't seen yet, many brothers and sisters I haven't yet met."

We walked in silence for a few minutes, feeling the soft grass caress our bare feet. "Tell me about Mom," I said. "I mean when she was little. What was she like?"

Grandma Catherine's blue eyes deepened with memories. "As you said earlier, I was forty when I had her. She was the last of seven children. My bonus baby. My next youngest was already nine. Your mother took us all by surprise."

"So the nine-year-old was Uncle Phil, my uncle that lives just two streets over with Aunt Lesa."

"No, Phil is your father's brother. I'm talking about Jonny."

"Oh, Uncle Jon. That's right." I felt a little stupid to have mixed up my relatives like that, but Grandmother just smiled.

"The mix-up is understandable. Jonny lives in Alaska, and you've only met him a few times. Anyway, when your mother was born, she looked just like a little angel—that's why I named her Angie. It was the closest I could come to angel without actually using the word. I took her everywhere with me, watched over her like a hawk. I even helped out in her kindergarten for the whole year. It was hard for me to let her grow up."

"Mom did that with Jacky—went to kindergarten with her, I mean." I chuckled in memory. "She's a big worrywart."

"Yes, she got it from me. Always a little worrywart, right from the start. Used to call me up when she was baby-sitting just to make sure I was all right. She was also the first one to notice if I ever felt ill."

"She hasn't changed much," I said with a laugh. "I used to wake up in the middle of the night and find her checking to see if I was still breathing."

Grandma Catherine chuckled. "She got that from me, too, I'm afraid. But I bet you had some really nice midnight chats with her, didn't you?"

"Oh, yeah. A couple of times we even got up and had hot chocolate." Just thinking about it made me happy.

"You see," my grandmother said, bending to pluck a strand of sweet grass and put it in her mouth. "The good times will bring the happiness back. Your family will begin to remember them soon. It's part of what will help them heal."

I stopped walking. "You're right, Grandma. I'm sorry for being such a baby. I just thought that since I was a spirit now, I would be able to change things faster."

"We can't. We can never interfere with their agency. It is one of our Father's most important gifts."

We began walking again, breaking from the trees and into the meadow where Grandma's house waited. "I know just the thing for you," she said.

"What?" I smiled at the mischief in her eyes. I reached out my thoughts to hers, trying to see what she was thinking, spirit to spirit, but she just laughed. "You'll have to wait." She pulled up her white dress a few inches. "Race you to the house."

If you would have told me before I died that I would be having races in Paradise, I would have thought you were crazy. If you had told me I'd be racing my grandmother who would have been seventy-eight if she had been still living on Earth, I would have deemed you completely insane. I always thought spirits were more refined, and certainly too dignified for such things. But here I was—racing my grandmother! Toward the end, I was actually flying through the air and laughing myself silly when she beat me to the door.

She allowed me to walk into the house first, and to my surprise the hall was bursting with people. They greeted me in chorus, their faces obviously happy to see me. Most were adults about my parents' ages, but some were younger and a few older. I knew the way they appeared was their choice, and it was how they felt most comfortable.

A man clasped my hand warmly. "I know you," I said, scanning the faces. "I know you all."

"Of course. This is your family." Grandma Catherine took my arm and walked with me as I greeted everyone. "At least the part of your family I could fit in the house. We go back all the way to Adam and Eve, you know."

" 'The hearts of the children shall turn to their fathers,' " I quoted. "We really are sealed."

As I hugged each member of my family, I felt their spirits and caught a glimpse of their lives. Many had been pioneers, some even traveling over the ocean, leaving families and all their possessions to join the Church. A few had known and walked with the prophets of old. Some had come to Paradise more recently, like my Alaskan cousin who had died when she was a newborn. I had never felt so loved and welcomed since I arrived in Paradise, except for with Jesus.

"We wanted to greet you when you first got here," said my fourth-great grandfather. "But Catherine wouldn't hear of it. Said she wanted to ease you in."

"It was because you were always her favorite grandchild," my fourth-great grandmother confided.

I looked at Grandma Catherine, who shrugged. "When you were born, your mother took ill. I took care of you for the first few months of your life. It was kind of like having my own little Angie back. But don't listen to these guys—I never play favorites."

But she did. I could see that from the twinkle in her eyes.

★ ★ ★

I met Randy Williams soon after that day. At first I didn't recognize him because he was older and I hadn't seen him for two Earth years. But he knew me.

I was in the Music Center where I was alone, soaking up heavenly hymns from the angel choir and meeting other spirits like George Washington and Flannery O'Conner (who had to introduce herself and to whom I had to confess that I hadn't yet read any of her books). I had even talked to a resurrected being—Ruth, the daughter-in-law of Naomi in the Bible. I'd read in the Book of Mormon that worthy members of Christ's Church who had died in the years before Christ had been resurrected at His resurrection because He had loosed the bands of death. I'd see a few of these beings around, but before today I hadn't talked to any other than Jesus Himself. In all, I was pretty pleased with the way things were going.

"Kristin!" A young man rushed up and hugged me, nearly knocking me over.

I was used to being hugged by people I didn't recognize right away. Some I had known on earth, and most of these appeared to me as I had last seen them. A few liked to make me guess. And of course, there were many I had known only in the Premortal Life. I reached out mentally to feel his spirit, certain I would recognize him.

"Randy? Is that really you?" For an instant he changed to the short, skinny, blonde-headed boy with freckles who had lived in my neighborhood, complete with the cut-off jeans he'd always worn and brown bare feet. Then he sort of grew up before my eyes into a very handsome man with brown hair and nice skin. His white pants and shirt didn't hide how well he'd filled out. "Wow, you've changed!"

"You haven't," he said, not taking his arms from around me. "You were always beautiful, though I do like you better grown-up." His face turned red. Really, it did. Though I wonder if it was only for show, because other than the color change he didn't act embarrassed.

"You drowned on your vacation," I said, frowning. "I was so sorry to hear it. Your parents were very upset."

"I know, they still have a tough time dealing with my death, even though it happened two years ago. But they're finally starting to accept it, I think."

I silently hoped my parents would be able to do the same.

"Come for a walk with me in the garden," he invited. "Tell me what's going on."

"Well, I died," I said for starters.

He snorted. "I can see your humor hasn't changed. Now tell me something I don't know."

So I did. I had the satisfaction of seeing him turn sober as I told him what happened and how my family was suffering. It was nice to know that everyone in Paradise—at least those outside the first few generations of my ancestors—didn't know all the details of my life on Earth.

Randy took my hand in what seemed like a natural gesture. I felt warmth run up my arm to my heart. I stopped and stared at him.

"What?" he asked. I felt his thoughts reach out, but I didn't let him in. This feeling of spiritual attraction was so new, I wanted to treasure it for a while to myself. Not even with the handsome Jay had I ever felt this way.

"Nothing," I said, talking a few unsteady steps forward. "So what is it that you do here?"

"I'm an astrophysicist."

I had no idea what that was, but now that my emotions were under control, I let his mind touch mine. Instantly, I saw stars and planets and endless amount of space. "Impressive," I said.

"Maybe you *have* changed," he said with a laugh. "Once you would have said 'cool.' "

I grinned. "That too."

We walked and talked for a long while, but at last I sighed and said, "I really need to go visit my family again. It's about time."

"Yeah, I'd better get back to work, too. I only came because I'd heard you were here."

"I'm glad you did." I meant it.

"I'll see you later," he said in a voice that told me he would. He tried to walk away, but couldn't because I was still holding his hand. Now it was my face that turned red. He laughed again and brushed my cheek with the lightest of kisses and was gone.

My whole spirit body tingled with life from his touch. This was some feeling! Did mortals experience anything remotely similar? Was this why my parents had married?

I envisioned myself back at my grandma's house, and instantly I was there. She was on the porch in a rocking chair, reading a book of poetry. Looking up, she smiled. "I used to dream of Heaven," she said. "I dreamed of sitting in a rocking chair reading all the poetry I never had time for since I was taking care of my husband, seven children, and a house."

"But I thought Mormons believed that when we died, we'd just go right to work," I said. "I remember one of my teachers saying so in church. I know you told me when I first got here that we could take time to rest or do whatever we wanted, even sitting around on a cloud, but I haven't seen much of that here."

"Oh, you will. Keep in mind that spirits work, progress, and do everything else at different rates. For me, reading is not only a joy, but a way to learn. And learning is fun—you've discovered that for yourself." She gave a contented sigh. "Yes, I have to say that Paradise is just as wonderful as I imagined it would be. It'll be even nicer when Merrill gets here."

"Will he come soon?" I asked, leaning against the porch railing opposite her.

"Not too much longer."

"I was thinking I should go back down," I said.

"Do you want me to come along?"

I did. But I remembered how awful I'd felt seeing my mom in such turmoil. Seeing my mom suffer couldn't be easy for Grandma. Better that she stay and peacefully read her poetry. This was my job, not hers.

"I'd better go alone," I said.

She arched one brow but didn't comment. I leaned forward and kissed her cheek.

"Wait," she said. "Before you go, there's something I need to tell you about your dad's brother. About how he grew up."

"Uncle Phil?" From the serious look in my grandmother's eyes, I wasn't sure I wanted to listen to what she had to say.

"Yes."

I pulled up her footstool and sat on it. "Okay," I said. "But I don't think anything you say will change how I feel about him."

I was wrong.

Chapter Six

Later, upstairs in my room, I turned on the Translator with a touch of my thoughts. I saw my house immediately. It was dark there, but that was a good time to visit. I didn't know if Dad had returned to work or not, but if he had he should be home by now.

I walked up the drive and onto the porch. As usual, I reached for the doorknob, but my hand went right through like some ghost in a movie. I laughed nervously before walking right through the door. Amazing! I had to try it twice more before I could remind myself why I was there.

At the kitchen counter, Jacky and Benjamin were doing homework, while my mom stared into empty space. Dad wasn't there and I couldn't see Meghan, but as I thought about her, my spirit was pulled to where she was. The rapid transition was frightening at first, as I rushed through doors, cars, and houses, but when I found my balance, I began to enjoy the journey.

Meghan was outside, a few blocks over, wandering aimlessly in the dark. She was barefooted and not wearing a coat, though it was raining lightly. "What are you doing out here?" I asked her. "Don't you know there's a murderer loose?" She didn't reply. "Oh, so now you've decided to become talkative," I added.

She walked on, and I walked silently with her. She was shivering from the cold. "It's all my fault," she muttered at one point. "Come and get me, you jerk. I'll kill you myself." I saw the flash of Dad's pocketknife in her hand.

"Meghan, this isn't like you. Go home. I'm fine. Please, Meghan! Mom needs you. If something happened to you now, she'd go insane."

We were passing my aunt and uncle's house now. Meghan turned up the walk.

"No!" I said. "Home. Meghan go home! You shouldn't come here now. Please!" She wasn't listening. I decided to go back to our house and see if I could get my mom to call my aunt before

Meghan took to the street again. I couldn't let anything happen to my sister.

I arrived at the house just as my father did. His deeply tanned face was haggard, his shirt stained with sweat, and his jeans powdered with dirt. My mother ran to meet him at the door as he pulled off muddy hiking boots. He shook his head and the flickering hope died in her face. I realized he had been out looking for me all day. He had lost about ten pounds since the vigil and his wrinkles were more pronounced. I wondered how much Earth time had passed. Peeking at Jacky's math paper I saw that another week had gone by. It had seemed much less than that for me.

My mom glanced over at the younger children, who were staring silently at our dad. Once, they would have run to him, and he would have gathered them laughingly into his arms. But there was no laughter now, and Dad looked like a hug might knock him over.

"That's enough homework," Mom said. "Go up and brush your teeth and get your pajamas on."

"But I'm not fin—" began Benjamin.

"Now." Mom's voice brooked no argument.

When the children were gone, Mom said, "Detective Lowder called again today. They found some of Kristin's hair in that boy Jay's car."

Dad sat down heavily at the kitchen table. "Have they arrested him?"

"No. The girls did talk to them outside the pool. Wade's little sister, Tamara, I think, said that Kristin leaned inside the car. It's possible some hair fell then."

"But Meghan said she was wearing a ponytail."

"I know. It's suspicious so they're questioning him." The whole time my mom had been speaking, her voice remained hard and emotionless, but the energy I felt coming from her belied that outer expression. Perhaps this was the only way she could survive.

"Detective Lowder said they also found some bones up Provo Canyon," she continued, "but not to worry when we heard about it on the news because they . . ." She stopped talking and took a deep breath. "They aren't Kristin's. There were also four more sightings—one in Idaho, one in Missouri, two in California. He's following up, but ..." She shook her head in resignation. Apparently, there had been many false sightings of me since my disappearance.

Dad put his elbows on the table and let his head drop into his hands. I noticed his hairline had receded more than I remembered. He was almost completely bald on top, like Uncle Phil. "I looked and looked today," he said, his voice raw and broken. "And I prayed so hard. I just want to find my little girl. I'm her father—I was supposed to protect her." My heart wrenched at the words because truly there was nothing he could have done to save me.

I looked toward my mother, expecting her to offer comfort, but she remained silent, her eyes veiled. Apparently, she had nothing left to give. Opening my arms wide, I spread myself over my father's back as he hunched over the table. I held onto him for a long time, breathing in his sweaty smell, until I felt his strength returning.

"Where's Meghan?" he asked Mom. I felt guilty at the words because I'd completely forgotten about her.

Mom blinked back sudden tears. "She walked out. I told her I was getting those locating watches I read about in the paper and that she'd have to wear one. She got angry—said that wouldn't bring Kristin back."

"You really think that's a good idea?" Dad asked. "I don't know that those things would stop anything from happening. Might even make them a target."

"If we'd bought them when I first read the article, Kristin might not be missing." Her voice was cold and accusing.

My dad's face slumped in defeat. "I'll go look for her," he said wearily.

"We already drove around the block five times. I think she might be at one of her friends'. I was calling them before you came in." She reached for the phone, just as it rang.

"It's Lesa," Mom said after a minute. "Meghan's there. Lesa can't run her home because Phil and Garen aren't home, and she doesn't want to leave the little kids asleep alone." Mom turned back to the phone. "Gary will come. Keep her there."

I was glad at least that Uncle Phil wasn't home.

Dad climbed slowly to his feet and walked out the door.

When he returned a short time later with Meghan, Mom bawled her out for twenty minutes, making everyone even more miserable and unhappy. Meghan slunk upstairs to her mattress on the floor in Mom's room. She didn't change her clothes or brush her teeth. I stayed watching over her all night.

For most of the next few days Meghan stayed on her bed in her own room, staring silently at the ceiling. Since she hadn't yet returned to school, Tamara and Wade brought her homework almost every day. She didn't even look at the assignments, but carelessly placed the papers in a growing pile of untouched work under her bed. This was not at all like Meghan. She had always been a good student who had enjoyed school. Of all my family, I worried about her the most.

* * *

I stayed with my family for several weeks, slowly growing accustomed to being invisible and unable to touch things or people. Everything was the opposite of what it had been when I was mortal. In Heaven, spirit things were real and solid to me, but here where things were supposed to be real or solid, my hands only passed right through. For instance, I had to learn to support myself instead of depending on chairs. The effort wasn't great, and after a while, doing so became natural to me. Not being seen by those I loved was much more difficult.

I watched Mom and Dad grow further apart, and Meghan more withdrawn. Our house had once been full of laughter and music, but now it seemed an empty shell. They didn't even read scriptures together in the morning anymore, though I read to them from my own spiritual copy while they ate. Sometimes Jacky would cock her ear in my direction, a bemused expression on her face as though she could almost hear my words, but the others continued whatever they were doing.

Only in Jacky and Benjamin did I find any joy at all, though Mom kept a prison guard's care of them. They had returned to school, but she walked them to class each day. She often drove up to the school at recess time to watch them play from her car, and she was waiting outside their classrooms when school was over. They couldn't go anywhere to play, except Aunt Lesa's, which in my view was the worst place she could let them go.

The police didn't have any leads on my kidnapper, though my mom called two or three times a day to ask. They were still questioning neighbors, searching houses, and doing background checks on everyone my parents knew and many they didn't know. So far, Jay and Wade were their only suspects, mostly because of the hair they'd found in Jay's car. One of the policemen had been assigned to check out similar abductions in Florida and Kansas where Jay had lived before moving here, and in Washington where Wade was from. They didn't have much hope for a history for abduction because the boys were both so young, but they looked for other indicators, such as violence and pornography addiction.

Three weeks after I had disappeared, Meghan had still not made any progress toward healing. I wondered what she thought about as she lay on her bed day after day, practically unmoving. She didn't read or listen to music. Sometimes she cried. At these times I talked to her. I begged her to pray, but I didn't see her praying even once, not even at night when everyone was asleep. Then one day Mom told Meghan she would have to go back to school. Meghan had a fit, and in retaliation she refused to sleep in my mother's room anymore, but I think she was secretly glad to return. At home she was bored and angry all the time; at least in school, she would have something to do.

If Meghan wouldn't pray, Mom seemed to be constantly on her knees, though I didn't know what she said. Whatever it was, it certainly didn't seem to be doing her any good. She let everything in her life go except checking up on the kids. The house needed cleaning, the refrigerator was empty, the laundry needed to be done, and if not for her visiting teachers and other ladies from church, I doubt my family would have eaten anything but frozen dinners from the freezer in the dusty garage.

Dad was even worse. He blamed himself for my abduction just as my mother seemed to do. He had turned a corner of my room into an office, and every hour he wasn't out searching for me, he was there, organizing clues, talking on the phone to the police or the media, and surfing the Internet for clues. He never seemed to find anything new, but he kept on with a doggedness that exceeded all reason. I could feel how much he missed me and how desperately guilty he felt for not being able to do anything to bring me home.

Eventually, he used up all his vacation and the extra days off the furniture manufacturing company had given him, and he had to return to work—someone had to pay the bills—though he kept searching the hills for me at night and on weekends. It was really pointless because he was so far away from the desert where I had been taken that it was almost funny. Or it would would have been if it hadn't been so tragic. Dumped where it was behind a hill, and covered by sand and rocks, my body might never be found.

Speaking of this, I did go once to the place where I was buried, just because I was curious. There was nothing to see. I went through the rocks and sandy dirt, but underneath it was dark and even my improved eyesight was useless. I felt no connection with my mortal self or desire to stay nearby, though I knew my body had been a most wonderful gift to me. I knew one day I would have it back again—glorified and resurrected like my older Brother's. Until then, I was content being a spirit in Paradise.

On the day Meghan returned to high school, Wade came up to her in the halls. "Hi Meghan," he said hesitantly. "I'm glad you're back." He looked around to make sure they were alone. "I've done a lot of thinking. I shouldn't have let him keep the magazines there. I should have told on him. And like my dad says, I shouldn't have had the temptation around. Jay might not have come to get them, and I might have broken down and taken a peek. To tell the truth, I'm glad the cops found them because I was kind of curious." He turned a bright red. "But I learned my lesson. I swear I did."

Meghan nodded but didn't smile. Though she tried hard to be impassive, I could see how much her heart hurt—would she ever smile again?

"And Jay, well, we're not buddies anymore," Wade continued. "I didn't know he was into that stuff. I really didn't."

Again Meghan's head went up and down, but the slight motion didn't even cause her long golden locks, now limp and unwashed, to move or slide against one another.

Wade's eyes were anxious. "Will you ever forgive me, Meghan? I should have waited there with you until your father came. Every day of my life I will be sorry for that."

In her dead-looking eyes a little life sparked. "You should have waited!" she returned venomously. "But you didn't, and now I'll have to pay for the rest of my life. And you know what? I deserve it. It's my fault Kristin's gone. My fault. I deserve to die myself!"

By the way Wade's mouth opened, I could tell he hadn't expected this. He grabbed her unresisting hands. "No. It's not your fault! It's no one's fault except the guy who did it!"

For a moment, I thought she might let him hug her, that she might let out tears where someone could hear and help, instead of silently in her room, but she jerked her hands from his. "Goodbye, Wade." Her voice had a finality to it that I knew well. Wade obviously didn't.

"Let me know if you need anything," he said to her retreating back.

She didn't acknowledge him.

I ran after her. "Meghan, I think you should talk to him. Meghan, stop!" Of course she didn't hear me. "Meghan, he didn't do it!"

But I knew that didn't matter now. Because she liked Wade, she would punish herself by not letting him get close to her. What better way to punish your imagined guilt than to deny yourself the very thing that might help you heal? My heart was so full of sadness that I didn't know what to do. I stayed by Meghan the rest of the day, seeing her somber face as she struggled through each class. The other kids were nice, but curious, and each question about me brought my sister closer to an explosion. Fortunately, her blank expression and frosty silence was enough to deter most people.

She didn't eat lunch since no one had reminded her to bring one or had given her money, but she didn't seem to care. She worked instead at her algebra. The going was tortuously slow for her although I grasped the concept instantly. Couldn't she see how it all fit together?

When school was over, Meghan walked home alone, even though Mom had told her to get a ride from our cousin, Garen. I noticed that Wade was following her from a distance in the old car his parents had given him to drive. His actions showed a responsibility and consideration I wouldn't have expected from a boy who wasn't quite eighteen. I felt a rush of sympathy and thankfulness toward him. I was glad he wasn't giving up on Meghan. She looked so small and so vulnerable right now—and I knew too well that this neighborhood was far from safe.

Then Garen's old green truck pulled up beside Meghan and she climbed inside with him and his girlfriend, Trish. Meghan hugged her backpack to her chest and didn't put on her safety belt, although there were enough to go around. I noticed Wade still behind them, following the truck. I thought that strange until I remembered he lived on our street.

Deciding Meghan was taken care of, I went to check on Mom, who should be about ready to pick up the other children from school. I found her sitting on the couch in our living room, talking to Brother Dale Loveridge, an old friend of Mom's from before she had married Dad. His wife had died of cancer some time back, and now he was renting a house in our neighborhood, sharing the place with a couple of young men everyone assumed were students. His two young boys had gone to live with his deceased wife's mother, presumably until he found better accommodations for them. Brother Loveridge attended our church, which was why we called him Brother, and up until recently, I had liked him. Now it made me furious to see him holding my mother's hand.

"I think I blame him, Dale," my mother was saying. "It's illogical, I know, but I blame him. I really do. May the Lord forgive me. He should have been there a minute earlier, waiting there outside like I always did. Then he could have made sure nothing happened."

Brother Loveridge patted her hand. "I felt that way after my wife died. I blamed her."

"But she couldn't help dying."

"I know that with my mind, but sometimes feelings don't have a connection to logic. Still all feelings have a basis. They always have a basis. Some reason why they exist."

"Are you saying I'm not wrong to feel this way?" Mom asked, her brows arching.

"No. I'm saying I understand, that's all. But we can't go back and change the past. If I'd had a clue about my wife's family history of breast cancer, I would have made her get a mammogram a lot sooner. For a long time, my sons were mad at me about that. I was mad at myself."

They were silent a long time, just holding hands. I felt like I could hardly breathe, which is pretty silly since spirits don't breathe air at all.

"It's nice to see you again, Dale," my mother finally said into the silence. "We dated for so long in high school—it's nice to know you again."

Dated? I hadn't known they'd been *that* close.

"You too." There was an expression in Brother Loveridge's eyes that I couldn't name, but recognized from the way Randy had looked at me in Heaven. I would have kicked him out of the house right then, and I tried, but he couldn't feel my foot. "I want you and Gary to know that I'm here for you. Whatever you need—just ask."

Mom didn't reply, and I wondered if—at least for a minute—she regretted her choice to marry my father. But would that have spared her this torture?

"Mom," I said, my voice all choked and full of tears.

Her head shifted, and she pulled her hand from Brother's Loveridge's tightened grasp. "I think that's Meghan." My sister hadn't come home yet. Had my mother somehow heard my plea? "I'd better go get the kids," she added, standing abruptly. "Lesa offered to pick them up, but I . . . I just need to be there."

Brother Loveridge nodded and stood next to her, with one hand on my Mom's shoulder. The touch was meant to be comforting, I knew, but it wasn't. Not for me anyway. "Don't touch her," I said crossly. He didn't remove his hand. That's one thing annoying about being a spirit. Mortals don't tend to listen to you at all.

Hurry up, Meghan, I thought.

I watched as Mom's gaze settled on Brother Loveridge's hand on her shoulder and then slid up his arm to his gray eyes.

"Let me know if you need anything at all," Brother Loveridge was saying. "I've given some of my classes to my graduate students so I can help with the search and to be here for you."

"Thank you," Mom murmured. "Everyone has been so nice."

Their words were normal and innocent, but I wondered if there was something more, something I couldn't see or feel. So what if he appeared to have a full head of hair, and his body was toned and well-formed compared with my father's grief-stricken, skeletal features? So what if he had once been in love with my mom? He had no right to be here. I wanted him gone.

The garage door slammed and relief washed over my mother's face. "There she is. Thank you again." She stepped away from him and opened the front door. As Brother Loveridge started to leave, a very pale Meghan came rushing in from the kitchen.

"Mom! Mom! Aunt Lesa just called Garen on his cell phone. Uncle Phil called her from the police station. They came and got him at work for questioning. She thinks they're going to arrest him!"

My mom looked aghast. "Whatever for?"

"They think . . ." Meghan paused, her lips trembling. "They think he had something to do with Kristin. Aunt Lesa said she already called Dad at work."

My mom left the door with Brother Loveridge still standing there. She flew to the kitchen and picked up a phone, dialing my father's number. "Gary?" she asked breathlessly. "I—I just heard about Phil. What's going on?" Then she fell quiet as he spoke.

I couldn't hear what she was saying so I pressed my face close to hers. She never felt me, but I could hear now.

"Lesa just barely called me," my dad said. "It seems the police have unearthed records of my brother being a convicted pedophile."

"A pedophile?" my mom's voice was scarcely a whisper.

"I can't believe it myself. I know we were never close until he married Lesa and moved to Utah—he was always so much older than me and we were in different phases of life." My father swallowed hard. "But to think that all this time . . . Look, I'm going down there right now to sort this out. I'll call you when I know what's going on."

"Gary, wait!" Mom's hand on the receiver was white from clutching it so tightly. "Could it be . . . do you think . . ." She left the sentence dangling, but I knew what she meant. Had Uncle Phil had something to do with my disappearance?

"I don't know," my father said. "I don't know anything anymore."

My mother hung up the phone. Her face was as rigid as white marble, yet I knew that inside her heart violent emotions battled.

Of course, the information about Uncle Phil came as no surprise to me. I was glad my parents finally knew.

"What did he say?" Meghan asked.

Mom shook her head, but then said, "I guess you'll find out anyway; it's bound to be in the papers. The police found . . . Well, your—your uncle has a history of molesting children. It must have been a very long time ago in another state because we never knew. Oh, I can't believe this is happening!" She paused. "Oh Meghan, he never touched you, did he?"

Meghan shook her head.

"Thank heaven for that!" Mom put her face in her hands and began to cry.

The news, the continual stress, and lack of food was too much for Meghan. Without a sound, her eyes rolled up in her head and she fell to the floor. Brother Loveridge barely prevented her head from cracking into the hard ceramic tile.

Chapter Seven

When he arrived at the police station, Gary Marshall was pulled aside by Detective Jim Lowder before being allowed to see his brother. "They've found a body found in Colorado. A young girl about Kristin's age. She's not been identified yet, and there'll be a lot of speculation, but the minute I heard I called and questioned the officers. From what they tell me, it can't be your daughter. I just wanted you to be aware in case the press calls for a comment. They'll likely try to connect it to our case."

"Thanks," Gary said past the lump in his throat. Detective Lowder had been thorough in warning them about these gruesome discoveries before they were public knowledge. He knew that by doing so the detective had saved them useless agonizing, and Gary was grateful.

Detective Lowder nodded. "You contact me anytime, understand? This case is a priority with our department and the FBI. You still have my cell phone number?"

Gary nodded. He didn't think he'd need it.

"I seriously want you to call me at any time." The detective's voice lowered and his blue eyes showed concern. "I can't pretend to know what you're feeling—I'm not married and I don't have children—but I have two nieces Kristin's age, and I know how I would feel if something ever happened to either of them."

"Thanks," Gary said again.

With a nod, Detective Lowder led him down a short hall to another room. "Your brother's in there. I've questioned him, and it's not . . . Well, I'll let you find out for yourself." He shook his head with sympathy. "I'm sorry, but the press is going to have a heyday with this when they find out."

Gary shrugged. He was accustomed to the press. In the beginning, there had even been stories about his own possible involvement with Kristin's disappearance—a bunch of utter nonsense. As a result, he didn't pay much attention to their assertions anymore.

Gary waited until Detective Lowder left the room before seating himself opposite his brother. A small rectangular table separated them. Its shiny surface reflected a man Gary hardly recognized as himself. Everything had changed since his Kristin, his sunshine, had disappeared.

"Have they arrested you?" Gary asked after a long silence.

His brother shifted uncomfortably, his big bulk barely fitting under the table. The balding top of his head shone with perspiration. "No. I'm just here for questioning. I—I had Lesa call you because I wanted you to know before the papers got hold of the story." After meeting his eyes briefly, Phil stared at the glossy surface of the table, too, and Gary wondered if his older brother could recognize himself there.

"It's true then." Gary had hoped it was all some terrible mistake.

Phil met his eyes. "I did have some problems in Texas—way before I moved to Florida and met Lesa. I didn't tell anyone, except for Mom."

Some problems? Some problems? Gary wanted to yell. Was that what he called destroying a child's life? Instead he mumbled, "She knew?" Their mother had never been the same after their father had walked out on them when Gary was a baby, but she had done her best to raise them in the Church. Gary felt close to her, yet all these years she had never alluded to any family secrets. Of course, they didn't see her much anymore since she had moved to North Carolina ten years ago with her new husband.

"Yes."

"Why?" Gary couldn't understand how his brother could hurt a child—any child.

Phil's hazel eyes filled with moisture. "There are a million reasons," he said dully. "But none of them mean anything in the end."

"They'd mean something to me." Gary's heart felt like it was in a vise and that every hope he had left was being squeezed slowly out.

Phil's fleshy lips twisted into an uncontrolled expression of disgust, the same disgust Gary was sure showed on his own face.

"Our father left when I was ten," Phil began, swallowing hard. "Mom had to go to work and left us with the neighbor lady. You— you were little, always with the sitter. But I had to hang out with her sons who were eleven and thirteen. They weren't good examples. They did things to me—I learned things I shouldn't have. I didn't tell Mom—I knew how much she needed the free baby-sitting. I didn't have anyone to go to. The experiences with them twisted my perceptions. I got more involved." He went on with details that sickened Gary further. He saw clearly how actions that might have begun as childish curiosity had become a perverse adult addiction.

Gary pressed his fingers into the table top. Had the entire world gone insane? Of course it had. That was the only explanation for everything that had occurred. He had believed that with Kristin's disappearance nothing could damage his heart further, not even his wife's turning away from him, not even her blame.

He was wrong.

Phil was his big brother, the man he'd looked up to and respected from a distance all his life. The man he had longed to be close to, the man who had become a good friend and guide these past few years. The knowledge of what his brother had done pierced deeply into his wounded soul.

He raised a hand and Phil's voice stopped. Gary made his expression hard. "Where's Kristin?"

Phil's eyes grew wide and hurt. "I knew you'd think that. That's why I had to bring you here. I didn't hurt Kristin." His voice grew stronger. "I swear to you, Gary—I never touched any of your girls, or mine. I did my time in jail twenty years ago. I haven't done anything wrong since. I've repented and have been forgiven. I still see a counselor every few weeks to make sure I stay well. Lesa helps me . . ."

Gary stood, knocking his chair backward with the violence of his motion. "You should have told me!" he snarled. "You had no right to put my children in that kind of danger. I should have known! Why do you expect me to believe you now?"

"I—I didn't hurt Kristin!" Phil was crying now, but his denial fell on deaf ears. Gary wondered how much his little girl had cried the night she had been taken.

"Don't!" Gary screamed. "Don't!" He shook his fist at his brother. "I have only one thing to say: if I find any proof that you had anything to do with Kristin's abduction, I will kill you with my bare hands!"

Gary left the police station feeling soiled and depressed. All the stuff he'd learned in church about forgiveness and judging others suddenly took on new, almost ominous meaning. His brother had molested children, had gone to jail for it. Who knew if he were really cured of this despicable tendency? From what Gary had read, less than a few percent of child molesters ever permanently reformed. If anything could change a man, the gospel could, and Phil appeared to be dedicated to the gospel, but how could Gary ever be sure of his heart? When he thought of all the many times his children had gone over to Phil's house, even slept over, he began to feel ill. As he reached his car, he leaned over near the pavement and retched.

Thoughts rocketed through his head. How could Phil, and especially Lesa, sit on the couch in their living room and offer comfort for Kristin's disappearance when they knew Phil's secret? Angie considered Lesa her best friend and she would feel betrayed—again. First by her husband for not keeping Kristin safe, and now by her best friend for allowing her children to be in a potentially dangerous situation without any warning.

How would he tell Angie this? The news would destroy her, or at the very least, put another wedge between them.

Gary sat in his car, head in his hands, and cried.

★ ★ ★

I could do nothing but watch helplessly as my father sobbed like a small child. I had never seen him this way. He had always been so strong and confident. Now here he was crying as though he would cry himself right out of existence. I wished I could tell him these terrible moments would pass. I wished I could tell him about Heaven and the joy that awaited. I wished I could transmit to him the feelings I'd experienced in Jesus' arms. Of course, I couldn't.

I knew he was furious. I was angry at Uncle Phil myself. But I was no longer mortal and my anger and suffering were tempered by my knowledge of Heaven and of the unconditional love of Jesus Christ.

I sat in the passenger seat by Dad, and as I did, I became aware of another presence in the car: the comforting Spirit of the Holy Ghost. The Spirit had been with him earlier but had left when he had become so full of hatred toward my uncle. Now He was back, and I knew Heavenly Father was aware of my earthly father's pain and loved him even more than I did.

Blinking back tears of thankfulness, I laid my head on my father's shoulder and sighed.

"It's going to be okay, Dad," I whispered. "It's going to be okay."

★ ★ ★

The next day was Meghan's sixteenth birthday. For a while, I thought everyone would forget, but Benjamin and Jacky got up early and blew up two packages of balloons—enough to fill Meghan's room so that she would be covered when she awoke. Mom made Meghan's favorite breakfast: waffles with fresh strawberries and whipped cream. Meghan actually smiled.

I hadn't really been tempted to taste food in all the times I'd visited my family. I mean, I'd had other things on my mind. But the waffles and fresh strawberries brought back so many wonderful memories that I reached out for one without thinking. My hand passed right through the stack. I had to laugh. I tried to lean over and take a bite from Meghan's plate, but I couldn't do that either.

"I made you a big card," Benjamin said, drawing my attention away from the waffles. "Since Kristin couldn't."

Meghan's face paled, but she accepted the card. For every birthday I always made a card for whoever's birthday it was, a card that specifically celebrated their past year. Well, it was more a scrap booklet than a card. It took me a long time, too. For Meghan's card, I'd been saving comic strips about meeting boys and secretly liking them. I'd found large lips that I'd planned to write "sweet sixteen and never been kissed" under. I'd also organized a list of new romance titles I knew she'd love, and had planned to put in highlights from our summer camping trip. Seemed sort of silly to me now, but I knew my family enjoyed my cards; they never threw them away, but brought out the old ones at every birthday.

"See, I used the things she had in that box under her bed," Benjamin said. "I don't know why she put these lips in, though."

I thought Meghan was going to cry, but she hugged Benjamin fiercely. "Thank you," she whispered. "Thank you." Dad and Mom were wiping away their own tears. I was smiling like crazy. It was my most triumphant card yet, and I hadn't even been the one to finish it.

"I like the cards she made for me the best," Jacky said, placing a box on the table. "Look at me playing the piano. And see that ghost she put over me? That's to show how really scared I was to play in that recital. But look, there's me playing with the ghost after." She giggled.

In a minute everyone else went to get their cards. They laughed and pointed out the highlights while I sat on the counter by the sink and watched them, feeling pleased. Maybe healing my family would be easier than I thought.

"Oh no," Mom said suddenly, glancing at the apple clock by the sink. "We have to get to school. Meghan, you're already late. Come on, kids, out to the car. Gary, you'll be late, too."

As the kids scrambled for books, Mom brought out a medium-sized package. Meghan's eyes lit up.

"Hey," Benjamin said, "she can't open presents until tonight."

"This isn't a present," Mom said. "It something I ordered for all of you. Came in the mail." Out of the box she drew cumbersome watches and strapped one to Benjamin's wrist. "They're called GPS personal locators."

"What's GPS mean?" Jacky asked, holding up her arm.

Mom put hers on. "Global Positioning System. They work through satellites. Very easy, really. I read all the instructions yesterday and got them set up. All we have to do it put them on, and your dad and I'll always know where you are if we need to. We can also page you with a short message."

"You mean like in *Spy Kids* or something?" Benjamin asked. "Cool."

"Sort of. I'm going to lock them on your wrists. If you get lost, we'll be able to find you. And if you ever feel you're in danger, push these two buttons at the same time. But don't use them unless you're really in danger because it'll contact the company, who will then call us and the police. But don't try to take them off unless you're home with us," Mom warned. "Or we'll be notified."

The younger children didn't mind the tracking devices, and in fact were excited about all the features, but the light in Meghan's eyes went completely out. "I don't want to wear one," she muttered, keeping her arms behind her.

Mom's face was like iron. "I don't care what you want," she said. "I won't lose another child."

"Honey," Dad began.

Mom whirled on him. "Make her put it on!" When he didn't answer, she added, "Please!"

Dad's gaze shifted to Meghan. "Your mother's right, Meg. We need to know that you're okay. Put this on for us. It won't be forever."

Meghan's eyes narrowed and her face flushed a deep red. "What if I want to be kidnapped!" she said tightly, her voice rising with each word. "What if I'd rather be kidnapped than stay here with all of you!" There was a stunned silence, then Meghan continued, "It's all my fault. I deserved to die, not her. I should have taken care of her!"

Dad's eyes opened wide in shock, and Mom made a little noise in her throat. She held out her arms but Meghan turned away. "If I'm going to be forced to wear that thing, I'm getting on long-sleeves. I don't want anyone to see it."

My parents watched her storm out, and only Jacky's sobs brought their attention back to the present. Dad picked up Jacky. "Come on, Ben. Let's get out to the car. Meghan's already late so I'm going to take you two and come back for her." He looked at my mom. "You stay with Meghan. I'll be right back."

"I'll take her," Mom said. "You don't need to come back. You don't want to be late for work."

Dad looked at her for a moment, undecided. I wanted to yell at my mom to let him help, to let him be her knight in shining armor, at least for that moment. Surely she could see how much he needed that.

"Okay," Dad said at last. "Call me if you need me."

Still carrying Jacky, he walked to the garage door. He didn't offer my mother a goodbye kiss and she didn't go after him to claim one. I wondered how long that had been going on. I hadn't paid close enough attention these past weeks.

I heaved a great sigh. "You are all so stubborn. Don't you know I just want you to be happy? Don't you know that?" I was yelling, but they couldn't hear; and if they could have heard, they wouldn't believe me because I was crying. Crying because of my frustration with their pain. I could feel so much of it right then. Yet it seemed I could give them little solace.

What a miserable failure! I couldn't even hug or hold them, not so they'd feel it. I decided then that sometimes being the only spirit in a roomful of mortals was about as much fun as watching four-year-olds play soccer.

Chapter Eight

I returned to Heaven after that because I'd had enough of Earth and all its mortal turmoil—for the moment anyway. Actually, wrestling alligators or facing a wild tiger sounded a lot more appealing.

Grandmother was swimming in the lake in back of our house, laughing with Merriam, my Alaskan cousin who had lived on Earth only a few short months.

I made my white robe change into a bathing suit and jumped in with them. "Hey, this water's clean!" Most lake water I'd swam in was hazy and full of fish and green growing things.

"Yeah, just the way I like it." Grandma stretched out in the water, floating on her back.

I laughed, lifting my face to the radiant sky. This was certainly Paradise!

After we'd had our fill, we lay on the soft grass to dry, which was funny because I knew my hair was only wet because I wanted it to be.

"Can we make anything happen here?" I asked.

"Well, yes, we can make it appear to happen," Grandma said. "But take alcohol for instance. There are a lot of people in Spirit Prison who were addicted on Earth. They can imagine up a nice fine goblet of wine to drink, but it won't satisfy their craving."

"But their bodies aren't here, so how can they have a craving?"

"Mortal addictions profoundly affect the spirit. It takes time to recover."

Merriam shivered. "One of the new arrivals in Spirit Prison who I was assigned to teach today is a big smoker. He's having a hard time of it. He wants to smoke—craves it desperately. He found he could whip up some cigarettes, but it wasn't the same at all. There was no nicotine in it to soothe his craving, and if there had been, he wouldn't have been able to ingest it anyway in spirit form. It was a terrible thing to watch."

"He'll be all right soon enough," Grandma said, placing a comforting hand on her shoulder. "He'll receive a lot of help, if he wants it." I laid my head on her lap, glad that I could feel her and she could feel me. Not being able to touch or be felt by my family back on Earth was very difficult, especially with Meghan, who wouldn't let anyone reach out to her.

I thought how odd it should have been, me lying on the grass with my grandmother, who didn't look like a grandmother, and my cousin, who should have been a baby. That made me ask, "Grandma, when the Millennium comes, they say mothers will be able to raise their babies and children—the ones who've died. But Merriam was a baby when she died. That means she'll have to start all over again. I don't know about her, but I sort of like being grown up."

"I think it'll be neat having all those experiences," Merriam said, tossing her dark hair. "I didn't get to really live the first time on Earth like you did. I mean, thirteen is pretty close to being an adult compared to my short two months."

Grandma's bright laughter rang out over the lake. "Well, I'm not sure exactly how it will work. There's still so much to get straight, and I have to confess this isn't something that's worried me. But I am sure that both you and Merriam will get to be with your families, one way or the other. We have the promise of that. It's not something we need to worry about."

"The Millennium would be a wonderful time to grow up," Merriam said. "Lambs lying down with the lion, and so forth."

"No kidnappers or child molesters," I added without thinking. When the others stared at me, I added, "Sorry, that just came out."

"You're thinking about your uncle," Grandma said.

I nodded. "This is ripping my family apart."

"They'll be okay. We are all praying for them."

Her words were a comfort. I knew our Father heard the prayers, because he'd sent the Comforter, the Holy Ghost, to be with my earthly father.

Merriam suddenly looked behind Grandmother. "Hey, look who's here."

I lifted my head from Grandmother's lap and saw Randy

coming toward us, dressed in brilliant white pants and shirt.

"He came by earlier, too," Grandma said, "but you weren't here."

"I needed to stay with my family," I murmured, coming to my feet.

Merriam arose, clad now in a bright yellow dress. "I'm going to check on that new spirit and see how he's doing," she said with a smile. "This outfit should cheer him up; yellow is his favorite color." She gave me a hug and disappeared. Grandma winked and followed her.

I felt awkward standing there alone in my swimming suit. Quickly, I willed a change to a dress of midnight blue. The color had always been my favorite, and it fit the melancholy I was feeling.

Randy didn't say anything, but took my hands and reached out his thoughts. I met him willingly. It was good to tell him all my doubts about my family ever recovering. "It all seems so odd," I mused aloud. "Almost like I'm being held to Earth. I love them so much, but right now . . ."

"You need a break," he said. "All work and no play, does not make a happy life. Even Alma in the *Book of Mormon* wrote about spirits taking rest in Paradise."

The verse came to me from his mind: "And then shall it come to pass, that the spirits of those who are righteous are received into a state of happiness, which is called paradise, a state of rest, a state of peace, where they shall rest from all their troubles and from all care, and sorrow."

"I thought that here, work *was* play," I said, giving him my best smirk.

His expression was serious. "For a lot of people. But come, I want to show you something."

He took my hand and we started walking . . . up. Then we were rushing through the infinity of space. It was wonderful, like I imagined it would be to zoom about in a spaceship. After a time, we poised over what looked like a huge mass of white sparkling clouds. "What is it?" I asked, gazing in awe and wonder.

"A nebula."

I made a face. "And what's a nebula exactly, Mr. Smarty-pants?

I haven't even finished eighth-grade science, if you'll remember, and this was never my field of study."

Randy let out a big laugh. "It's a nursery. A star nursery. The helium is fusing together to create hydrogen and so on—that's why all the light. Thermonuclear reactions. Very violent, released as light. There'll be another star here soon. It's actually in its second cycle. A star was here once many, many years ago that blew up and this is what's left. That's why some heavier elements are present. Come on, let's get closer."

We zoomed closer until we were engulfed in sparkling clouds. There seemed to be no beginning or end to them. I focused my attention on the clouds, my spirit eyes seeing things I wouldn't have been able to with ordinary mortal eyes. I could actually experience the reactions taking place, all in order and according to the Father's plan. I wanted to cry in wonder. "I want to know everything," I whispered.

Randy laughed again. "I know. That's just how I felt the first time I saw one of these. This will be new solar system some day, complete with planets, a star, and asteroids. Like the solar system where Earth is."

"Let's go there," I suggested. "To the Moon and the Sun. And I always wanted to see if my science teacher was right when he said that modern astronomers believe Pluto is only one big asteroid in a field of asteroids instead of a planet like my parents were taught."

He took my hand again and we went together. It was undescribable. I mean, I could try, but words can't suffice for something so extraordinary. I understood now what it meant when people said that the glory of God was intelligence. It was light, it was truth. All truths—physics, biology, religion. Everything is connected.

"It's so organized," I said at one point. "Just like Heaven."

Randy nodded. "Yep. Everything has its purpose and its reason for being. Like you and me. The only real confusion we have in the Afterlife is in the Spirit Prison, where people really aren't sure what they want."

"But what does God do with spirits who never want to work or learn?"

Randy's face grew thoughtful. "You have to remember that

after resurrection and judgment, we'll be assigned to different kingdoms. Wherever that is, it will be where we would be the most comfortable."

That was a big comfort. I'd met so many people in Heaven and it was hard for me, with my limited experience, to understand how order was maintained. I wondered which kingdom of Heaven was the one where people lay around all day doing nothing. I knew that wherever it was, I didn't want to be there. No, I wanted to achieve the Celestial Glory, the top Kingdom, so that I could be with my family forever, and so that I could progress and learn enough to be like my Father in Heaven. I craved knowledge and learning as I had never imagined possible. I sincerely wished that back on Earth I had paid more attention to school than I had to daydreams.

All in all, it was some field trip. When we returned, I suspected that I was already half in love with Randy, but I wasn't about to admit it. I wanted time to meet others and to see the rest of Heaven. Meanwhile Randy and I would date. The thought made me laugh so much that I accidentally fell into the lake behind Grandmother's when we appeared. My dress didn't even get wet, but it was funny. I noticed the dress was white now, as brilliant as Randy's outfit. So was my mood.

"I guess it's time to go back to work," I said, feeling as though I could single-handedly change the entire world.

Randy nodded, his eyes never leaving mine. "My thoughts and prayers will be with you."

I'd heard people say that on Earth before, and have to admit that I seriously thought they sounded fake. But I *felt* Randy's sincerity, and I knew prayers were answered.

"Thank you," I said.

He leaned over and kissed me softly on the lips—my first real kiss. I had never experienced anything so deeply.

I remembered learning in church that those who died without a chance to marry on Earth would have the chance afterward. How grateful I was to know that now! I knew the emotions I was beginning to feel for Randy were intense and far-reaching—the beginning of a true relationship.

Smiling to myself, I walked slowly up to the house.

Chapter Nine

Lesa had tried to call uncounted times over the five months since Phil was first questioned. Angie had let the answering machine pick up each time. She missed Lesa more than she would admit, but she couldn't forgive her either. Since the newspapers had picked up the story about Phil, two neighborhood children and their parents had brought charges against him for molestation. The entire Orem neighborhood reeled with shock. At church things were even worse. Nobody knew what to believe, though Phil was quietly released from his calling as a Boy Scout leader. Phil adamantly denied the new charges, and as far as Angie knew, Lesa had stood by him.

Angie honestly didn't know if Phil had anything to do with Kristin's disappearance. The police had no solid proof either way. They had checked out every place that Phil, Jay, and Wade had lived. In Washington, the only state where Wade had lived besides Utah, there had been nothing suspicious. In Angie's mind and in the view of the police, Wade was no longer a suspect.

In Florida, where Phil and Jay had both spent several years, there had been four unsolved kidnappings and killings of young girls that police thought might have been committed by the same man. In all of the instances, the girls had been abducted from or near a swimming pool, and later their bodies had been found in a deserted place clad only in thin white nightgowns. They had been raped, abused, and even tortured in ways that made Angie cringe.

But the first of these deaths had taken place before Phil had moved there from Texas, and the last had taken place after Jay had moved to Kansas before coming to Utah. Police figured that Jay could have returned to Florida to commit a crime to throw off suspicion, or Phil could have gone earlier than believed, but neither idea could be verified.

In Texas, where Phil had lived before moving to Florida, there was a lengthy list of Phil's victims, but he had served time in prison for those offenses. The biggest surprise was in Kansas where police found that Jay had been accused of raping a young neighbor girl. He had eventually been acquitted. Neither Phil nor Jay had alibis for the night Kristin was missing, since Jay had decided not to go to the movie he and Wade had planned to see, and Phil had been at work alone. Jay's young age—he would have been about eight years old at the time of the first killing—made it unlikely that he could be the perpetrator, so Phil remained the top suspect. The idea of Phil hurting Kristin brought both and Angie and Gary endless pain.

Gary spent less time out searching now, but when he wasn't at work he was in Kristin's room on the Internet, tracking down cases of missing girls and trying to make some reasonable connection. He believed Kristin had been taken by the same man who committed the swimming pool kidnappings in Florida, though he hadn't yet found anything solid to prove his theory—or the man's identity.

"I don't know who to believe anymore," Angie murmured. She was staring out her front window at the dancing curtains of bright March snow. Her lawn and driveway were completely covered now and the street showed only a spot or two of blacktop. A lone figure toiled along the sidewalk, bent forward into the wind. Angie turned away, sinking to the couch. Her eyes looked out onto her living room, but in her mind she still saw the thick flurries of white flakes. Her mind and body felt numb.

The ringing of the doorbell shook her from her reverie. Plastering a smile on her face, she went to the door. "Hi, Dale. Nice to see you." Or it would have been, if she could feel anything beyond the numbness.

"I came to check on how you were doing."

A rush of half-expected agony came coursing from her heart up to her throat where she squashed it with a tight swallow. "I'm fine."

His glance was sympathetic. "Do you want to talk?"

"Actually, I'm going to get Meghan from school. Her cousin moved to Salt Lake to live with friends. He goes to high school there now." Not that she would have allowed him to give Meghan a ride home anyway, after the revelation of his father's record. Though Garen was actually Lesa's son from her first marriage before she was a member of the Church, Angie no longer trusted him or what Phil may have taught him over the years.

"I wondered if the kids would hassle him," Dale commented.

Angie nodded. "Meghan said they did."

"Did he get along well with Phil?"

She nodded, clenching her lips so they wouldn't curl with the bitterness her brother-in-law's name dredged up from the depths of her stomach.

"I heard that Lesa was teaching the other two children at home."

Angie shrugged. She hadn't known that, but as always, she hardened herself against any softening she might feel toward Lesa.

"At least they're still young," Dale said. "It's easier to teach them in grade school. It's worse when they get to high school. Or college. I can tell you that. My students are so thirsty for knowledge, it's about all I can do to give them what they want each morning."

Silence fell between them, but it was comfortable, without the terrible, aching loss that marked Angie's relationship with her husband. The realization made her look at Dale objectively.

He was a good-looking man. Though not as tall as Gary, he had a head full of wavy dark brown hair, expressive gray eyes, and smooth, almost perfect facial features, except for a slightly narrow chin. Once, in what seemed like another lifetime, Angie had thought herself in love with him. She wondered where she would be now if she had never met Gary. Would a life with Dale have spared them both pain?

Perhaps. But could she trade her children for a pain-free existence? No. A fierce love for both her husband and her children leapt to life in her broken heart. She knew she wouldn't change the past. How could she wish she had never known Kristin?

Oh, she cried in silence. *Oh, I just want to find her!*

"It's pretty hairy out there," Dale was saying. "I could drive you."

"Well, I was going to stop by my mechanic's shop after. He fixed my car when Kristin—" She swallowed hard. "A while ago. But the engine light went right back on the next day. I never had time to go and see what was wrong. It's running pretty badly now. Gary's out of town for business—they gave him a promotion, you know, and I guess I could use his car until he gets home, but I like my van."

"I could take it in for you." Dale gazed at her earnestly, and she could see how much he wanted to help. Everyone in the neighborhood had been just as kind. Oh, if only her heart could gain more comfort from their sincere offerings!

"Well, I was just going to stop by in between picking up Meghan and the others. I wasn't going to leave the van or anything. Just talk to him. He said last time that I wouldn't likely have any more problems."

Dale nodded decisively. "This is what we'll do. You pick up Meghan and stop by the shop. I'll follow you so that if your mechanic needs to keep the van I can drive you to pick up Benjamin and Jacky."

Angie felt tension ease out of her body, as though a burden had been lifted from her shoulders. It was easier to let Dale take over, and his wanting to do so made her feel cared for. Gary usually offered to see to the car, but between working, business trips, and the endless search for Kristin's kidnapper, he had spent little time talking with her in the past months. She knew much of that was her fault. Since discovering Phil's past, their relationship had become even more strained.

At the high school, Meghan was waiting outside in the snow. Angie had told her not to, fearing her daughter would come down with an illness, but Meghan didn't listen to her anymore. She was constantly sullen and morose, withdrawn. At school she had started hanging out with friends Angie didn't approve of, and at home they had to constantly tell her to turn her music down.

At least Meghan had her coat on. She always wore that to hide the GPS locator they forced her to wear. Angie still didn't understand her daughter's reluctance to wear the device. In fact, she didn't understand anything about her daughter. They had been seeing a grief counselor for the past five months, but Meghan hadn't opened up. Angie had told Meghan repeatedly that she hadn't been responsible for Kristin's disappearance, and she hoped Meghan believed her. But how could she, when deep inside Angie did partly blame Meghan? It was stupid, terribly stupid, and infantile, but no matter how she repressed the emotions, they remained. *If only they'd stayed together*, she thought. *If only Gary had been a minute earlier.*

Angie dug her fingernails into the palm of her hand, cutting off the emotions. What mattered now was Meghan, not Angie's irrational feelings.

"What's *he* doing here?" Meghan said as she caught sight of Dale in the car behind them.

"Put your safety belt on please." Angie slipped the van into gear. "Brother Loveridge is going with us to the mechanic's in case we need to leave the van."

"Why couldn't Dad do it?"

"He hasn't come home from the sales trip yet."

"Oh."

"Did you have a nice day?" Angie asked.

Meghan pushed up her coat sleeve and pointedly rubbed at the skin around the GPS device. "I guess."

"Anything fun happen?"

"No."

Angie sighed. Once they had talked about everything, but now there seemed to be nothing left for them to say. Like with her and Gary, miles seemed to separate them. She wasn't even sure where in the house Gary was sleeping at night.

At the mechanic shop, Big Ned Lyman scratched the base of the grizzled beard on his lower cheek. "The engine light again?" he asked. "And you say it went on right after you last brought it in. Well, that shouldn't be. I mean somethin' coulda happened—there's about a million things it could be, but happenin' that soon . . . we've replaced all your sensors in the last year . . . hmm." His eyes lifted to the passenger side of the van where Meghan was talking to one of the mechanics. "My nephew there was supposed to take care of it. But I have to tell you the truth, Angie, he ain't that reliable. He's a good mechanic and all. I taught him good enough. But he's sort of a scatterbrain, like his old man. Why, the other day he was supposed to do a lady's brakes and he just forgot. She was so mad, I had to give her a discount. That boy's always got his head in the clouds."

Angie frowned. That "boy" as Big Ned called him had to be

over thirty, despite his baby face. "That's tough," she commented. "You'd think he'd learn responsibility at his age."

Big Ned nodded, shifting his bulk. "He was okay at first—very responsible, quick learner—but it's getting to be a bit of a problem lately. I might have to let him go. But he's family, and you know how that is. I think his heart's good, though. He was just never taught how to work. Been fired a lot. Girlfriend left him some years back. His mom said that hurt him pretty bad. I keep thinking if I can help him succeed, it'll make a difference."

Angie noticed Dale coming into the shop. He pointed at his watch. "Oh, I've got to go pick up my kids from the elementary school. Should I bring it back or leave it?"

"Leave it, if you can. I'll look at it myself right away. And if it's the sensors or something we already fixed, there'll be no charge."

Angie smiled one of her now-rare smiles. "I knew that, Big Ned. You're the most honest mechanic I know."

He took a cigarette from his pocket. "You take care now." His eyes flicked over Dale Loveridge, but he didn't ask the question in his brown eyes.

"This is our neighbor," Angie felt compelled to explain. "He offered to help me—us—bring down the van. Gary's out of town."

"Nice to meet you." Big Ned transferred his cigarette to his other fingers and shook Dale's proffered hand.

"Meghan, get your books," Angie called. "We're leaving the van."

★ ★ ★

Meghan was trying to make sense of her math assignment when a man appeared at the car window. She recognized Big Ned's nephew, the mechanic who had thought she was seventeen. She reached over and twisted her mother's key once so that she had power to roll down the window.

"Hi," he said.

"Hi." Meghan waited for him to ask about Kristin. Everyone always did. And she hated it. Did they think she wouldn't tell them if Kristin came home? Or maybe they never liked Meghan. Maybe it was only Kristin they cared about. The thought consumed her with guilt, and she felt a telltale redness seep into her face.

He smiled at her gently, his light brown eyes seeming to delve into her heart. "It's nice to see you again."

"You too." He was still good-looking, but Meghan noticed his face under the disorderly brown hair was rounder than she remembered, and except for the square chin, which looked strong and competent, she might have thought him too baby-faced to be handsome. She wondered how old he was.

"You're Meghan, right?"

She was flattered that he remembered. "And you're Lucas."

"Call me Lu," he said. "Just thought I'd come over to say hello. Sorry you're having trouble with the van again."

Meghan shrugged. "It's okay." She waited for the inevitable question about Kristin. Lu knew about her. Like all of her mom's friends, his uncle, Big Ned, had been at the candlelight service. She didn't know if Lu had been there, but he would have at least heard about the kidnapping.

His eyes went to her math book in her lap. "Algebra?" he asked.

"Yeeees," she groaned.

He reached for the book. "I can help you, if you want. Which problem are you on?"

Meghan pointed, and Lu studied her attempt to solve the problem. "Hey that's easy. Just think of it like this. If the whole cubed or squared number is negative, it'll have parenthesis around it so then the final answer of the square would be positive and the cubed negative. But if you don't have parenthesis, it just means the whole thing is negative or if something's before it, treat it like a minus."

"Could you say that again?" she asked.

He explained it once more, reaching for the pencil in her lap to show her on paper. Meghan blushed as his hand touched her leg, but he didn't seem to notice. After three times explaining the concept, Meghan began to understand.

"Thanks," she said with a smile. "That makes sense—finally."

He stared at her. "You should smile more often. You're a very pretty girl."

Meghan felt her face growing red again. She glanced down at her math book and didn't reply.

His hand covered hers where she balanced the math book on the window opening of the door. "Look, I know you've been through a lot," he said. "I know exactly what that's like. And I just wanted to tell you to hold on, that it does get better. I been through it before. I once lost someone very close to me."

"You did?" Her eyes met his.

"Fiancé. She died. Broke me up for a long time."

"I'm sorry."

"Me, too."

Just then Angie called her over. Lu smiled and withdrew his hand, leaving her flesh suddenly cold where he had been touching her.

"Thanks," she told Lu. "For help with the math. And everything else."

"You take care." With another boyish grin he was gone.

Meghan collected her books and joined her mother and Brother Loveridge. "I see you were talking to Mr. Lyman's nephew," her mom said as they walked outside into the snow.

"He's nice. He helped me with my math." Meghan wondered if her mom would have a problem with that; she seemed to have a problem with almost everything these days.

"I'm pretty good at math." Brother Loveridge opened the front passenger side door for Angie. Meghan tugged the back door open before he could offer. She liked Brother Loveridge but felt uncomfortable around him. "I could help you if you want."

"Thanks," Meghan mumbled. "But my dad usually helps me. When does he get home, Mom?"

"Not till tomorrow."

"Oh."

While Brother Loveridge and her mom talked in the front seat, Meghan stared silently out her window. The passing world looked strangely unfamiliar with its blanket of snow. Slowly, she became aware of her reflection in the window, but for a moment she thought it was Kristin. *Where are you now?* she thought. *Are you cold? Is your heart as numb as mine is without you?* A tear rolled down her cheek before she could stop it. Impatiently, she wiped it away. But the vision of her sister lying beneath a layer of harsh, unforgiving snow didn't leave her mind.

It's all my fault, she thought. *It's still all my fault.* She absently fiddled with the GPS locator watch on her arm, secretly glad for the safety it represented, but also feeling deeply guilty for having it when Kristin had been the one who'd needed it most.

★ ★ ★

I willed Meghan to see me in the car, but she didn't. She stared out the window and rubbed a tear from her cheek. I reached for her hand, but mine passed right through hers. That's right, I was back in the physical world, where I was only a spirit. What I wouldn't give for a body right then! My body.

"Meghan, you have to listen to me," I said. "You're in danger." I glanced at Brother Loveridge and then at my mom. They were still happily talking.

I turned back to Meghan. "Can you hear me? Meghan? Oh, please listen!" She didn't. I sat back in the seat, a little perturbed at being so ignored. I forgot to keep my spirit moving with the car and I came out the back end, floating in a seated position over the white road. I stared after the car and the black tire marks it sliced into the fresh snow. The car behind theirs drove through me, and for a brief instance, I was seated on a man's lap before I was in the road again.

"Drat!" I almost went back to Heaven, but I knew that my family was my job, however out of tune with me they were at the moment, and I did want to see them happy again.

"I wonder what Dad's doing." I willed myself to find him and again I began to rush through the intervening solid objects. I had learned to control my flight better in the past months, though, and I only saw snatches of people and places before I arrived next to my father, who was sitting on a barstool with a drink in front of him.

"A sales convention," he was saying to a long-haired brunette sitting next to him. "I work as a manager for a furniture company and we're here to show our new products."

I had no idea where "here" was except a bar—probably in the hotel where he was staying. He was slowly sipping a dark liquid in a clear mug.

"You here alone?" The woman asked, lowering her eyes to her wine glass. Her thick lashes made shadows on her white, delicate cheeks. There was no lipstick on her glass, but her lips were obviously painted. I would have wondered more about how she achieved that moist, perfect look, if I hadn't been gawking at the amount of cleavage she was showing from the front of her sleeveless black dress.

I saw my dad noticing this very thing. He glanced determinedly back to his mug. Were he and Mom still in separate bedrooms? Had they become even further apart during these past months? Would he be able to reject this woman's obvious advances?

"Well, I'm here with some others in the company," he mumbled.

Glancing around, I saw that I was not the only spirit in the bar. Three others sat next to men who appeared half drunk. As the men lifted their beers, they tried to drink from the mugs, sometimes half disappearing into the drunken mortal bodies. I wasn't sure what joy the spirits derived from the experience, but it made me sick to watch. I also saw other spirits who seemed to be urging the men to drink more. Were these Satan's followers, the ones who had never been given a body but were allowed on Earth to tempt mortal men?

And what about my father? Sure enough, there were four spirits near him, but they backed off as I approached, muttering and sneering at me. Another faceless spirit whispered in the woman's ear like an intimate friend.

The bartender, a small-headed, big-chested man with shaggy brown hair nearly down to his shoulders, sidled up to the other side of the bar. "Need anything?" he asked, leering at the brunette. She smiled and tucked her hair behind her ears in a gesture much like my mother used. I saw with small triumph that her earlobes were connected to the side of her head instead of swinging free like my mother's. I knew my dad had a preference for my mom's ears, and that he had noticed the brunette's gesture.

"I'll have another and—" she glanced at my dad "—another for him—whatever he's having. My treat."

With a rude smirk on his thin lips, the bartender pulled out a bottle of rootbeer and began to open it.

My dad stood up suddenly, downing the rest of his soft drink. "No, thanks. Really, I have to get going. I need to check in with my wife and children. Nice to meet you, though. See you around." Face blushing crimson, he fled.

I watched him go, as did the brunette and the bartender. But while they were obviously astounded and a little disgusted, I was bursting with pride at my father's actions. It couldn't have been an easy thing for him, but he hadn't stayed and flirted like many men might have done—or worse. He had fled like Joseph in the Bible. Like he'd always taught us to do.

I started to follow him, but ran into another spirit I hadn't noticed before, who smiled at me and radiated a sense of well-being. "All is well. He listened."

I realized the Father had sent another to warn my dad of the danger here. "Thank you," I said.

"He's a good man."

I knew that. My mother was good, too. What I didn't understand was why they couldn't go on with their lives. Grandmother thought it was because they were too caught up with my death and not focusing on the reality of eternal families, but I didn't know what to think. If only they could pray to accept the Lord's will—and honestly mean it—maybe then I could ease their pain.

Chapter Ten

After checking on Dad and seeing him at work with his fellow employees—all male to my relief—I returned to Mom and Meghan. The girls were doing their homework at the kitchen counter and Benjamin was banging out his half hour of piano practice in the adjoining family room. I was glad to see they had started lessons again. I'd been the best at it, but the others had to take lessons, too. Mom said it was to teach us responsibility and how to work, and since we didn't have a farm, the piano would teach us that. Meghan had groaned that she would rather plow a field or bale hay any day.

I found I missed practicing and vowed to start doing it again once I went back to Paradise. The concertos would likely be easier to learn there. Maybe they'd even let me play in the Music Center with the angel choir.

I sat down by Benjamin. "No, no," I said. "It's this finger. There you go. See how much smoother that is? Good. Now go through it again . . . Okay, don't," I said as he shut the book. "Then how about that sonata by Beethoven?" Dad had printed off the "Sonata in F minor" by Beethoven from the Internet over a year ago, and it had always been one of my favorites. *Beethoven*, I thought absently. *I wonder if he's in Paradise.*

To my surprise, Benjamin pulled out that very sheet. "All right!" I said. "Now remember to count correctly."

He began to play, making a lot of mistakes at first, but I leaned over and put my hands over his, willing them to guide his moves. I'm not sure how much I influenced him, if any, but I could tell he had been practicing at least some on the song.

Suddenly, I became aware of my mother standing over us. My hands fell still and after a few more notes, the music ceased. Benjamin stared up at my mother.

"I've never heard you play so well," she said. "You're as good as—you sound great. Thank you for playing that."

Benjamin stood and hugged her. "I was practicing it as a surprise for you."

Mom wiped a tear with the back of her forefinger. "Look, I'm going to pick up the car. Big Ned called and said it was just the sensor they were supposed to have fixed the last time."

"He'd better not be charging us," Meghan said from her stool at the counter.

"He's not. It was just a misunderstanding apparently. His nephew thought he was supposed to reset it instead of replace it. Anyway, they dropped everything to fix it, and it'll be ready by the time I get there. Brother Loveridge has been kind enough to offer to drive me to get the car."

Not him again! I thought.

"Will you be okay here?" Mom went on. "Meghan, will you watch the kids?"

"I can watch myself," Benjamin said.

Jacky nodded. "Me too. And don't worry. We got our watches on." She lifted her skinny arm which looked really small under the bulk of the GPS locator.

I went with Mom because at that moment I was worried more about her being with Brother Loveridge than anything else. But nothing happened and she was home within a half hour.

"Dad called while you were out," Meghan told her from the piano where she was practicing.

"What did he say?"

"He'll be home late tomorrow."

My mother's brow creased, and I wondered if she would have preferred a more romantic message. What was it with these two? Once they grossed us kids out kissing in front of us, and now they could barely talk to each other.

"Look, I'm going to lie down for a while," my mother said. "After my nap, I'll make dinner. What do you want to eat?"

"Macaroni and cheese!" shouted Benjamin and Jacky. Meghan grimaced and shrugged.

"Okay." Mom turned to leave. "Finish your homework and chores, and I'll be down in an hour to make it."

"Macaroni and cheese?" I asked following her. "Macaroni and

cheese? You never let us eat that when I was here. You said it wasn't healthy." She didn't reply.

In her room, she slipped to her knees. I couldn't hear her thoughts, but I knew they were about me. I imagined she either pictured me alive somewhere as a prisoner in a foreign brothel or in a house with a man who abused me daily. Both of these possibilities would be pure torture for her. "Please bless my baby," she began to moan. She muttered the words over and over.

"Mom, I'm here," I said, "Mom."

She stopped crying, though she still couldn't see me. I wondered if part of her spirit didn't want to see me; then she would have to admit I was dead.

I held her hand as she fell asleep on her knees.

I left Mom and went downstairs. Actually, I floated down through the ceiling. Never would I have to use stairs again! Meghan had finished her piano practice and was going to empty the garbage into the bin outside. I went with her. The snow had stopped, but it showed no signs of melting yet. Meghan's breath made clouds in the crisp air.

She padded barefoot into the snow on her way to the bin that stood on the side of the house near the garage. My sister, the girl who normally had to wear boots, a sweater, and a coat in order to carry out the trash in the snow, not to mention checking her make-up and making sure her hair looked good under her hood. She said you never knew who might be out there to see you.

This time she was right.

"Meghan," hissed a voice.

She glanced up, face paling. My own blood ran cold, or it would have if I'd had any blood. Uncle Phil came from the garage near the newly-repaired van. I knew my father had forbidden his brother to come near my family. Why was he here?

I stood between them. "Just go in the house, Meghan," I ordered.

Uncle Phil walked right through me, larger than I remembered him, and made even more so by the bulky coat and gloves he wore.

"You're not supposed to be here," Meghan said, looking small and uncertain in her jeans and long-sleeved shirt. She held the plastic kitchen garbage can in front of her, poised to toss it at him.

"I want to talk to your mother, but she won't answer my calls. Or Lesa's. It's killing Lesa for your mom not to talk to her."

"I can't do anything about that," Meghan said. "I think you should go."

"But the case has been dropped—the one those kids brought against me. My lawyer told me yesterday that there wasn't enough evidence. He believes they're making it all up—and I swear they did. I never touched those kids. They were just mad because they wanted to cut through my yard on the way to the bus stop. Never mind that they ruined Lesa's garden. You should have seen how they smashed her tomato wires when she wasn't using them."

"That's good they dropped the case," Meghan said.

"My life is still ruined," Uncle Phil continued, barely seeming to notice her comment. His hazel eyes were slightly glazed. "Everyone thinks I did it. Garen wouldn't even come to see Lesa anymore with me there, so she made me move out for a while. She won't listen to me when I say we're going to have to leave the state to get any peace at all."

He was so pathetic that, believe it or not, I actually felt a touch of sadness for him.

"I have to go in." Meghan looked pointedly at her bare feet, now reddened from the snow. She stepped sideways around his bulk so she could enter the garage. I doubted the cold cement was any more comfortable for her feet than the snow.

"Please tell your mom what I said."

"I will." Meghan hurried to the two steps that led to the kitchen. When Uncle Phil followed her to the base of the stairs, she whirled around and held out the garbage can in front of her. "Don't!"

"What's the matter, Meghan?" Uncle Phil said, rubbing his balding head with his gloved fingers. "You know I would never hurt you. How could you think I would hurt you?"

There were tears in Meghan's eyes. She shook her head mutely.

"Oh honey, I know how it looks, but I'm innocent. You don't have to be afraid of me. No matter what happens, I'll always be your uncle. I love you."

Meghan's breathing was coming fast, and she was looking anywhere but at Uncle Phil's face. I know she felt uncomfortable around him, just as I did. Knowing about his past had changed everything.

I had to stop this. "Leave her alone!" I shouted. "Can't you see you're upsetting her? Go away!" I beat at Uncle Phil repeatedly with my fists. "Meghan, just go in the house and lock the door!" She didn't follow my request, but stood there as though frozen to the spot. "Please, someone help me," I muttered.

Help came in the form I least expected. Wade's old friend Jay, the infamous owner of the dirty magazines, came walking by and looked up the drive with interest. "Hey," he said in way of greeting.

"Oh, not you," I muttered. No matter what I did it seemed I couldn't keep Meghan away from people who might hurt her.

"Hi, Jay!" Meghan said a little too eagerly. Uncle Phil stepped away from Meghan. "Just remember what I said, honey. Tell your mom that Lesa really needs her. Please." With a last pleading look, he jogged down the drive to the neighbor's where he had parked his car.

Meghan shifted from foot to foot as Jay reached her side. "Hey, you're not wearing shoes," he said.

"No."

Jay glanced over his shoulder. "Who was that guy anyway?"

"My uncle." Her voice broke on the words.

"Oh, that's why he's so strange."

His lame attempt at humor brought a smile to her face.

"Don't listen to him," I warned Meghan. "He has a record—attempted rape, remember?"

"Do you want to talk about it?" Jay asked.

Meghan shrugged, but before I knew it, she had opened the door to the unlocked van and they were inside. She pulled the blanket Mom always kept there for emergencies around her. "It's just my uncle's a . . ."

"A creep," he finished for her. "I know. I read about it." He ran a hand through his blonde hair. "I have to tell you—I was a little relieved the papers started hounding him. The police haven't been on my case so much since then."

I snorted from my seat in the back. "Oh yeah, think of yourself, Jay. I don't know what I ever saw in you."

"I didn't do it, you know." Jay leaned back on his seat and put his arm along the edge behind Meghan, though not touching her. "I mean, what they said I did in Kansas. That girl, she and I were dating. We were really close, planning to get married even. But her dad didn't like me. He tore us apart. I hated him." There was sincerity in Jay's eyes. Either he was a really good actor, or he was telling the truth. I voted for the former. "He tried to say I took advantage of her, but I didn't. We were in love."

Meghan looked at him, her own troubles momentarily forgotten. "Do you still love her?"

Jay's mouth twisted bitterly. "We moved, they moved. I don't know where she is. But, no, I think it's over between us. If she had fought as hard as I did . . . Well, it's time to go on with my life. I know I've made some mistakes in the past. I know I was wrong—very wrong. But believe me, I've paid for those mistakes."

"I never knew that about you," Meghan said. I could see Jay had moved from acquitted rapist to a tragic, misunderstood figure in one of her novels.

"I suppose you also have an explanation for the dirty magazines you gave to Wade," I said, but as usual, neither of them paid attention to me.

Jay took her hand. "I can't imagine what you've been going through, but I also lost someone I loved."

"You're not the first one who's said that to me today," my sister said softly.

Jay tried to kiss her then, and darn it all if she didn't allow the brief touch. My heart filled with sadness because I knew how heartbroken she must have been to even think of being there with Jay.

"I have to go in," she said, pulling away and opening the door.

To my relief, he let her go. "I gotta get to work anyway. I moved out with some friends down the street in the old Giles place—my mom was always on my back, you know."

"That's why you haven't been around at school."

"I don't go anymore. I wondered if anyone would notice."

She nodded without replying. In a few steps she was at the door to the house.

"See you around?"

"Yeah." She picked up the garbage can, twisted the doorknob, and slipped inside the house.

★ ★ ★

It wasn't until the next day Jacky found my CTR ring under the middle seat of the van. "Did anybody lose a ring?" she asked. We were on the way to pick up Dad from the airport.

Seated next to her, Meghan paled. She grabbed the ring. "That's Kristin's."

Mom glanced back. "Are you sure?"

"She never went anywhere without it," Meghan said. "Not even the pool. She was wearing it that night. I saw her."

Mom drove to the side of the road. "Let me see it." She took the silver ring with the sparkling dark blue face in her hand. "It's hers all right. She must have taken it off when we took the van into the shop that night."

Meghan shook her head. "No, she was wearing it."

"But that would mean someone put it there later." Mom's eyes were kind, but her expression was one of disbelief.

"I know my sister, and she was wearing it!" Meghan practically yelled. She leaned forward, snatched the ring from Mom's hand, and put it on her finger next to her own purple CTR ring. After a moment of tense silence, Mom put the van into gear and pulled onto the road.

Meghan was right. I had been wearing the ring that night exactly six months before. I didn't know why he had put it there. I didn't think he'd done anything like that with his other victims. What did he mean by it? For the first time I think I was truly scared for the physical well-being of my family.

Chapter Eleven

He had lost the only woman he had loved—Lilet. After he had dedicated his entire life to her, she had turned on him Well, he'd shown her. She was gone and he was free to do whatever he wanted. So far what he'd wanted had brought him fabulous success.

Unfortunately, he couldn't tell anyone what a success he'd been. And because of that, people didn't treat him with the respect he should be given. No, he was in a dead-end job that was beneath him, living in a dump he didn't have money to pay for. At least it was better than living with family. Here he could take out the pictures and remember. He put on thin rubber gloves before reaching under the bed and pulling out a metal box. Opening it with a key, he pulled out a stack of pictures, shutting the box again quickly. Then he lined up the pictures upright on the twin bed so the backs of the photographs were supported by the wall. In the candlelight, the figures in the pictures seemed almost alive.

He knelt on the floor and sprawled his upper half over the bed. Gently, he stroked the face in the last picture. He didn't know why that case was different, but he thought about the girl all the time, about the fear in her eyes. Yet the power he'd experienced with the others hadn't come. Somehow she'd cheated him. He blamed her for the disaster of his life—police sniffing around, a boss that was worse than a nagging relative, and unspoken accusations. Well, he'd gotten her back with the ring, returned to her family on the six-month anniversary of her disappearance.

He laughed aloud. That would show them who was in charge—him. He would taunt and tease them as though they were nothing but a bunch of idiots. They were all so stupid, so far beneath him.

On the dresser and the nightstand in his rented room, the candles flickered and the pictures seemed to move. The girls would be with him always. He smiled.

Suddenly, the darkness in the corners of the room lunged at

him from all sides. The blackness wanted his soul—or was it coming from his soul? He couldn't tell.

Occasionally, he had moments like this—though very fleeting and rare—where there seemed to him a different way of looking at his triumphs—a cold, horrifying, unspeakable way that to him had no bearing on reality. For one clear second, he knew that there could be nothing more in life for him. Only the ultimate darkness of death would set him free from the torment he suffered. Torment that was like burning alive but never dying. A raging that made him oblivious to human suffering.

He pushed it back and then he was himself again—confident, mocking, enjoying his superiority. Gathering the photographs, he shoved them into the metal case under the bed. He threw away the rubber gloves.

I am the best, he thought. *My next case will be even better. More lovely. More satisfying. Too bad I have to wait for the right conditions. Maybe I should change the parameters—do something different.* No, if he did that they wouldn't know to connect the killings. They wouldn't know how great he was. They didn't know it enough now. He would have to think about that carefully and maybe do something about it.

Greed and desire feasted in his mind, reaching into every cell of his body and beyond that to the part that made up his very essence. He went to the bed and crouched there, laughing and shaking like a creature that was only half human.

★ ★ ★

I knew I shouldn't have come to see him. Grandmother had said it wouldn't do me any good. You'd think that seeing him on the bed laughing maniacally would have made me angry for all he had done to me and my family. Instead, I felt sad beyond anything I'd ever experienced. This man had given himself completely to evil. Here was truly one of the devil's own. I could barely put my face through his door to see him because the feeling inside was so oppressive and depraved. So depraved in fact, that I glimpsed only one evil spirit there tempting him, and it was obviously not working very hard. Apparently, my kidnapper needed only a little encouragement. The evil spirit caught sight of me and grinned with triumph.

Yet my kidnapper, too, had been a child of God. When he died, he would go to Spirit Prison, to the terrible part of it where visitors and preaching were rare. There, he would await and suffer until judgment.

Oh, I thought, *then he will be forever excluded from the Glory of God.* Having experienced the joy that came from association with my Savior, I knew that was the most terrible fate anyone could ever face.

I had never desired to have pity for such a person, but I felt pity now. Horror, yes—he'd stolen so much from innocent people, broken so many spiritual commandments and earthly laws. But all at once I could understand the Savior's compassion for those who had sinned. There was no help for this man that I could see, but I was infinitely grateful I would not have to be the one to mete out his terrible punishment. When the devil took his own, I would be safe with my family in Paradise.

My grandmother was right in a way. Now that I had visited him and felt the evil that controlled his soul, I felt soiled. I couldn't wait to leave.

He would have to pay for what he had done; I had no doubt of that. And I was determined to be a part of bringing him to justice on Earth, if I could. My family and the families of the other girls he'd taken needed closure. More importantly, he needed to be stopped before he killed again.

But how could I do such a thing?

I would watch and I would pray, and somehow a way would be opened.

Chapter Twelve

I spent the next six months learning new songs on the piano and reading all of Flannery O'Connor's books. I found it interesting that redemption played a very large part of her work. The sinner would invariably be saved as he accepted Christ. I knew there were some things that couldn't be forgiven easily, and her ideas were at times simplistic to my growing spirit, but they did help me realize how important accepting the Lord was and following His will. Flannery let me read a few chapters from the book she was currently writing, and I found it better than anything she'd ever written on Earth.

There were many other books to read as well, from the current writings of old prophets, to the new books being published on Earth and the many other inhabited worlds—plus all the books from the past. I was content to explore and learn from all good books.

That wasn't all I did, of course. I was seeing a lot of Randy. I also made many trips to the Spirit Prison where I helped missionaries teach the gospel. I even ventured into the darker parts, hoping to discover some information to aid me in my quest to bring my killer to justice, but I could never stay there for long. It was too horrible—no hope, no repentance, no love. Only selfishness and a delight in doing evil. I sorrowed for the loss of souls and did not go there after the first few times. At the same time, I noticed there were missionaries who didn't give up, who were tireless in their preaching and in their selfless service. Every now and then, a soul that could be saved was discovered, and all the holy angels would burst into beautiful song. We all wept with joy.

I also saw my Father in Heaven, but I am not permitted to tell you about that. Suffice to say that every hardship and effort is worth having Him look into your eyes and place His arms around you. If you could only feel a millionth part of the joy I felt, you would give all your life to Him with gratitude in your heart for the opportunity.

After my experience with Him, I went again to stay with my family on Earth. I had visited them often during the past months, but never for very long. They were continuing in the same pattern of numb hope which seemed to paralyze my own happiness and progression. I hated seeing them so miserable; it hurt me deeply as nothing else could. Though they put on a good outer face, my parents were as far apart as ever. Even worse, Meghan was now regularly sneaking out of class to see Jay.

Still, there was at least some progress. There were fewer arguments, and if there were also fewer smiles, no one mentioned it, but instead kept busy. During my visits, I concentrated my efforts on Mom because I felt that if she could heal the rest would follow. She was both the pulse and the heart of our home. At times I could see she was almost edging to acceptance, maybe even to a peace of sorts—a gossamer thread of peace yet too small to be seen.

Then he called, and the fragile thread snapped.

★ ★ ★

"Mom," Benjamin said as he and Jacky climbed into the van after a Saturday morning primary activity. "Robby's having a big birthday party next Saturday and I'm invited. I can't wait!" Then he frowned. "You are going to let me go, aren't you?"

"Who's Robby?" Angie asked warily. She was having a terrible day already, what with today marking the one-year anniversary of the day they had lost Kristin. How could a year have gone by so quickly? *Oh, Kristin, where are you?*

"That new boy I told you about. He says he's got a cool back-yard with this line that you can glide on—all the way across. And his grandparents have a pool at their house, and they think since it's been so hot that we'll be able to go swimming there and then go back to his house for the rest of the party. The pool is even heated, and they have a hot tub."

"Cool," Jacky said from the far back seat, but Angie didn't miss the uncertain glance sent her way. Jacky didn't think Angie would let him go.

"Put on your seatbelts," Angie said, glancing into the rearview mirror.

"Please, Mom? Can I go? All the kids are going to be there."

"I don't know," Angie hedged. The fear she'd been fighting down over the past months came rushing back. *I can't lose him*, her heart cried.

"Mom?" from the tone of Benjamin's voice she could tell he was becoming angry.

"Let me think about it."

Benjamin scowled. "You always say that! Always! And then you say no. When's Dad getting home anyway? At least with him I'd have a chance!"

"Benjamin!" Angie said too loudly. That had been another problem between her and Gary. Lately he had allowed Benjamin to go places she didn't think he should go alone—like to a Boy Scout Merit Badge Pow Wow or to the park with his friends. Each time had infuriated her and made her more bitter toward her husband. Couldn't he understand that nowhere was safe? Gary's own brother had been a child molester. Might still be a child molester.

"Look," she offered, trying to sound reasonable, "I don't know Robby's parents. Don't you see? I can't let you go with people I don't know."

Both children were quiet for the rest of the drive home, though the occasional sniffle told her Benjamin was fighting tears. Angie was glad Meghan wasn't there so she couldn't take Benjamin's side. There was already too much anger between mother and daughter.

When they emerged from the van, Benjamin hurried to the cement steps leading into the kitchen. He stopped on the top step and turned, eyes even with Angie's. "It's because of Kristin, isn't it? It always comes back to Kristin!" He was yelling now and his furious expression frightened Angie. "Well, I wish I'd never heard of stupid Kristin. Never! I hate her—it's all her fault. I'm glad she's dead!"

Angie's hand whipped out and slapped Benjamin across the face. His hazel eyes grew large and angry, yet at the same time spoke of a hurt too terrible to name.

"I hate you, too, Mom!" he yelled before darting into the house, clutching a hand to his cheek.

Angie sank onto the steps, her purse sliding down her leg to the cement. *Oh, God,* she thought. *Dear God—please help me! Please just let me die so I won't feel this pain any more!* Tears trickled down her cheeks, though she had thought there were none left to cry.

"It is because of Kristin, isn't it?" Jacky was standing in front of her, deep blue eyes intent, her hair the color of sunshine—oh, how much she resembled Kristin! "But I thought she was okay, Mom. I thought you said you feel she's okay."

Angie blinked hard. "I do feel that way. I really do."

"Then why don't you let her go?"

A thousand answers sprang to mind. *Because I miss her too much. Because she's only thirteen—no, fourteen now—and still needs me. Because she's a part of me. Because I'm not ready to believe she's dead, though the alternative is even worse.*

And yet . . .

There had been moments when she had felt Kristin near. For instance, she could almost imagine Kristin at her side right now, hugging her and stroking her arm. Often when she prayed, she felt warmness on her hands as though . . . As though what?

Angie groaned silently in frustration. When it came down to it, Jacky was right. There had to come a point when she had to let go.

But not after only a year! her heart cried. More tears came—a wild, raging surge she couldn't control. "Oh, Jacky. I miss her so much. I couldn't bear to lose any more of my children."

Jacky hugged her tightly, and for a long moment neither spoke or moved. Then Angie drew back and wiped her face. "Come on. I'll listen to you read while I start dinner."

As she worked, she thought about what Jacky had said. Maybe it was time to go on with her life. And maybe it was time to see if it wasn't too late to heal the breach between her and Gary.

★ ★ ★

I left Mom and Jacky in the kitchen and went upstairs to check on Benjamin. He was lying on his back in bed. Tears streaked his face, and there was an angry welt on his cheek where Mom had hit him. He was mumbling under his breath and glaring at the ceiling.

"Better be careful or your face will freeze that way," I said. In the past, the words had always made him laugh, no matter what kind of mood he was in. My heart ached that he couldn't hear them.

I stroked his arm as I had Mother's. "I know you didn't mean what you said. Don't worry, things will get better. I promise."

He sat up suddenly and picked up one of his toy cars from the shelf by his bed. I recognized it as the Jeep I had moved around for him more than a year ago when he was sick. "I love you, Kristin," he whispered. "No matter what I said to Mom."

"I love you, too," I told him.

He jiggled the Jeep around in his hand, a small smile forming on his face.

I left him there and went to check on Meghan.

★ ★ ★

One year, thought Meghan. *It happened one year ago today.* Her heart refused to believe. In a year everything should have been different. Kristin should have been found and life should have returned to normal.

She glanced down at the CTR rings she wore on the same finger on her right hand next to the little pinky. Hers was the sparkly purple one on the bottom, Kristin's was the top deep blue one. Many people asked her why she wore the two rings—especially on the same finger. Meghan never told them. She didn't even understand it herself except that this was the only part of Kristin she could still touch. Somehow, the rings shoved together on her finger made her feel closer to Kristin. Maybe she even was Kristin—or living the life Kristin had wanted.

Her hand fell to her biology book. She had to understand this if she was going to be a heart surgeon like Kristin would have been had she lived. Only if she achieved her sister's goal could Meghan make a real difference. The world certainly wouldn't notice one less romance novelist.

Against her will, her eyes sought out the books on her shelf. How long had it been since she'd touched them? Even now her fingers ached to run lovingly over the worn spines, to caress each page as her mind soaked up the stories. But no, that wouldn't help her reach Kristin's goal. She couldn't allow herself to indulge.

With a decided flick, she turned on the music to her stereo. She didn't know who the group was and didn't care to know. She didn't care about anything except that the music had a beat, and when she turned it up loud, all her troubling thoughts and longings were blotted out. Yes, the thoughts of Kristin, and how Meghan had failed her. Thoughts of Uncle Phil, who gave her nightmares. Of Wade who graduated last May and was talking about sending in his mission papers in a few months, and who was so nice to her every time she saw him that her heart ached for what might have been. And most of all the thoughts of Jay, who kept inviting her out alone, but whom she had kept refusing. She was fascinated with him, it was true, but at the same time repulsed. One more thing to puzzle her. Her parents knew he had dropped out of school, but they didn't know she often skipped class to see him at McDonald's where he had recently found a new job. Once they found out, there would be more trouble.

Meghan's attention returned to Kristin's CTR ring. She had convinced her mother to tell at least one policeman about the ring, but he had not believed the kidnapper had put it in the van. She remembered the detective's name—Jim Lowder—and secretly hated him. After that, no one believed her, not even Jacky, who was usually easy to convince. But Meghan knew she was right; Kristin had been wearing it the night she'd been taken, and the kidnapper had somehow returned to place the ring in the car. Many had the opportunity that day—her uncle, Brother Loveridge, Big Ned, and even Jay. Or anyone who'd passed on the street since the garage had been open much of the day and the van left unlocked.

Meghan put her finger on the first paragraph in the biology chapter she was reading. Yes, this music would help her focus on the parts of a cell. She would get it right, and somehow that would make it up to Kristin for not protecting her.

But after a time, Meghan stopped trying to read and stared into space.

★ ★ ★

I tried to enter the room to see Meghan, but the blaring music forced me out into the hall. "What?" I tried again and managed to stand at the door for a minute before leaving again.

"Turn it off!" I shouted at Meghan from the hall. Ignoring me, she continued staring at something only she could see.

I didn't like this at all. Couldn't she hear the awful things the singers were enticing her to do? She had never listened to that sort of music when I was alive, and I hadn't noticed it during my previous visits. Of course, I usually visited her at school or at night during dinner.

I stuck my face through her closed door. She was twirling the CTR rings on her finger. Tears had formed in her eyes.

I couldn't stay. The music beat at me, creeping into all parts of my soul, making me feel as if at any moment I would fly apart into a million pieces. I could see the edges of her room and how holes seemed to appear in the cloak of my father's priesthood that covered the entire house. Through those holes, I glimpsed spirit followers of Satan, struggling to burst inside. I looked for the Holy Ghost, whom I usually sensed here with my family, but He was not in Meghan's room.

"Please turn it off," I begged.

Nothing.

Disappointed, I returned to Mom to see if I could get her to help Meghan.

* * *

Though Angie had been listening for the sound, she started when Gary's car pulled into the driveway. *Good, he's home safe*, she thought. After the promotion when the business trips first began, she had picked him up from the airport, but now he drove himself and left the car there to save her the trip.

The younger children were already asleep, and she had finally made Meghan turn off that awful music and go to bed as well. Though Angie was exhausted, she waited up for Gary, anxious to talk to him about Kristin.

For some reason she had felt Kristin close all day. Perhaps

because today marked the anniversary of the kidnapping, or perhaps because of what had happened earlier with Benjamin. She wasn't sure. But she did know that she and Gary couldn't continue pretending everything was normal—smiling and acting as though they were the perfect models for parents coping with grief. Either she had to admit to the world that she no longer wanted to live herself, or she had to let Kristin go and learn to live again.

When Gary came in, Angie almost didn't recognize him. How long had it been since she actually gazed into his eyes? He was spending as much time as possible working, and since spring he spent the hours he couldn't work combing another section of the mountains or the desert, hoping for a clue to Kristin's disappearance. Guilt crept into Angie's mind. She had spurred him on, even making an enormous map and tacking it up in the family room, marking off each mile covered.

"Gary," she said.

He looked at her, surprise covering his face. More guilt seeped through Angie's heart. How many nights had she not waited up for him? How many nights had he come home to a dark house and no dinner?

She swallowed hard and tried to speak.

He beat her to it. "I'm thinking I'll try a bit south this weekend. And I met someone on this trip who travels a lot to Europe. She has connections and can set us up with a private investigator who has access to the brothels."

"She's not there," Angie said. "She can't be." She tried to say more—about how they needed to accept Kristin's death and go on with their lives, but the crushed look on his face brought an immediate and unexpected desire to hold him, to smooth away the agony, the responsibility, the guilt. She held out her arms, and he came to them, not like a man, but as a child, long starved for attention. His arms pulled her tightly against him, strong despite his emaciated appearance. Angie breathed in the familiar fragrance of him—a fragrance that brought back memories of much better days.

"Angie," he muttered hoarsely in her hair. "Oh, Angie." He drew back slightly. One of his hands cupped her neck, drew her face up to his. Their mouths met in a familiar yet strangely new way.

Emotions surged through Angie. Did love still bind them together after all that had happened?

The ringing of the phone forced them apart. For a moment, Angie was tempted to ignore the sound, but out of habit, she broke away from Gary and picked it up.

"Hello?"

For a moment there was silence, and then a low voice spoke, "I wanted to let you know that your daughter is just fine. I'm keeping her safe. Don't worry."

Angie choked, and then her breath came in rapids gulps. "You have her?" No answer. "Is she okay? Let me talk to her!"

There was a brief, jangling laughter. Angie thought she heard a child's voice in the background. Then there was a loud click.

"No!" Angie screamed. She grasped the phone with both hands, pressing it hard to her ear. "Who are you! Let me talk to her! Please!" She repeated the last word a few times before Gary pried the phone from her grasp.

"Dial tone," he said gently. "No one's there."

Angie gave an agonizing moan, doubling over as though someone had punched her in the stomach.

Gary made her sit on the couch while he called the cell number Detective Lowder had given him. It would save much time and explanation if he could reach the detective directly. He answered on the third ring. Gary could hear a TV blaring in the background.

"Lowder here."

"It's Gary Marshall. We need to talk to you. A man just called here. Said he had Kristin."

"I'll be right there." The phone went dead.

* * *

Within minutes Detective Jim Lowder arrived on the Marshall's doorstep. He had changed into uniform to look professional, but he had driven his own truck. Gary Marshall opened the door as he approached. Immediately Lowder felt a tug of compassion for the other man, whose stress was obvious by the haunted expression in his eyes. To hide this flood of emotion, the detective wiped his feet methodically on the doormat before stepping inside the living room that seemed hot compared to the cool September night air outside.

"Tell me what happened," he said, seating himself on the couch where Mr. Marshall indicated.

Mr. Marshall remained standing as he briefly described the phone call. Lowder noticed that his breath was coming faster as he progressed and that his eyes kept darting worriedly to his wife, who sat on the couch looking pale and shaken. He also recognized the hope in their hearts but understood the impossibility of it. There was simply no way their daughter could be alive after all this time. The chances were less than one percent. He took a deep breath, knowing he would have to be the one to put an end to the hope before it broke their hearts all over again.

"The police are checking the phone company now to see if there's anything we can do to find the caller," he said. "But my best bet is that this is some sicko calling from a local phone booth who thought he'd get his jollies by claiming responsibility." He shook his head, trying to make his words calm and his expression caring, without exposing too much of the deep pity he felt. They needed so much he could not give them. "I'm really sorry about this, Mr. and Mrs. Marshall. Heaven knows you've endured enough for one year. I promise, I'll do what I can to make sure calls like this don't happen again."

They stared at him blankly for a moment as the information registered. He wondered if they doubted his words. Or perhaps his commitment to the case. They didn't need to. Since Kristin's disappearance, he had worked each day on her case, and put in a lot of overtime he wasn't paid for. More than anything he wanted some resolution—some peace—for this poor couple.

"Thank you," Mr. Marshall said.

"Yes, thank you," Mrs. Marshall echoed, coming to her feet unsteadily. "I appreciate your being honest with us. You have always been direct, and we are truly grateful for that—and for everything else you've done."

Lowder arose and moved toward the door. "Glad to be of service. I'm just sorry it had to be under these conditions."

Mr. Marshall started to open the front door, but then hesitated. "Look, is there any possible way this guy really could have our daughter? Angie thought she heard a girl's voice in the background."

Mrs. Marshall made a noise in her throat and sat abruptly once more on the couch.

Lowder met the father's tortured eyes gravely. "Anything is always possible, Mr. Marshall. However, it could have been any girl in the background. Anyone. Meanwhile, I suggest you get caller ID. It probably won't help because whoever called likely used a phone that's either not his or not listed, but you never know when someone will slip up."

He left them and walked slowly to his blue truck, which appeared black under the thin glow of the streetlight. Pausing, he gazed up at the sky. "I believe You know what You're doing," he prayed. "I just hope I can be of use to You in finding the man who has hurt these people." He nodded once, then added, "If it be Thy will, of course. Amen."

He climbed into his truck and drove away.

★ ★ ★

Gary watched the officer walk to his truck, and Angie watched Gary. From her seat on the couch she see a slice of deep blue night sky and the twinkling stars hundreds of light years away.

Maybe she'd been wrong today, giving up on Kristin. Maybe it wasn't time to seek peace but to pray harder for her return.

When Gary came to the couch, Angie arose. "Call that woman you met tomorrow, Gary. Maybe she can help us find Kristin."

He silently held out a hand to her but she turned toward the hall, pretending not to see it. She couldn't—she simply couldn't take his hand and go on as though nothing had happened. "Good night, Gary."

For a long time she lay in bed next to Jacky, who still slept with her, listening for Gary. She hoped he would come in, and yet prayed that he wouldn't. She knew then that she wasn't ready to open her heart to him yet; she wasn't ready to go on with their lives. She had to concentrate on Kristin. Somewhere, her baby was alive and wanting her. The call had proven that.

Gary didn't come in. After a while, when she heard the room to Kristin's door shut, Angie slid silently from bed. On bare feet she crept quietly down the hall, first into Meghan's room, and then into Benjamin's. Both were sleeping safely and soundly. Angie pulled Benjamin's blanket up around his neck and kissed his soft cheek. He had only returned to his bed last month, and it had been hard for her to let him go.

On the way back to her own room, she paused at Kristin's door, placing her hand against the wood at though to feel the beat of the life within. Her heart ached.

"I'm sorry, Gary," she whispered so softly he would not have heard had he been standing next to her. "So sorry."

★ ★ ★

I was furious. I don't think I've ever been so furious in my entire existence. Not even when Satan enticed away one third of the hosts of Heaven do I remember being so angry. I couldn't believe he was toying with my family in this manner. All my efforts at healing their hearts had dissolved in a few fatal seconds.

After seeing my family to their beds, I went to him. He was in his ramshackle room, pacing before the pictures on his bed, occasionally cackling like a sick crone.

"Ha! I did it. If only they knew. But they will never be able to trace that call. Never." He bent his head back and laughed. He spoke to the pictures, but mostly to mine. I couldn't understand his fascination.

"Maybe it's time to use the suits," he said. In an instant, he was on his knees, drawing out the small metal box where he kept the photographs. I noticed he was wearing rubber gloves again. I watched with interest because I had never seen what else was inside the box. I gasped as he pulled out swimming suits of various colors and styles. One was mine.

A knock at the door startled him. Swiftly, he gathered up the suits and pictures and shoved them into the metal box, kicking it under the bed. With a fluid, almost dancing motion, he blew out the candles on the nightstand and then on the dresser before ripping off his gloves and depositing them in the small trash between the bed and the nightstand. He turned on the light when he got to the door, blinking at the hall light which was much brighter than the candles had been. One hand stole up to check the position of his toupee.

"Yes?" he asked as he opened the door.

"Hey, we're going up the canyon to party," said a young man with shaggy hair. I recognized him as a man who rented one of the other rooms in the house. "Want to come?"

"Sure."

"But only if you got some booze. Guy's gonna drive and I'm payin' for the weed."

"I'll get the booze. Don't worry."

The shaggy man clapped him on the back. "Knew we could count on you, man."

They went out together, but my kidnapper stopped and carefully locked the door behind him. "Hey, Barry," he said, "what do they do to serial killers in Utah?"

"Kill 'em, I think."

"That's what I thought."

"Why, you thinking on becoming a serial killer?" joked Barry. "You're too clean-looking for a serial killer. Besides, that would kinda interfere with your work for the FBI."

My kidnapper gave him an enigmatic smile. "If I were a killer, the cops and the feds would be too stupid to find me anyway."

"You can say that again. Them cops is nothin' if they ain't stupid. Hey, what's wrong?"

My kidnapper had begun to rub the base of his head. "Nothing," he muttered. "Just a headache. Been getting 'em lately. Got an appointment Monday with the doc."

"Hey, you don't need no doctor—I got somethin' for that. For someone who does such important work as you do for this country, you deserve it. You just come with me." Barry put an arm around my kidnapper. He shrugged it off immediately, but Barry didn't seem to notice.

I didn't go with them, but watched as they climbed in their friend's car and sped out of sight. Coming here had been a useless waste of time. How was I going to help my family see the truth?

Chapter Thirteen

"Grandmother," I said when I arrived back at her house in Paradise and found her once again on the front porch in her rocker. "When I first came here—I mean after Earth—you took me to see Jesus. Well, I remember you saying that He was right about something that had to do with me. Do you remember?" This had been bothering me for some time now, and since I really didn't want to talk about what happened with my family, now seemed the time to ask—especially since the experience was indirectly related to my own work.

She looked up from her needlepoint—something she claimed relaxed her after hours of teaching the gospel in Spirit Prison. "Oh yes. You'd think I'd learn. You see, we were talking about you before you came. He was briefing me on what you'd be thinking and feeling, and the reluctance you would have to leave your parents. He also told me you wouldn't recognize me at first or believe that you were dead."

"He was right."

"Of course He was. But after hearing from Him that you would have trouble adjusting—I believed it when He said that—I decided to do to everything in my power to help you. So I thought He hadn't figured in my presence, or how much I would help you adjust."

"But He's Jesus," I said, leaning against the porch railing. "He's always going to figure in everything. *Of course* He would have known how much you would help me."

"Well, I know that *logically*, I guess." She sighed and shook her head. "But I still had to see for myself."

"But didn't Jesus tell you that He'd be right?" It didn't make sense to me. If I was always right, I'd be sure to let everyone know.

Grandmother's brows rose in surprise. "He knows how important it is for us to learn for ourselves, even here. It's a lesson we humans have a hard time learning, both here and on Earth. And we still have our agency, after all. He's not going to force us to see things His way. He tells us how things are, and we believe or we don't."

"He told me I was going to help heal my parents' hearts," I said, staring at my hands so she wouldn't see in my eyes how miserably I'd failed. "So I guess if I've learned anything here, I should know to trust Him." I lowered my voice. "I have to believe I'll be successful. But I have to confess that sometimes it seems impossible, given my limitations. If I could appear to them, it would be easier, but so far that ability hasn't been given to me, though I did put in a request."

"Well, stop worrying about it." Grandmother gave me a little shove in the direction of the steps. "You're younger than I am, and you should learn to trust Him more easily than I did. Go on—you have work to do. And remember, trust in Him."

I drifted along, at first not knowing where I should go. I'd rather be with Randy, exploring the Universe, or maybe teaching a few discussions to the newly arrived spirits, or learning at the feet of one of the resurrected beings who occasionally visited. I even considered going to see my older Brother for advice, but I put that aside for now. I hadn't yet given my best, so how could I ask for His assistance?

Then suddenly I knew where to go.

They weren't hard to find. I had seen the names of the four other victims in my father's makeshift office many times. I simply asked the Translator to find them, and I was drawn to where they were—Spirit Prison. I was startled at first to have been taken there, but I quickly realized that none of their families had been members of the Church. Of course they hadn't yet been baptized.

I found the first two women, Patricia and Rosemary, together, teaching a beginning doctrine class for new Spirit Prison arrivals, overseen by missionaries from Paradise. I could feel their own yearning as they taught the importance of baptism. They had obviously accepted the gospel and were waiting for their work to be done on Earth.

I listened until the class was over and then introduced myself.

"We know who you are," Rosemary said gently. Her smile made me feel welcome.

Patricia nodded. "I've been wondering how long it would be before you came to talk with us."

I felt embarrassed. "Well, I didn't really think of it before—I've been so busy. But just now when he called my parents and ruined everything—" Here I had to sidetrack to explain what happened before rushing on. "And then seeing those swimming suits . . . I guess you suddenly became real to me. I mean, I realized that there was a lot more involved here, and I thought you might be able to help me somehow. But I want to get the others, Lilet and Melanie, as well. If that's okay."

"I can get Melanie," Patricia volunteered. "But we'll have to wait awhile for Lilet." She exchanged a knowing smile with Rosemary.

Rosemary noticed my curious stare and explained, "She's down on Earth right now."

"Oh?" This was interesting. I wondered what Lilet's business there could be—especially since she was supposed to be in Spirit Prison.

"She's getting baptized!" Rosemary fairly burst with the news. I stared.

Patricia nodded. "It's true. Her cousin was converted last year and she's doing Lilet's temple work. We're so happy for her; she's been waiting here a long time."

Their excitement and obvious desire to follow Lilet's footsteps made me want to cry. How many times had I taken my baptism for granted? How many times had I gone to the temple to do baptisms for the dead and not realized the importance?

"Look, you go on down and wait at the temple for Lilet—her cousin lives in L.A. so that's where she'll be, and we'll go get Melanie. We'll meet you at Lilet's place—she'll take you there."

I agreed and left them, curious to meet this spirit who would soon be one of the newest members of Christ's Church. I arrived at the Los Angeles Temple in seconds and was amazed by the number of spirits guarding the place—literally thousands of angels with glittering swords of truth girded around their waists. I knew instantly that they were there to fend off the minions of Satan—to prevent them from entering the temple. I could see dark spirits turned away at the doors, peeling away from the humans they were trying to tempt. I was on holy ground.

I made my dress white and entered the front doors, allowed inside by a smiling spirit angel. Opening my heart and eyes so I could see beyond the physical walls, I saw that the hosts of angels surrounding the temple weren't the only spirits here. Hundreds of others waited in different parts of the temple for their work to be done. Some stood behind the chairs of those doing their work, others hovered near the walls or in the open space at the front of the rooms. There was a hushed reverence and an amazing sensation of love that filled my entire being. I stood silently just inside the temple for a long time, a witness to the happiness on the spirits' faces as they emerged from the different rooms as fully covenanted members of the Church of the Lamb.

Since I had been too young to enter anywhere other than the baptismal area during my time on Earth, I'd never had my temple work done. But I knew that someday I'd be given the chance to make further covenants with my Heavenly Father, and to marry a special companion. Gratitude swelled in my heart. I thought of Randy and what he had begun to mean to me. To have the chance to be sealed with him forever was something I had not really contemplated before. A longing sprang to life in my heart.

"Hello, Kristin."

I turned and saw a woman dressed in white coming from the baptismal area into the lobby where I stood. A group of spirits that had been with her stayed behind as she flowed toward me with a grace that was unusual even for a spirit. "Lilet," I said, recognizing her from the Translator.

The smile on her small face was radiant and there were tears in her blue eyes. She touched my hand and feelings raced between us. How happy she was to finally be baptized! How eager she was to enter Paradise!

"I'm so glad for you," I whispered.

"It has been a long wait," she said regally. "Even so, I am lucky. There are others who have been waiting hundreds of Earth years."

We went silently from the temple. I knew we'd both return one day when it was time for us to make other covenants and to receive additional blessings.

Lilet took me to a stretch of beach outside a small cabin, where she'd been living. The place was peaceful and beautiful, though it did not come near the exquisite brightness or beauty of the beaches I had seen in Paradise. I knew Lilet was anxious to go there, but the other women were as yet forbidden to enter, so she had to content herself to wait a while longer. I was grateful to her for her patience.

Rosemary, Patricia, and Melanie were seated on the sand in a loose circle near the water. They all wore white, though in different styles. I was the only one wearing the color of the evening sky—I had changed it again after leaving the temple.

As I dropped to the sand, I realized how similar we all looked. We had blonde hair, blue eyes, slender bone structure, and our faces were oval. Lilet was by far the most beautiful, however. There was something in the combination of her high cheek bones and shape of her eyes that called attention even here—not that it was much of a concern. We were different; a particular kind of beauty was not a requirement or even sought as it had been on Earth. It simply existed. I wondered, though, if Lilet's radiant beauty had something to do with her baptism, for all the spirits I had met in Paradise seemed beautiful to me. I hoped I emanated the same radiance.

Over the continuous rumbling of the waves that thundered up to the shore, I began to tell the other women my story. Lilet was lying flat on her back in the sand, soaking up the brightness that came from the light of Christ and illuminated the sky even here, but now she drew to a sitting position, her long golden tresses flowing down her back. Her pressed temple dress had changed to a gauzy, cap-sleeved dress of white with a wrinkled look that was modest but perfectly right for beachwear. "I knew he'd kill again," she said. A deep sorrow came through with the words.

"We all did," said Melanie, the second victim, she was wearing white overalls that were a trifle too large. She stared at the sand she cupped in her fingers, not meeting my gaze. "But what could I do to stop him? What could any of us do? He has done us all so much damage. Once I asked for permission to visit my parents, to try to help them recover from my death. It was granted, but they wouldn't listen to the inspiration I tried to give them. They divorced right after I died. My dad became an alcoholic, and my mom remarried a man who beat her so badly she finally had to leave. They never did get back on their feet. Now they are so miserable."

I stared at her. My parents, too, seemed headed in a similar direction, though I couldn't imagine either of them becoming drunks or marrying anyone else. Of course, I didn't know that for sure. Brother Loveridge was way too nice for comfort.

When Melanie's blue eyes finally met mine, they were filled with tears. "I'm happy here. I believe I'll be baptized one day. Like Rosemary and Patricia, I have accepted the gospel. I only wish my parents would have been members before it all happened. Maybe then they'd still be together. Maybe they'd be happy."

I didn't know what to say. Lilet touched Melanie's arm. "We'll never give up hope. Never. The Father will answer our prayers. We just need a little patience."

As we continued to talk, I discovered that none of their parents had been active in any church, except Lilet's mother, who had killed herself for her grief and had since been unable to come to terms with her own death or her daughter's. She would remain in Spirit Prison because unlike Lilet, she had not accepted the baptism Lilet's cousin had done on her behalf in the temple that day.

"My father became a ruthless businessman," Lilet added. "He's been so miserable. But he'll be coming here soon. I'll meet him when he does and take him to my mother. I only hope it doesn't take him too long to listen to the missionaries. Maybe he can help her. I think he will."

Patricia's and Rosemary's parents were still living on Earth and were still together. Each couple had other children and had a semblance of a normal life, but neither were very happy. Since they worked in a group to help prevent abductions, they knew each other and had become good friends, just as their daughters had in the Afterlife.

"My parents don't believe in God." Patricia ran a hand through her short blonde hair. She and Rosemary were both wearing the usual silky white robes that we used in most of our official capacities here, but Rosemary's had white roses embroidered up the sleeves. "I think that's why they can't be happy."

"I've been told my parents are going to meet the missionaries soon," Rosemary put in. "But I worry that they might not listen. It will have to be a very special missionary to reach them."

"You don't know who yet?" I asked.

Rosemary shook her head.

Lilet's gaze settled on me again. "You're really lucky, Kristin. Your family will be together forever. They already have that promise."

A protest rose to my lips. I wanted to tell them everything that was going wrong and how helpless I felt. Yet how could I complain when my family still had so much going for them?

"So how can we help you?" Rosemary asked with her customary gentleness. "That is why you asked us here, isn't it?"

I nodded slowly, appreciating her sensitivity. "He called my family on the one-year anniversary of the day he took me. He said I was okay. Well, I am, but not in the way he means for them to believe. It really shook my parents—and just when they were on the verge of coming to terms with what happened. I want to know if he did that with any of your families. And I guess I want to know if you think there's any way we can help stop him."

They shook their heads. "Would have been pretty pointless of him to call our families," Lilet said, "since our bodies had all been found."

"Oh, that's right." I hadn't thought it through quite that far.

"You might ask the others," Lilet added.

I blinked. "Others?"

Melanie nodded. "There are three more—we thought you knew. Their bodies were never found."

Never found, never found, never found. The words reverberated in my head.

"Well, one of the remains were found, but never identified," Rosemary put in. "Or connected to our cases. That was Jayna. A runaway then—fifteen years old—but a really responsible woman now. She works as a sort of grief counselor with people like Lilet's mother. She's hoping her remains are identified soon so that her brother can get her temple work done. He's become a member since. I was going to ask Jayna to come here when we went to get Melanie, but she was occupied. Besides, we didn't know if you wanted the others to be here—you hadn't mentioned their names."

I felt chilled, though the sea breeze was warm. Now that they mentioned the others, I remembered there had been more than four pictures in my kidnapper's possession, though I hadn't actually counted them or studied them during the two brief times I'd visited. "I didn't know there were more," I said.

"Besides Jayna, there are two more—Sandra and Jenni," Melanie continued. "We don't know either of them well, but Jenni's in Paradise. Apparently, one of the foster families who raised her were believers, and she was baptized as a young teenager. Sandra, though, is here. Another runaway. Like Jayna, her family doesn't know for sure that she's even dead. "

"Where do they fit in?" I asked. "Timewise, I mean." Inside I was angry at myself for not being more alert to this possibility. My father had a list of kidnappings and had been doing research on them; I should have been doing the same instead of reading novels and visiting nebulae. That is, if I wanted to help my family. If all of these cases could somehow be connected on Earth, the police might find a trail leading straight to the kidnapper.

Lilet dug her bare feet into the sand. "I was first. Melanie was second. Two of the others we told you about—Jayna and Sandra, the runaways—were third and fourth. Then there came Rosemary and Patricia here—fifth and sixth. And last there was Jenni—the one who was baptized by her foster family. She was seventh—just before you."

"How long before me?" My mind reeled with the information. "I mean when exactly did each of the kidnappings happen?"

With their information, I quickly put together what they already knew: the killings were occurring every seventeen months. Or every year and five months.

"We don't know about any phone calls," Rosemary said. "But you might ask the others."

After a moment of silence we bid solemn farewells, and everyone left except for Lilet and me. "How did it all begin?" I asked quietly.

Her blue eyes seemed to hold as many memories as the ocean behind her held drops of water. She smiled wistfully. "He was my boyfriend. But you have to understand—he was so different then, and I was only fifteen. I had no one to tell me I shouldn't date that young. I thought for a time that I really loved him. He was smart, funny, and good-looking." She shook her head. "But I found out that he was into a lot of weird stuff, too—like porn and these stupid rituals. He became obsessed with what I wore or who I talked to. He made me feel creepy, so I broke up with him. I knew it was the right thing to do, but he was angry. Then one night I went to a swimming party given by a mutual acquaintance. He came, too. Asked to talk to me alone. I refused, but later, after the party, he was waiting for me." She sighed and threw a handful of sand at the oncoming waves. The grains fell short of their intended destination. "I guess you know the rest. I wondered for a long time if it was my fault—all that he did afterward."

"Of course it wasn't," I said, blinking back tears.

Lilet arose, shaking sand from the gauzy skirt of her dress. "Yes, I know that now, and I know how grateful I am to the Lord for allowing me to be here. The gospel, the Plan of Salvation, is the most beautiful thing in the world. I never knew that someone— even the Son of God—could love another person enough to suffer all the sins and torments of the world to bring us back to Heaven."

Our eyes met with complete understanding. I, too, had been amazed at the Savior's love and how He had willingly experienced my pain—and marveled even more at how much both He and my Father loved me.

"Tell me," I asked, forcing my mind back to the issue at hand. "How long did you date him?"

She gave me a wry smile. "One wonderful year and five long, horrible months."

I left her standing there, staring out to sea, and went to visit the other three women.

★ ★ ★

Soon I returned to my Grandmother's house in the meadow

and found it different than before—very different. Houses had sprung up next to ours, many complete with white picket fences.

"I thought it was time to have neighbors," Grandma said as I looked around. "So now we do."

"Great!" I said with enthusiasm. I had only been back in Paradise a short time since staying with my family, and I was always grateful to be surrounded by tangible spirits after a stint in the physical world.

Randy came up beside me, a smile in his eyes. "I'm one of your new neighbors."

"Even better." I took his hand and our thoughts touched. Joy and light and laughter rose in my heart, partially blocking out the upset of my new discovery.

He frowned. "What's wrong? Do you want to talk about it?"

"No," I said quickly. "Well, maybe. I'm not sure."

Grandmother smiled indulgently. "You two young 'uns go off for a spell. I'm gonna sit in my rocking chair and watch my new neighbors. I done had a difficult day today." Her voice had an accent I didn't recognize, and I knew she was trying to make me laugh, so I did.

"Imagine calling me a young 'un when she's as old as I am here," I said to Randy.

He chuckled. "Old habits die hard."

"I'll say. Right now, I just want to curl up in my mother's arms."

"Will mine do?" He held out his arms, and I sensed his energy radiating toward me. A shiver of delight traveled up my spine and deep inside to the inner part of my soul that was growing more and more attached to Randy each day. Sometimes it was as if I didn't know where I left off and he began. Not in a losing yourself kind of way, but rather a finding of self, of true purpose. I had never understood the meaning of two becoming one through marriage, but now it had a very clear meaning, one that went far beyond any physical expression. Of course, Randy and I weren't married yet, and we had only just embarked upon our adventures together.

"It's not really for me that I want to be with my mother," I said, snuggling into him. "It's for her. For both of my parents. They're together, yet there could be oceans between them for all the communicating they do."

He didn't say anything. He didn't have to—I could feel his sympathy. If only my parents could communicate like this, spirit to spirit. An idea sparked in my mind. Maybe somehow I could help them, if only I could get them close enough.

Chapter Fourteen

Gary studied the information on his computer all the next day before and after church. There were some clues here that he just wasn't connecting. Somehow he had to find a way to prove his brother's guilt or innocence. If Kristin were still alive, her life might depend on it.

More and more, Gary didn't see how his brother could be involved, not if the four other kidnappings and murders in Florida were connected. The first few had occurred when he was newly married to Lesa and eagerly awaiting the birth of their first child. Gary didn't think he would have had the time to plan a kidnapping, much less a murder. If the kidnappings had started earlier, or a year after, he might be more inclined to believe Phil had been involved. As it was, Gary vividly remembered visiting the newlywed couple and seeing their devotion. They had been inseparable in those days.

But how well did he know his brother? The charges the boy and girl had brought against him had been dropped and Lesa had allowed him to return to the house. Garen, Lesa's son from her first marriage, was making more visits. Rumor had it that since his graduation from high school, he had become more forgiving toward Phil. But Gary had also heard that Phil had lost his job because of the incident and was working at a restaurant to make ends meet. Still, all in all, it appeared the family might just survive intact. Maybe better than Gary's own.

Of course, it was all rumor. Gary had no contact with Phil or his family, though they lived in the same area. Lesa often made an effort to call them, but Angie would never answer the phone if their number came up on the caller ID, and she would delete the messages immediately from the answering machine without listening to them.

Gary forced his mind back to the information at hand. He thought he was seeing a pattern here that he had missed before. Perhaps he should share the information with Detective Lowder. It might be worth a call. He hesitantly dialed the detective's cell number and was referred to his voice-mail. Gary left a message. In less than a half hour, Detective Lowder returned his call. Gary guessed that he had been in church.

"What's up?" Detective Lowder asked.

"I've been looking at the previous kidnapping cases—you know, the Florida ones. And I know it might sound strange, but I've been feeling that we're overlooking something. The feeling's stayed with me all day—I can't shake it."

Lowder was silent, and for a moment Gary thought the man must think he was crazy. Then the detective said, "You know, I've had that same feeling. Like someone's sitting beside me trying to get me to look at the facts again."

Gary sent up a little prayer of thanks for what might just be divine help. "Well, I keep thinking—what if that call last night was really from the kidnapper? So I wanted to ask you if any of the other victims' families received calls like that."

"I don't think so," Lowder said. "Besides, what would be the point? The girls were all found within a week. A call like that wouldn't have meant anything."

"Oh, you're right." Gary had been pacing Kristin's room with the portable phone, but now he sat down and looked at the information on his screen. "So what makes Kristin's case different is that she hasn't been found. So either she's alive, or she's dead and the kidnapper wants to toy with us. I think we both know how unlikely it is that she's—" Gary stopped swallowed hard "—safe, though I'm not exactly giving up hope quite yet." He didn't want to admit how many times during his searching for Kristin he had found himself looking for fresh mounds of dirt, or piles of rocks that might hide her remains. It was a private torture he didn't share with anyone—especially not Angie.

Gary shook the thoughts away. "Anyway, I got to thinking that maybe he's killed more girls than we know about, and that he's made other phone calls so he can get noticed."

"Well the consensus in our department is that the phone call to your house was likely a hoax, but such a call would actually fit the FBI profiler's reports on the Florida kidnapper," Lowder said. "The guy obviously has something to prove, and it must be frustrating him not to be able to take credit for his deeds—especially if the body was never found. Still, the fact that the police haven't been able to catch him also means that he's one smart cookie."

One that I'm going to crumble, Gary vowed silently. He took a deep breath. "A little earlier today, I set up a timeline with the other four kidnappings in Florida and put Kristin's at the end. As we already know, all these girls were taken from a place where they had been swimming or sunbathing. They were all wearing swimsuits so presumably the kidnapper had been at those pools or beaches or whatever, checking the girls out and then following them as they left."

"Yes," the detective said encouragingly.

"Well, on this timeline I was talking about, it seems there's a year and five months difference between the first and second cases. Then we have a big gap of four years and three months. Then we have another gap of a year and five months until the next killing, followed by two years and ten months break—give or take a few days—before Kristin was taken. It occurred to me just before I called you that there's a pattern here that might be important. All of these kidnappings are divisible by a year and five months."

"Yes, I came to that conclusion as well. In fact, everyone working on the Florida cases has. And that led them to believe that there might be other victims. But they never found any other kidnapping cases that linked up."

"Years have passed," Gary reminded him. "Maybe there are new developments we could connect if we had the information. Maybe some girls who weren't reported missing at the time are now considered officially missing."

Detective Lowder was silent for a minute. Then he said, "Maybe a runaway."

"That's what I was thinking."

"To tell you the truth, I've thought a lot about runaways being connected in the past month," Detective Lowder said. "I've done some checking for girls who meet the criteria—young, blonde hair, blue eyes, slender—but the number of missing teens is rather long. It'll take awhile to research each case. But there is one thing I discovered. There were some bones found in southern Alabama about four years back. They belong to a young female who was never identified. But there are so many ways to trace remains available now that weren't available even then—DNA, facial reconstruction, and the like—and I've put in a request for additional research as a possible connection to the Florida cases."

"So we're looking for how many missing victims?" Gary asked. "Three, isn't it? That's what I figure."

"Yes. But only if the one year, five month theory is correct— and if they were committed by the same nut. Three missing in a series of eight victims. They would have been numbers three, four, and seven."

There was a pause and Gary wondered if Detective Lowder had purposefully avoided identifying Kristin as number eight—the fourth missing victim. He held his hand over his heart and forced himself to speak. "So if we find anyone who came up missing anywhere near these times, and who match the other criteria, couldn't we find out if their parents received a call?"

"It's worth a shot." Lowder's voice was hurried now as though he was anxious to return to work. "I've talked with the detectives in Florida already, so I know who to call. But I need to run this by my superiors and the FBI. It'll probably take a few days. I'll get back with you when and if I have any information."

"I know. You always have. But there's one more thing I wanted to tell you."

"What's that?"

"My daughter was taken a year ago. And if I'm right about this time period thing—and I believe I am, especially after talking with you today—in five months there will be another victim."

"Then we'll have to make sure that doesn't happen." Lowder clicked off.

Gary hung up, feeling for the first time in a year that he had actually done something to help bring his daughter home. It might not be the reunion he had hoped for, but at least they would finally know what happened to Kristin.

★ ★ ★

He believed that seeing the doctor was a waste of time, but the over-the-counter drugs were proving useless for the increasing pain in his head. Once it had come only occasionally, but lately it happened with more and more frequency. He simply couldn't stand the agony anymore. That was when he made the appointment.

"These headaches really have me worried," the doctor said after a only few minutes of examination.

Yeah, right. Like you really care.

"Alone they wouldn't be such a concern, but your coordination seems to be a little off. How's your memory?"

"Memory?" Yes, that had been disturbing him. Lately, when he tried to remember the nights with the girls, a few of the scenes were missing. Usually, he could remember better after the headaches were gone, but the lapses made him furious.

"Having a little trouble," he said aloud.

"Job give you a lot of pressure?"

He thought a moment before replying. "Well, I work under-cover—you know, for the FBI. So I do get a lot of pressure."

The doctor's eyes widened, obviously impressed with his confession. Or was that doubt in his eyes? The possibility infuriated him. He wished he could rip off the doctor's mustache and shove it down his throat.

"That could explain it, then," the doctor said. "I'll give you a prescription for a painkiller, but we'd better do some more tests. How does Thursday look for you?"

"Great." He pointed to the picture on the wall. "That your family?"

The doctor smiled. "Yes."

"Any swimmers?" He laughed, trying to smooth over his abruptness. "I mean with all that blonde hair, there's got to be a swimmer there."

"That's right." The doctor motioned to a girl with golden yellow hair. "Youngest daughter there—Courtney—swims like a fish. Used to be on the swim team, but she gave it up two years ago for dance. Now she breathes, eats, and sleeps dance."

He nodded congenially at the information, but it was an effort to hide his disappointment. He shook the doctor's hand. "Thanks. See you next Thursday."

Chapter Fifteen

Months slipped by. I watched Detective Lowder urge his colleagues in Florida to track girls who had turned up missing around the correct dates. He also worked with authorities in Alabama on the bones found there. The going was slow. I went to Florida to push things along myself, but the foul language, cigarettes, and alcohol the detectives used forced me away. They had to be left to their own devices, which was frustrating for me because I knew exactly who the unclaimed bones belonged to, exactly which runaways had been victims to my kidnapper, and where to find their families.

"Remember, it was to our family that our Brother sent you," Grandma told me. "Not to those detectives. Even when they find this guy, if they find him, your family will have some healing to do. That's your real job."

Christmas came and went—all in an outward semblance of normality. If there were fewer presents under the tree, no one mentioned it. If the decorations weren't as elaborate in past years, at least Mother put them up, as she hadn't the first year of my absence.

Birthdays also came and went. No one made special cards anymore, and Mother bought the cake instead of making it, but they still had birthday breakfasts and the younger children didn't seem to notice the somber overtones.

Dad and Mom began to fight more about which activities the outgoing Benjamin would be allowed to participate in. Mom pleaded, cried, and raged, but Dad held firm. "We cannot keep him in a prison. He's a child, he needs friends, he needs to have fun." Mom retaliated by going with Benjamin to his friends' houses and hanging out until she felt there was no danger, and then hurrying back to pick him up before the event was over. She never let him walk home, unless it was across the street, and then she'd watch from the window. Nor did she allow him go to the pool, the movies, or the skating rink with a group of friends the way some of the parents did, but would go with him and stay the entire time. Almost twelve in her mind was way too young to be on his own. I happened to agree with her on this, though Benjamin bucked at her authority. I talked to him for hours about how he should respect her, and after a while I think some of it got through because he seemed to resign himself to her presence. At least he got to go with his friends.

Another thing my mother did for Benjamin was to enroll him in a Taekwondo class four nights a week so that he would be too busy to ask to go anywhere else. In the end, this was probably the best thing she could have done for him. He adored martial arts, and there were a lot of boys in the class that he liked. It didn't escape anyone that the lessons would also help him defend himself . . . just in case.

There were other changes in our family. Jacky had discovered art at school and began drawing everything she could see as well as many things from her fertile imagination. Dad brought her a water-color art set on one of his business trips, and she used her old plastic Little Tikes easel to paint in front of the sliding glass door in the kitchen. She never went anywhere except school and church, but stayed close to Mother. I think in a big way, she was trying desperately to ease my mother's pain. And she did a good job.

On the other hand, Meghan continued to sneak out of class to see Jay, and her grades dropped to barely passing. She didn't care— not even when Mom cried and raged at her. One day I saw Meghan try to smoke a cigarette in the back of the school. She didn't like it, and she refused another drag, but her actions and the company she had begun keeping made it uncomfortable for me to get close to her. I knew she still blamed herself for my disappear-ance, and that her sadness was growing instead of abating. I think it was because I couldn't get closer to her that she worsened. I wished I had stayed with her more at first, before she fell into this horrible routine of survival.

Then came the day before Valentine's when Detective Lowder finally had some news and called Dad at work. I immediately went there. You see, I'd learned to keep track of all my family in the way that only spirits can. As a spirit, I could divide my attention between them, no matter where I was. I couldn't do it as well as the Holy Ghost, or with anyone outside my family, but it was enough. If they needed me, I could immediately go to them.

Dad was clutching the phone eagerly. I glided closer and leaned my ear into the receiver so that it was practically buried in my head. My hearing was better as a spirit than it had been on Earth, but I wasn't taking chances of missing anything.

"It's been really slow going," Detective Lowder was saying. "We've had one delay after another. But the missing bones found in southern Alabama were used to reconstruct the face of the victim. When they ran the image in the paper, a family in southern Florida came forward, saying the face resembled their missing daughter, Jayna Craft, who ran away from home about the same time of the second kidnapping and murder. Over the next year or so the family managed to track her to northeastern Florida, but there the trail ended. The last place they tracked her was to a canyon where a group of friends were having a party—near a stream, I might add. She was likely wearing a bathing suit which would fit the killer's MO. DNA results came through yesterday, and it is their daughter. The police there think this is likely connected to our other cases. What's more, the family does remember receiving a strange phone call. They figured their daughter asked someone to let them know she was all right. They had no way then of knowing the call came an entire year after her actual death."

"So the timing is right for her to be victim number three?" my father asked. He held his breath for the reply.

"Yes. The police there believe he went over the border to Alabama to hide the remains in the hopes they wouldn't be connected to the two previous incidents."

"Or maybe it was to show how smart he was." Gary was beginning to feel he knew the kidnapper too well. "Maybe he was trying to taunt the Florida police by getting another state involved."

"Could be."

"What about the other missing victims?"

"They've narrowed a large list down to five runaways that could be victim four. They're asking the families about any strange phone calls now. I'll let you know."

"And number seven?" My father brought out a crumpled paper

from his pocket—notes he didn't need because he had long since memorized them. "The victim before Kristin."

"There are no runaways for that period who fit the our description—young, blonde hair, blue eyes, possibly wearing a swimming suit. The only thing I dug up was an odd report about a woman in northern Florida who lived on her own. Her name was Jenni Wright, age eighteen. Didn't have any family and was apparently in the process of moving because she'd gotten a new job in South Carolina. According to the police record, she packed up and moved. Only the strange thing is that she left her dog. The neighbor who reported it to the police said she was really attached to him, that she'd never leave without him, but police decided that's exactly what she had done. They gave the dog to a shelter and forgot the whole incident. But since our inquiries, the police contacted the company where she was supposed to have gone. They said she must have changed her mind because she never showed up for work."

"Because he got to her first!" I said, forgetting they couldn't hear me. "He was the neighbor, don't you see? They lived in a complex with a pool. And later he told the police about the dog to taunt them."

"She was never found?" Dad asked.

"No. Not her or her car or anything in it. According to the IRS, she hasn't filed a tax return since the year prior to her disappearance."

"So we have victim number seven." My father's voice was heavy.

"Maybe," Lowder replied. "She might have purposely disappeared, changed her name. People do that."

"I don't think so. It's too much of a coincidence."

"You may be right. She had lived with a foster family for three or four years, and she promised to keep in contact. But six months after she left their home, she stopped calling. They tried contacting her a few times, but the number had changed. They figured she had moved and gotten too busy to call."

"Is there any connection between any of the cases? I mean other than the fact that they were all kidnapped. Any mutual friend or other similarity?"

"None so far. They're still working on it. But there is something more you should know. Your brother had moved to Utah by the time of our supposed seventh disappearance, but he was there on vacation to Disney World with his family during that time."

Dad shut his eyes and sighed. I noticed more wrinkles around his eyes than ever. "Thanks for telling me," he finally managed to say.

"You're welcome. I'll keep you posted."

"Thanks."

My father hung up. I could tell that though he was glad they had found two of the missing victims, he was depressed by the news about Uncle Phil. He was also unhappy that the investigation hadn't led to a direct connection to my disappearance. Nearly five months had passed since the anniversary of my kidnapping. As always, looming above my father's urgent desire to find me was the knowledge that if the kidnapper held to his schedule, another girl would soon fall victim.

My father also had other challenges to think about. "Oh, Kristin," he said, rubbing his eyes. "If only I could find you. I think then I might win back your mother before it's too late."

I patted his back so hard, my hand disappeared inside him. "Oops. Sorry." Not that he noticed. "You're not going to lose Mom," I told him. "Even if you never find me. You're sealed—we're going to be an eternal family. It's true. You just have to get through this."

Dad smiled at something and warmth infused me. Somehow his inner spirit had understood my message! With a sudden snap of his fingers, he left his small office and went to his boss to ask to leave work an hour early. Since he was leaving on another sales trip the next day and would miss spending most of Valentine's Day with his family, his boss was only too happy to let him go.

But what he found at home was not something either of us had anticipated.

* * *

Angie opened the door to Dale Loveridge with more than a little trepidation; she enjoyed seeing him altogether too much. Today he brought with him the fresh clean scent of the snow outside and a bouquet of bright flowers. There seemed to be one of every variety she recognized, and a few she didn't.

"Come into the kitchen while I put these in water," she invited.

In the kitchen, Jacky was at her easel, brush in hand. "My, what a nice painting," Dale said, admiring it. "How old are you now, anyway?"

"I'm gonna be ten soon," Jacky said. "I'm the best artist in my class."

"I'll bet. You paint more like a sixteen-year-old, I'd say."

She giggled. "I'm making my teacher a Valentine. It's tomorrow, you know. Valentine's Day."

"I know." Dale sat on a stool at the counter, his gaze going to Angie as she arranged the flowers in a vase. His stare was intense, as though drinking in every detail of her. She felt herself blushing. Why did he affect her so? She liked him, but it didn't go beyond that. It never could. He was only a neighbor and a friend.

They talked about inconsequential things like how his classes were going and how Valentine's Day was really getting too commercial. Angie's eyes slid to the beautiful flowers, whose aroma she could smell even though they were several feet away. Had Dale brought them for Valentine's? Yet in the world of adults Valentine's Day was reserved for people in love—had he brought the flowers early so that his attention wouldn't appear too unseemly?

Stop it, she thought. *He's just a nice friend.*

Yes, one who's always there, answered a voice. *Not like Gary. He doesn't seem to want to be with you.*

That's partly my fault, she countered.

Is it? He could open up to you. He could fight for your relationship.

Angie begged the voice to stop. How could she expect Gary to fight for them when she could barely stand to be with him because of the memories?

"Are you all right?" Dale was beside her, gray eyes concerned. Angie could almost imagine losing herself in their depths. Anything not to think about what she had lost.

"I—I'm fine." She glanced over to where Jacky had been, but she wasn't there. Benjamin was at Taekwondo, and Meghan was up in her room—probably staring at her books or listening to wild music with the headphones a friend had given her. Somewhere outside a car's engine sounded, then faded away.

Angie was aware that she and Dale were completely alone. There was no one to overhear them or to question their actions. Panic ensued in Angie's heart. She was a married woman and Dale's presence shouldn't be an issue, but he seemed to represent all the hopes and dreams she'd had as a young girl. For an instant she wanted it all back—all the innocence, the freedom from pain.

The intensity in Dale's eyes deepened. Angie couldn't drag her eyes away.

"I wish I could help you be happy again," he said.

She tried to make a joke of it. "So do I."

"I'd better go."

She nodded and walked with him to the front door.

"What happened to us, Dale?" she whispered as he opened the door. "I mean all those years ago." She wasn't trying to flirt with him or to be improper, she just wanted to know how her life had begun down this path.

"You met Gary." With that simple answer, Dale dipped his head and walked out the door.

There was a sound behind her and she turned to see Gary standing in the hallway. She wondered how long he'd been there and how much he'd heard. In one hand he held a bouquet of flowers, pointing dejectedly toward the ground. They were large white daisies with sunshine middles—her favorite.

"Gary, I . . ."

He shook his head, tears shimmering in his pale blue eyes. "I don't know if I can go on this way. I don't want to give up on us, but I can't do this alone. You can't do it alone. We have to be together, or we aren't going to make it."

"Of course we'll make it!" she cried, taking a step toward him.

"Will we?" His chin raised in direction of the door. "Tell me, wouldn't you rather run after him right now? To get away from it all?" He blinked rapidly several times. "Face it, Angie, we've been living apart for over a year now. But us not being together won't bring Kristin back. Only our staying together will—whether it's now or in eternity."

"I—I know that." Angie was crying now.

"Do you? Do you really? Because sometimes I have a hard time believing. Sometimes I think it would be easier to walk away."

Angie could barely see through the tears. What was he saying? Did he want to leave her? "What do you mean?" she finally managed.

His shoulders lifted in a careless shrug, but his eyes echoed her pain. "I don't know. I only know that something has got to change."

"It will—when we find Kristin."

"And if we don't?"

"He said she was alive."

"It could be a hoax—that's what the police believe."

She wiped away more tears. "I don't think it is. It's him. And I think I know him. The voice—I think he tried to change it, but it was familiar. I just can't place it."

"Even if it was the kidnapper, he could be lying. He didn't ask for ransom—nothing like that. He might be taunting us. He might not have her anymore. So where do we go from here?"

It was something they had to face. They might never find Kristin—either dead or alive.

Angie swallowed hard. "I don't know."

"Neither do I."

Angie wanted to go to him, or have him come to her. To hold her tightly, to make the nightmares leave. But there was a wall between them, a seemingly impassable barrier that neither could penetrate.

"Since I came home early, I might as well get your van inspected today," Gary said into the silence. "I have to leave on my trip tomorrow, and there will likely be another trip later this month. I may not get another chance to do it."

And you know how much I hate getting the car inspected, she thought with a pang. Had she ever given him enough credit for the things he did for her?

"We can talk about this when I come back from the trip," he continued. There was a finality to his voice that shook her. Without another word he turned and went into kitchen. After a few more seconds, Angie heard a door slam.

She retraced her steps. In the kitchen, Dale's flowers beckoned to her brightly on the counter, a bitter contrast to the turmoil in her heart. She walked around the counter to the sink and automatically began to load the dishwasher. There were some bits of plastic in the sink from the can of frozen juice concentrate she had opened that afternoon. She bent to put it under the garbage in the sink. The can was full so she pulled it out and started for the door.

Gary had left the garage open, just as she had when she had come from taking Benjamin to his taekwondo class. If she had closed it, she would have heard him come home, and then he wouldn't have seen . . . Seen what? Nothing had happened. Nothing.

Yet in her heart she knew that she had begun down a new path. She had the choice now to stop and go back or maybe to choose another one. Would it include Gary? The gospel should be enough to keep them together, shouldn't it? Surely her covenants with him were more important than escaping from pain. Tears slipped down Angie's cheeks.

As she lifted the lid to their outside garbage bin, she saw something that cut into her heart. The happy-looking daisies Gary had bought were lying abandoned inside. With trembling fingers, she reached in and rescued them, their delicate blossoms already wilting from the cold.

She took them inside and put them in a vase. There was a small envelope, and she pulled out a card that read *Happy Valentine's Day. I love you, Gary.*

Blinking away more tears, Angie laid her head on her arms and cried.

★ ★ ★

Gary drove the van slowly to the garage. He hadn't planned on getting the inspection done today, but he couldn't stay there with Angie. His arms ached to hold her—it had been so long!—but she couldn't seem to forgive him for losing Kristin.

For that he didn't blame her. When did you finally give up hope for a child? When were you able to pack the memories away and face the future? When was it okay to laugh again?

Gary didn't know. He did know that his marriage was in serious trouble. He didn't blame Dale Loveridge; in fact, he was glad Angie had a friend who could help her take her mind off her pain. Bereft of Lesa, where else did she have to turn?

Me, he thought. *She should turn to me.*

Why she couldn't do that was a constant source of pain for him. He had done everything he could to find Kristin. That obviously didn't make a difference to Angie, and his presence seemed only to bring her more pain—pain that he couldn't bear to inflict on her anymore.

He would have to leave. All along he had been fooling himself into thinking Angie could love him again, but now he could see clearly where they were headed—drifting further apart until there was nothing left. But it shouldn't be this way! *Trials are to make us strong*, he thought, *not to break us apart*. Anger rose in his heart. He wanted to get the man who had done this to him! The man who had robbed him of everything.

But who could it be? Anybody, really. If not his brother, then another crazy who had nothing to offer anyone except fear and hatred. It could be the banker, the mechanic, or even his neighbor, Dale Loveridge. How much did Angie really know about Dale? He said he taught at the college, but for all they knew it could be a lie. Why didn't he buy a house instead of sharing rent with a couple of students? Maybe *he* was behind Kristin's disappearance. Maybe he was trying to pay Angie back for rejecting him all those years ago.

Stop it, Gary told himself as he pulled up at the auto mechanic's garage. Next he would be suspecting Big Ned Lyman of something. Still, it wouldn't hurt to do a check on Brother Loveridge. Angie meant too much to Gary to give up without a fight.

Big Ned was talking with someone in the back of his shop when Gary entered. The big man's face was flushed and his graying beard moved as he spoke urgently. Gary studied the other man and recognized the unruly brown hair and short build as belonging to Lucas, Big Ned's nephew, and he was obviously agitated as well. Big Ned finally reached into his pocket, pulled out a few bills, and shoved them into his nephew's hand. Without a word, the nephew turned on his heel and sauntered toward Gary.

Gary's eyes were drawn to him. There was something odd about this guy—perhaps the swaggering way he walked after so obviously begging for a handout. His unfocused eyes met Gary's as he passed, and after a brief moment of recognition, he stopped and held out his hand.

"Nice to see you, Mr. Marshall. How is everything with your family?" His light brown eyes narrowed, as though trying to focus.

"Doing well, thanks," Gary responded automatically.

"I won't be working on your car—I'm sure you'll be glad to know that." Lucas flashed Gary a winning smile. "I was never really good at it. But I have a new job, you know. I'm a manager at a construction site. Pays good."

Gary's eyes went instinctively to the man's left pocket, where he had put the money Big Ned had given him.

"That's for my mother," Lucas said, noticing his glance. "She's in a rest home, you know. My dad left my uncle money to care for her, but it's like squeezing blood from a turnip, he's so tight. He's a good mechanic, mind—the best. But very tight. I wouldn't have even asked, except that I'm planning to buy a house and couldn't afford both the down payment and the rest home fees this month."

Gary nodded politely.

"How's Meghan doing with math?" Lucas asked.

Gary didn't know Meghan was even having trouble with math, though her grades were generally low, and he felt annoyed that this man knew more about it than he did. "She's doing fine," he said, taking a step away from Lucas. "Thanks for asking."

Lucas looked as though he wanted to say more, but Gary took another step away. The other man left the garage.

Big Ned came toward him, looking after his nephew with an air of disgust. "That boy's more trouble than he's worth. He was here for money. Probably lost his job—says it was at some construction site, but I don't believe him. More 'n likely, it was somethin' that gets him minimum wage. But it looks like he can't keep even that. If he hasn't lost it yet, I bet he will. Meanwhile, he's always at me for money. I told him he can sleep in the back room if he needs to for a while to save up a bit, but he ain't gettin' any more from me."

Gary couldn't hide his surprise. Big Ned laughed. "You didn't believe him about that bit about his dad being dead and his mother being in a rest home. Bunch of bull. He's been tellin' that story since he was a teenager. The real story is that both his parents are fine 'cept they divorced when he was young. My brother remarried and has three more kids. Lucas never forgave him for that. As for his mother, she has grown a little odd, but she's been taken good care of—a nurse comes to her apartment a couple times a week. My brother still sends her money. I do too, when she asks."

Gary smiled sheepishly. Right, of course Big Ned wouldn't hold out on his sister-in-law.

Big Ned turned to the van. "So what can I do for you?"

"Inspection. Do you have time for it today?"

Big Ned boomed a laugh. "For you and Angie I got all the time in the world."

Chapter Sixteen

Nearly five months had passed since his appointment with the doctor. He hadn't kept the second appointment. When the prescription painkillers wore off, he bought more through one of his housemate's friends. How they got the pills, he didn't care. Nor was price a factor. That the pain abated was the important thing. But now the headaches were worse, interfering with his normal routine, and he'd been warned at work that if he didn't do his part, he'd be fired. Imagine, fired from a dead-end fast food job. He was smarter than the owner, smarter than the teenaged girls and boys who worked the counters. He was the best. Yet even he had to admit the pain got in the way of his work. So though he really detested the doctor, he made a new appointment for the tests. He should do it before he got fired again and the insurance ran out.

Besides, it was about time. He smiled to himself. *Yes, about time.*

When he wasn't at work, he was hanging out at area pools, trying to be as inconspicuous as possible. It wasn't hard. The intelligence of the average person didn't begin to match his. Sure, February wasn't a good time for this kind of thing—Utah weather wasn't as mild as it was in Florida—but at least it was a challenge. Maybe this time he should try to raise his sights a bit. Maybe kidnapping the child of a prominent citizen would show everyone how smart he really was. Maybe he would write a letter like other prominent killers had done. The phone calls he had made and the regular body count didn't seem to help the police any.

Dumb as mud, he thought. Pain sliced through his brain and he fumbled for the bottle of pills in his pocket. The prescription drug had been made out in the name of some woman; he bet the kid he'd bought them from had stolen them. The bottle was empty. Enraged he threw it across his room and fumbled in his drawer in search of another.

That was when Barry knocked on the door. "Hey man, phone's for you."

Pushing back the pain, he went into the shared living room and picked up the receiver, trying to sound bold and assured. The facade shattered almost instantly. "No!" he yelled. "No! You're lying, you . . ." He let out a string of swear words. Then he slammed the receiver down.

"What's wrong?" Barry asked, staring at him. "You look like you've seen a ghost. Are you being called into action? What is it—drug bust, arms stings? Tell me, man."

"No, it's my mother." He didn't know why he was telling this kid anything. "She's dead."

"Sorry, man. That's tough. What happened?"

"Car accident." No way would he tell this jerk that she had swallowed too many sleeping pills.

Turning abruptly, he went to his room. Carefully, methodically, he locked the door. Then he pulled out the metal box under his bed and fumbled in his pocket for the key.

He'd almost forgotten the gloves. He pulled them on and wiped the metal case with a cloth before opening it. The pictures were there, beckoning.

It was time. His world might be falling apart, but he'd make it all come back under his control. This time he'd take two. One for Lilet and one for Mother.

Chapter Seventeen

I was worried. Mom and Dad scarcely exchanged a word before Dad left for his trip on Valentine's Day. He had seen the flowers she'd rescued, but he had also noticed the ones Dale had brought. The two vases stood side by side like a decision my mother would have to make. I tried in vain to knock Dale's flowers over, but the power to move physical objects was never granted me. I think probably because it would have been more temptation than I could have resisted.

Meghan was more alert and nervous than usual, and I realized today was Valentine's Day. Who was she expecting a Valentine from? I followed her to school to find out.

She was greeted at her locker by Tamara, Wade's little sister, who was in the tenth grade now. "Hi, Meghan. I'm glad I ran into you. I wanted to invite you to a little get-together we're having for Wade. I would've told you sooner, but I only decided to do it yesterday. We thought a Valentine's party would be the perfect opportunity to kind of celebrate his mission call with all our friends."

Meghan froze, as though slowly digesting the information. I hadn't thought it would make a difference to her what Wade did. Since he had begun attending Utah Valley State College the past fall, she had seen him only a few times. Each time he'd hinted about asking her out, but she had never given him any encouragement. Sometimes I thought a lot about where they would be now if I hadn't been kidnapped. He had grown into a thoughtful young man, a side of him I had only glimpsed during my probation on Earth.

"I didn't know he'd gotten his call," Meghan said. That wasn't surprising. She had faked sick at the last moment on the Sunday the Bishop had announced the call and caused the entire family to be late for services.

"Yeah, weeks ago. I'm surprised you didn't hear."

I snorted. "Well, if she'd actually go to her Sunday classes she might have."

"Anyway," Tamara continued, as though I weren't there—which I wasn't for them. "He's going to Florida! He'll be leaving as soon as his block classes are out at school at the end of the month—about two weeks. He's so excited!"

"Tell him congratulations," Meghan said dully.

Tamara beamed, her short, dark curls perfectly framing her bright face. "You can tell him yourself, if you want. I would love for you to show up tonight. He's coming over from his apartment, but he doesn't know I've invited people. It'll be a complete surprise! We have plenty to eat—I made heart cookies all day yesterday."

Meghan hesitated, and I wondered if Tamara could read the longing in her eyes as well as I could. "Maybe," Meghan said finally, the word obviously hard for her.

"Good. I know he'd want you there." Tamara continued down the hall. She was so happy and, well, radiant with the goodness and cleanliness of her spirit that I felt a desire to go with her. But I stayed with my sister, whose spirit had been weighed down by events Tamara couldn't begin to comprehend.

Some of Meghan's questionable friends approached. One was Charity, a girl with too-short, bright red hair. Another girl, whose name I didn't know, sported shoulder-length black hair that did not match her dark blonde eyebrows and hazel eyes. Lastly came a mud-haired boy named Robb, whose dilated pupils made me suspect he'd been drinking.

"Go away!" I said. But unlike Satan's spirit hosts, they weren't repelled by my presence. To my surprise each of the three had brought Meghan some small candy token for Valentine's Day.

"Thanks, guys." Meghan blushed with pleasure, while I wiped a tear from my left eye, which tended to leak more than it should, even in spirit form.

Despite my resolve to dislike her friends, I said, "Okay maybe, just maybe, I'll try to put in a good word for you. Get you some help. I'm sure you all have relatives somewhere in Paradise who would be willing to work with you from the other side. Hey, wait for me!" They had taken off down the hall, sweeping Meghan along with them.

"So, you gonna see Jay?" the black-haired girl asked.

Meghan shrugged. "I want to go later. You think you could give me a ride at lunch time?"

"Sure. No problem."

Great, I thought with a sigh. It looked like I had my day cut out for me.

★ ★ ★

Meghan stared at her GPS locator as she sat at a table in McDonald's waiting for Jay to come over. Her friends had dropped her off and would be back to pick her up in a half hour. She usually didn't notice the locator anymore and no longer minded if people saw it. No one had ever suspected it was anything other than a big, fancy watch full of gadgets.

Strangely, as she waited, it was Wade she thought about, not Jay. What would Wade say if he could see her wearing this tight top that practically showed half her belly? The top had been a birthday gift from one of her new friends, but she kept it at school. As distracted as Mom was these days, she would never let Meghan wear something so immodest. Jay didn't think it was immodest. Would Wade? Meghan already knew the answer.

She couldn't believe he was going on a mission. Yes, he'd talked about it for the past year, but she hadn't imagined it actually happening. He would be completely out of her life now; she knew that once he returned it would be too late for them. He would be a man of God and she would be . . .

What?

Shutting her eyes, she felt tears squeeze out the corners. She swung her head forward, hiding her face with her long hair. More tears burned a path down her cheeks. She wasn't good enough for Wade. She had known that for a long time. Twisting Kristin's CTR ring on her hand, she tried to gain control. She couldn't let Jay see her this way. What was taking him so long anyway? He knew she was coming today.

Meghan wished she could talk to her mom about the feelings she had for Jay. Her emotions were so volatile. One minute she wanted him to kiss her, as he did occasionally as they sat at the booth, and the next she wanted to kill him. In the past few months, she had gone on several double dates with him that her parents didn't know about. Those had been both exhilarating and scary. He kept pestering her to go out with him alone, but she wasn't sure of him. Sometimes his hands roamed way too much and she was embarrassed. Her new girlfriends didn't understand her reluctance to become intimate with Jay, but Meghan held in her heart a vision of the temple. She knew Wade would never have expected her to do anything that would prevent her from marrying there.

Stupid, she thought. *Wade doesn't think that way about you. He has college girlfriends now, ones who aren't as stupid and immature as you are.*

Meghan sighed. She felt someone stroke her hair and looked up, expecting Jay, but no one was there. Unbidden, a memory came to her. A memory of Kristin. They had been reading the same book together one night in her room with the flashlight. It was a weekend and her parents wouldn't have minded them staying up later if they'd asked, but it had been fun to do something out of the ordinary.

When the hero had knelt down in front of the heroine and had begged her to become his wife in the temple, Kristin had turned to Meghan, blue eyes grave in the dim light. She held up her pinky. "Let's promise never to get married outside the temple, okay?"

"That doesn't always guarantee everything," Meghan reminded her. Though Meghan had always dreamed that her knight in shining armor would take her to the temple, she had seen a lot of marriages in their ward fall apart lately.

"Oh, I know," Kristin said. "But it's our promise to God, you know. We'll do our part and trust in Him for the rest. Besides, marrying someone in the temple is a real commitment, not just an 'until death to you part' sort of thing. I want a marriage like Mom and Dad have, don't you?"

"Of course I do. With all my heart."

"Then pinky promise." Kristin held up her pinky again and Meghan did the same. The two fingers met and entwined, and as they shook solemnly, Kristin added. "We will save ourselves for marriage in the temple."

"Deal," Meghan added. Then they had laughed and told secrets for another hour. That had been the first night Meghan had admitted to liking Wade, long before his growth spurt and acceptance on the basketball team.

"Hi, Meghan."

She looked up to see Jay slide into the seat opposite her. The memory of her sister had been so real that she had almost expected to see Kristin. "Hi," she said, surreptitiously touching her face to make sure her tears were dried.

"Where were you?" Jay leaned back, hands behind his blonde head, looking at her quizzically.

"Right here."

He leaned forward suddenly and grabbed her right hand. "I mean in your mind. What were you thinking? Of me, I hope."

For some reason Meghan was reluctant to tell him about her experience. "Yeah," she said.

He pulled her halfway across the table, where he met her with a kiss. "So, are you going out with me tonight? I have a present for you."

She had thought he'd give it to her now, if he had one. "Tamara invited me to her house," she mumbled. "She's having a little get together because Wade got his mission call. We could meet there."

Jay sat back again abruptly, releasing her hand. "When are we going to start dating alone? This is so weird, meeting like this all the time, or having your friends around. Do you still have a thing for Wade?"

She stared down at the table. "No, it's just that he got his mission call."

"Well, Wade and I don't talk anymore." Jay leaned forward again. "Look, Meg, you know how I feel about you. It makes me crazy to see you with him."

The admission warmed her heart. "You don't ever see me with him," she reminded him. "He graduated almost a year ago—you know that—and he doesn't even live at home. I only see him every now and then at church when he comes home to visit. Tonight I'll just go over for a few minutes to say hello. You pick me up there, and then we'll go out—alone." She glanced at the GPS locator on her left arm. "But we'll have to stay really close. It's a school night, I can't be out long." *And I can't risk my parents looking on the Internet and seeing I'm not where I said I'd be.*

"Okay." Jay took her hand again. "Look, I've got to get back to work. You can see we're swamped." He kissed her again briefly, and then stood. "I'll see you tonight."

She put on her blue coat while he walked back to the counter. He turned around and mouthed, "I love you." She smiled and waved. He'd said that to her the last few times they'd gone out, and it made her feel warm inside that someone as good-looking at Jay could feel that way about her. He always looked at her expectantly, but she didn't say it back. She didn't know if she loved him. Maybe her ability to love had vanished with Kristin.

Outside the restaurant, she pulled her coat tightly around her to ward off the crisp February breeze. Where were her friends? Lunch hour was nearly over and she needed to get back to biology class. One more absence and the teacher would probably make her parents come in for one of his infamous chats.

As her friends drove up in a little gray Mazda, Meghan gave a last glance into the restaurant, hoping to catch sight of Jay. He was in the drive up window, waiting for the next customer. A girl with long dark hair, was standing very close to him, her hand on his arm in an intimate gesture which Jay didn't shake off. Jealously surged through Meghan. She wanted to keep watching, to see what might happen, but the car at the ordering window moved forward, and Jay began talking to them. The girl let him go, watching with a smile on her red-painted lips. Meghan felt sick.

"Get in, Meghan. You know we can't be late again for biology," Charity called from the car.

Meghan slid into the back seat, trying to recall what she had seen. Had the girl's gesture really been intimate? Did Jay really care for Meghan, or was he leading her on?

She and Charity walked into biology class without a second to spare. They found their seats, and as the bald Mr. Cardley launched into another long-winded lecture about evolution, Charity leaned over, the movement hardly rustling her spikey, red hair. "Hey, I've been meaning to tell ya something. Did you see that girl in the drive-up with Jay?"

Meghan nodded numbly, feeling her face flush.

"Well, I don't wanna worry ya none, but I saw her and Jay last night when I went there to eat. They was sitting in a booth. Looked too cozy, if you ask me. I think she's out for him. You might want to warn Jay about her. You two are too cute together to let that witch ruin things."

Meghan couldn't find words to make a reply. She felt as though the well-meaning Charity had punched her in the stomach. She was infinitely grateful when Mr. Cardley turned out the lights to show a film. Tears stung the backs of her eyes. Was she losing Jay? Did she ever have him? Why, oh, why didn't she ever feel that she was enough?

★ ★ ★

Meghan went out to the car after school where her mother was waiting. She sat in the front passenger seat, putting on her safety belt and pulling her coat shut in front. She had forgotten to change back into her other top. If Mom saw her wearing this one there would be a long lecture. Never mind that she hadn't tried the marijuana Charity had brought to school, or taken any of the alcohol that Robb consistently carried in his backpack. Those things didn't appeal to her; they would make her forget her pain—and she never wanted to forget.

She rubbed at Kristin's CTR ring which had pinched a small piece of skin against her own ring. A red blister had begun, hurting more than expected. Yet she left the rings on her finger; the ache was nothing compared to the pain in her heart.

Her mother was talking about a Valentine's Day cake she planned to make as a surprise for Benjamin and Jacky. Meghan nodded without really listening. How could she care about a stupid pink-frosted cake when what she really needed was to figure out what to do about Jay?

"Is something wrong, Meghan?" Angie asked.

Meghan blinked. Had the woman gone insane? Of course there was something wrong. A lot of somethings. Like, duh, Kristin was gone. How could anything be right after that? Not to mention that Jay was putting pressure on her to become more physically affectionate, and now there was this dark-haired girl who had her claws out for him.

"Meghan? Did you hear me?"

"Nothing's wrong," Meghan managed.

For an instant, she thought she saw a sadness in her mother's eyes that begged for the truth. But Meghan couldn't talk to her; there was too much resentment in her heart. Her mother partially blamed her for what happened—she knew it—and Meghan felt that was something they could never get beyond. Besides, what did her mother know about relationships? She couldn't seem to make Meghan's dad happy, or get rid of that annoying Brother Loveridge who kept slobbering like a dog waiting for a juicy bone. Nor could she admit Kristin was gone for keeps.

In silence, they drove to the elementary school to pick up the younger children. Meghan's mother said, "I'll be right back." Then she locked the door and ran inside.

Meghan shook her head. What did her mother think was going to happen to her? She was wearing the GPS tracking device, and if something happened, she could push the two buttons that would notify the company of an emergency. Sometimes she toyed with the idea of pushing them just to see what would happen, but she had never dared.

When they arrived home, Benjamin and Jacky dumped out their loads of Valentine's treats onto the table. "Want some gum?" Jacky offered Meghan a pack. "I got about six of 'em. And I painted you a heart, Meghan. Want to see?"

Meghan didn't want another of Jacky's paintings, but she couldn't bear to break her little sister's heart. Jacky smiled up at her radiantly as she handed the picture over. A fist tightened about Meghan's heart; there was altogether too much of Kristin in that smile.

The picture was a surprisingly well-shaped heart that had a

ragged red slash in the middle. Through slits on either side of the heart came a navy strip of construction paper which crossed and glued in the front to resemble a cloth bandage. The words *You make my heart whole* were painted in blue lettering.

Meghan stared at the heart, thinking it could be a mirror image of her own—only without the bandage. Was this how Jacky felt—that Meghan made her heart intact? She looked at Jacky again. If the truth be told, she hadn't tried to be close to Jacky since the kidnapping. It just hurt too much. She loved Jacky, but she could never take Kristin's place.

"Thanks, Jacky," Meghan said, nearly choking on the words.

"Here, have a candy bar," Benjamin said, not to be outdone. He threw her one.

For some reason, Meghan felt tears behind her eyes. "Thanks." To hide her emotions, she turned to their mother. "Mom, Tamara said they're having a party for Wade. He got his mission call like last month or something."

Angie dragged her eyes from the two vases of flowers on the counter, her face breaking into a bright smile. "How wonderful! I thought I heard something about that in church. I'm glad he's going on a mission. He always was a nice boy."

"Where's he going?" Jacky asked.

"Oh yeah—where?" Angie echoed, her smile still plastered on her face.

"To Florida, I think."

Angie's smile died. "Oh. To Florida." Meghan knew she was thinking about the other kidnapped girls there.

"So can I drop by and congratulate him? Oh, and we might go out for ice cream or something after," Meghan hurried to add in case her mother was going to spy on her whereabouts via the Internet and the tracking device. "But I promise I'll stay right with someone." *Jay*, she amended silently.

Angie studied her for a moment. Then she sighed. "Okay, but be careful."

Meghan didn't remind her mother that she was seventeen now. She just nodded. "Okay."

"No fair," Benjamin whined. "I never get to go anywhere."

"No?" Angie asked. "Seems to me that you have to go to Taekwondo in a few minutes. Come on, go get on your outfit."

"It's a uniform," Benjamin said with exaggerated disgust as he rolled his eyes.

Jacky giggled. "Whatever, Ben. Better be careful or your face'll freeze that way."

Benjamin laughed, but Meghan felt a cold hand close over her heart. Hearing Jacky say that was like hearing Kristin's voice all over again. Holding her breath to stave off the pain, she quickly left the kitchen.

★ ★ ★

Meghan walked down the street to the Burke's house, where the windows were alight with a cheerful glow. The night was very cold, and a thin layer of snow clung tenaciously to the wide lawns. She didn't turn around to see if her mother was still watching her from the door. She probably was. For some reason that made her very sad. Why couldn't Meghan's father stop her from acting that way? Meghan knew the reason: he wasn't around enough to do much of anything.

She slowly walked up the steps to the Burke home. Happy music came from inside. Not the kind she listened to, the kind that blotted out all feeling, but the kind that made you want to laugh and dance.

Meghan didn't feel like dancing. She hesitated, staring silently up into the bright windows. She glanced back at her own house and saw her mother duck inside.

She was watching.

Meghan was at the door now but her hand suddenly felt heavy. Who was she kidding? She didn't belong here. She would just sit on the curb behind those bushes so her mother couldn't see her if she peered out the door again. Jay would be along soon, and she would try to forget she had ever hoped to see Wade tonight.

Chapter Eighteen

I didn't stay with Meghan. Knowing I only had a little bit of time before she left with Jay, I hurried into Wade's house. My momentum drove me through the door, past the entryway, into their family room, and through a half dozen people before I skidded to a stop in front of Wade.

He was surrounded by well-wishers, mostly youth from our area, kids I recognized from church. I was surprised at how they had grown the past year and five months since I'd been gone. How odd it was to see them so changed when my family seemed stagnant. Oh, I know my siblings had grown, but I'd been with them so much I hadn't seen it happening.

"Wade," I said. "Meghan's outside. Please go talk to her. I have this horrible feeling about her and Jay. Please." I placed my hand on his arm, feeling nothing tangible. I stepped back and frowned at how frustrating it was to be in the mortal world where I was nothing more than spirit matter no one could see.

"Don't give up," came a voice.

I looked around the room in surprise. In the corner I spied a small group of spirits watching me with interest.

"We're Wade's great grandparents," explained a woman with black hair and beautiful olive skin. "We're so happy for him—and proud. We received permission to come and celebrate with his family."

I drifted past heart decorations and bowls of red candy to stand near them. "My sister . . ." I began. But words were not enough, and I opened my thoughts, communicating spirit to spirit. I felt their positive responses.

"Try again," said a man with a dark hair and fabulous brown eyes that were obviously his legacy to Wade. "He cares for her, that's clear, and he's very in tune with the Spirit at this time in his life."

Smiling gratefully, I turned back to Wade. I prayed with my whole heart as I begged him to go outside—just for a moment. I thought I had lost, but then he stiffened. My eyes flew to his face, and I saw the dark brown pools of his eyes glisten as he scanned the crowd. Had he missed Meghan?

Oh please, Father. Let him find her.

★ ★ ★

Wade had hoped she'd be here, but he looked through the crowd in vain. Tamara had told him she'd invited her; if she didn't come, did that mean she still wanted nothing to do with him? Would she ever forgive him for that night at the pool? Would she ever let him back into her life? Would she even write when he was gone?

Sometimes he didn't understand why he cared so much. Why he kept track of her, though mostly from afar. After all, he and Meghan had never dated. *But we would have.* He remembered most vividly that last night at the pool—oh, how much he'd enjoyed being with her! He'd felt a connection with her then, something special he'd never felt with any other girl. And now, though it was over before it began, he felt a deep sadness that somehow they had lost something very precious.

Everybody else was here. His friends, relatives, his immediate family. His dad was beaming, and Wade was happy he could bring that proud smile to his father's face. There was a lot to be happy for. Wade felt honored to be worthy to serve a mission, to be a soldier in the army of the Lord. He knew there were people out there waiting to be baptized, people only he could reach.

A warm feeling filled Wade's heart. He recognized the confirmation of the Spirit testifying that his thoughts were correct. Serving a mission would help many people, and he vowed to give his entire heart, might, mind, and soul to the Lord.

But what about Meghan? Where did she fit in, if at all? The last time he'd seen her was at church when he had come to visit his parents' ward two weeks ago. During the sacrament, their eyes had met. Hers had been so vulnerable, giving him the impression that she had seen too much pain. He'd so wanted to put his arms around her and comfort her. She had looked away, and though he'd searched for her after the meeting, he had never found her.

Feeling suddenly stifled amidst the throng of well-wishers, Wade threaded his way through the group, gently pushing aside a bouquet of heart-shaped balloons that had drifted into his path. No one seemed to notice his departure.

Out on the front porch, he breathed in the crisp night air. His eyes wandered of their own accord to stare down the street at Meghan's house. Was she there? Should he walk over and ask to talk with her? What would he say? He raised his eyes to the dark sky where stars gleamed faintly, their light seemingly dimmed by the nearer light of the street lamps. *Father,* he prayed, *help me to know what I should do.*

He saw her then, sitting on the curb next to his mother's bare shrubs. His heart leapt and he started forward silently. She was hunched over as though cold, and her breath came out in wisps of white. She didn't look his way, so either she hadn't heard the front door or was hoping not to be noticed.

He was nearly to her when she turned toward him. Fear flashed across her face, then smoothed as she recognized him. Sympathy welled up in his chest. Had she thought he was someone who meant her harm? And did her mind go to Kristin as his did, wondering how fearful she had been the night she disappeared? Wade swallowed hard.

"Hi, Meghan," he said, shoving his hands into the pockets of his jeans to ward off the cold. He was wearing a gray cotton sweater, but it wasn't enough for this frosty night.

She stood, gathering her blue coat around her slim body. "Hi." Her eyes met his briefly, and he thought he saw a trace of tears. His heart lurched. What could he do to help?

"I was hoping you'd come tonight," he said. "I wanted to see you before I left."

"Well, you're speaking in church here before you leave, aren't you?" She moved the tip of her leather shoe along the crusty snow covering the grass.

He nodded. "Yes, but that's in two weeks. I know it'll be a crazy time. Besides, I wanted to start working on you now."

At that she raised her eyes to his again. He was pleased at the surprise and curiosity of her stare. "What do you mean?"

"You know, to get you to write to me while I'm out on my mission. You always said you wanted to be a writer. You can practice on me."

Her face went utterly still, hiding any emotion she might feel at his comment. She looked casually—too casually?—out over the street. "I don't write anymore. I'm going to become a doctor."

"Hey, I thought that was Kristin's thing." The words came out before he had taken time to think about them, leaving him feeling as he always did in basketball when he'd shot for the hoop before he was in position.

"It was." Meghan's cool voice was as emotionless as her face.

"I'd really love it if you'd write." He was pushing, trying to patch the damage he didn't really understand but clearly recognized.

She shrugged. "I don't know, Wade. You and I—we're going up two different paths."

"What do you mean?" Anger flared inside him, but he fought it down. "Meghan, I've known you for almost three years. I know your heart and it's every bit as good as mine."

She opened her mouth to say something, then shut it again.

"What?" he asked. "What were you going to say?"

Her blue eyes looked suddenly very weary. "It doesn't matter, Wade. It was nothing."

At least the expression in her face was back. "Please, won't you come into the house? My parents and Tamara would really love to see you."

She shook her head. "I'm glad you came out. I wanted to say congratulations about your mission, but I think I'll head back home now. I'm a little tired, and I have biology homework."

He felt there was more she wasn't telling him, but he couldn't very well call her on it or she might shut him out again with that cool, expressionless stare. "Okay, I'll walk you home."

"No." she said quickly.

"Come on, I want to be sure you're safe."

She pulled up her left coat sleeve and showed him the tracking device. "Wade, I'm always safe with this thing on—my parents' idea of a baby-sitter. Besides, it's just a few houses away. I can go myself. Thanks anyway."

Questions about the odd-looking watch came to his lips. He had noticed it before, but then, as now, her expression forbade his curiosity. There was nothing more to say; he couldn't force himself on her. "Well, thanks for coming." He offered his hand, missionary style.

An unexpected smile came to her lips. "You're welcome, Elder."

He smiled back at her. She turned and walked away. He stared after her, thinking how wraithlike and beautiful she appeared in the dark.

"I'll expect a letter," he called.

Her head turned and her hand raised in a wave. Not exactly agreement, or a promise, but at least a beginning.

He watched her until she arrived at her own door and then went back inside to his party.

* * *

Meghan stayed on her porch until she was sure Wade had gone inside. Her heart was beating heavily. He seemed to become more handsome each day. She had so wanted to go inside his house with him—why hadn't she? It wasn't as if people would ask about Kristin anymore. They had all given up on her long ago. Still, there would have been questions and interested stares. Yet she could have gone in and borne it for his sake. She had seen how much it meant to him, though for the life of her, she couldn't fathom why.

But every feeling she had about him always came down to the bottom line: he was to be a missionary, and she didn't want to be alone. At least Jay would be around for the next two years, instead of in another state teaching people she didn't know. Of course, she did know a lot of people in Florida—or at least she knew of them from her dad—and though she had never spoken to them person-ally, she silently shared their pain of losing a loved one to a kidnapper.

Meghan walked back down the street to wait for Jay. She hadn't even reached Wade's when he drove up in his red Porsche.

"Hey babe," he said over the blaring music.

She smiled and climbed in the seat next to him. As he drove off, she said, "Remember, we can't go far. I promised I'd be back really soon."

"Oh, Meg. Why'd you do that?" he said with a frown. "I finally get you alone, and you say you'll be home early."

"It's my mom, you know. She worries a lot."

"I thought you were sick of her smothering you."

"I am, it's just . . ." She trailed off.

"What's wrong with you tonight?" Jay demanded. "You're acting like your best friend died."

She did, Meghan thought, biting back sudden tears. Jay could be so cruel at times.

"Is it Wade?" he asked. "Are you sad he's leaving?"

"I didn't go to the party."

"That wasn't what I asked." Jay pulled into the nearly deserted church parking lot and drove to the far side away from the chapel. He let the engine die.

"Wade has nothing to do with me or with you." Meghan was hot so she removed her coat.

"Good, that's more like it." Jay reached for her, sliding his arms around her body. Meghan allowed the contact. How good it felt to be held by someone!

After a few moments of silence, Jay began to kiss her. At first she enjoyed it, but then his hands began to roam. She pulled back. "Stop it, Jay."

"What?" he asked.

"Let's go somewhere else," she said. *Somewhere with people.*

"I can't help it if I want to be alone with you, Meghan. I love you."

This time the words didn't warm her. "Jay, I—"

"What are you afraid of?" Moonlight coming in from the window, made his blonde hair shine. He had never looked so gorgeous. "I'll take care of you, Meghan."

"Who's that girl you work with?"

"What girl?"

"The one with dark hair. The one in the drive up with you today."

He shrugged. "Nobody—just a girl. Name's Sherrisa. She's nobody."

He tried to kiss her again, but she turned her face away. More than anything, she wanted to go home.

"Come on, sweetie, tell me. What is it? Don't you love me?"

She squeezed herself tightly against the passenger side door. Suddenly the idea of him touching her made her want to scream. Fear pulsed through her, seemingly penetrating each cell.

She held up her hand to ward him off. "Okay, there is something." She was relieved when he backed away slightly. "You know when you asked me what I was thinking about this afternoon? Well, it was about Kristin and how we promised each other to marry only in the temple."

"I don't even go to church anymore." Jay leaned forward, taking her reluctant hands in his. "I can't go to the temple. And you don't even want to go yourself. You've left that old life behind, haven't you? Can't you see how much I love you, Meghan? How much I need you?"

His words sliced through Meghan. He had utterly dismissed her promise to her sister, the deepest wish of her heart, as being "old."

"Next month it'll be a year that we've been dating," he continued, pushing the levers to incline their seats. "Don't you think it's time to move up to a new level of commitment?" Without waiting for her answer, he pulled her tightly to him, kissing her with more passion.

Fear overcame all her other emotions. "No! Stop, Jay. Jay!"

Jay's expression twisted, making him a total stranger. His hand shot out and tugged at the snap on her jeans. With dawning horror, Meghan realized what Jay intended. "I—I thought you loved me, Jay! Please."

"Love you?" he said softly, dangerously, squeezing into her seat with her. "I'll show you how much I love you. But forget all your talk about marrying in the temple. What makes you think you're even worthy to go to the temple? Ha! I assure you that's one place you'll never go inside, especially after tonight. God would strike you dead. Relax, you'll enjoy this."

"No!" Meghan fought him, but he held her with his body. She heard a rip as some of her clothing gave way.

A million thoughts went through Meghan's head—how she never should have believed in Jay, how she might actually deserve punishment for not being there for Kristin, and how terribly much she missed her sister—but not once did she think of pushing the panic buttons on her tracking device.

★ ★ ★

I had gone through a lot of emotions as I first cheered for Wade when he found Meghan in front of his house, and then cried as she left. When Jay showed up in his Porsche, I was frantic. There was a different feeling about him tonight, a determination I knew didn't bode well for my sister. She was so blind about him, a real innocent.

When Meghan drove off with Jay, I went toward my house, hoping to alert my mother, then changed my mind and returned to Wade's. Maybe he could help. I found him standing outside his garage. Apparently, Meghan hadn't fooled him as she had thought. He had come out to check on her again and had seen her leave with Jay.

"Go after her," I urged as the car disappeared. "Please, Wade. You know him. He raped a girl in Texas. You can't let that happen to my sister! She's been through too much already."

Wade stared up at the sky. "Father," he whispered aloud. "What should I do? Please let me know. Meghan's special—I want to help her."

My heart was one with his as he prayed; his words became my own. "Go after her," I said.

"Kristin? Is that you?"

I stared at him. "You can hear me?"

"Yes. Is that you, Kristin?"

I nodded, but he didn't react so I knew he couldn't see me, only hear me. I felt like celebrating. Instead, I looked through the surrounding houses and their occupants, at last finding Jay's car in the church parking lot. "They're at the church. Hurry."

Wade took off running. I wondered why he didn't go inside for his keys and take his car, but a glance inside his house showed me his parents were looking for him. No, running to the church would be faster than explanations.

He ran across the street to his neighbor's backyard, where he scaled the fence easily. I was glad he'd played basketball in high school and was accustomed to jumping so high. I glided along ahead of him, reaching Meghan first and then going back to urge him on. I didn't think he could hear me anymore, but I didn't care. He was going in the right direction.

I worried that he would be too late, but I underestimated my sister. From somewhere in her slight body, she found the strength to fend off Jay. I was proud of her.

At last, Wade rounded the church and charged Jay's Porsche. He ripped the door open. Meghan screamed in relief. Wade grabbed Jay and hauled him off Meghan and out of the car. Jay wrenched free, glaring.

"Oh, big hero coming to save the day," Jay sneered, putting up his fists. "Well, she's mine. You can't have her."

Wade gave an angry grunt and attacked, fists clenched, arms flailing. I had to give him points for heart and intent, but Wade wasn't much of a fighter. Jay easily ducked his shots and in turn slammed Wade with a hard upper cut to the stomach. Wade heaved as he felt to the ground. I knew that had to hurt, and when I heard his head crack on the blacktop, I was even more worried. Jay wasn't above playing dirty. He kicked at Wade several times before he realized he was unconscious.

"Wade!" Meghan screamed.

"Run, Meghan!" I shouted.

She did, but only as far as Wade's body. Jay pounced on her, dragging her back to the car to finish whatever he had in mind. I was terrified. Now he had a witness. He couldn't claim Meghan had been a willing participant as he had with his former girlfriend. He would have to come up with another plan—one that might mean even more trouble for Meghan.

All at once, Wade jumped to his feet. *So, you were only pretending to be knocked out*, I thought admiringly. *Good for you.*

Blood pulsed from the wound on the back of Wade's head, matting in his hair, but he didn't seem to notice any pain. He rammed into Jay's back, knocking him to the ground. "Run, Meghan!" Wade shouted. "Go to Sister Apgood's."

She picked herself up from the ground, took a few steps, then hesitated.

"Go!" screamed Wade. "Call the police!" Jay's fist slammed into Wade's jaw, garbling the last words.

Ignoring him, Meghan jumped on Jay's back and began strangling him. Jay gagged loudly before yanking her off and throwing her roughly to the blacktop. "You can have her," he said scornfully. "I've got better things to do." With that he sprinted to his car, tripping as his baggy pants slid down past his hips. He jumped back to his feet, hitched up his pants, and made it to the car barely before Wade caught up with him again.

As the Porsche sped from the church parking lot, Wade went to his knees at Meghan's side. She was lying face-down on the blacktop. He touched her gingerly on the back. "Are you okay?"

She nodded, but there was a dazed expression in her eyes. Her hand went uncertainly to the left side of her forehead where an ugly gash oozed a steady stream of blood. Wade helped her sit up. Instinctively, she began arranging her clothing, which was torn in several places. Wade peeled off his gray sweater, leaving himself wearing only a T-shirt, and slipped it over her head, avoiding her injury.

"Do you hurt anywhere besides your head?" he asked.

She shrugged. "It doesn't matter."

"Yes, it does. Come on, you're shivering. I'm going to get you to Sister Apgood's. It's the closest house, and we can call the police from there."

"No!"

"What do you mean? Jay just tried to rape you! He hurt you. He had no right to do that. I'm going to see that he pays."

Her hand wiped at the blood coming from her wound, smearing it over her cheek. "I deserve it," she said in a thin, aching voice.

"No, you don't." Wade had to stop and clear his throat before going on.

"I shouldn't have let Kristin walk off alone."

That made Wade pause. "Oh Meghan, you aren't responsible. You aren't! You have to believe me."

"I'm not who you think I am."

"Then who are you?"

Her tears began to fall in torrents. "I don't know. I think I died with Kristin." She paused and then came a rush of words to match the rush of tears. "Oh, I wish Mom would admit that she's dead. I wish she could see me. I wish she could love me." These last words were said into Wade's T-shirt as his arms went around her. He didn't seem to mind the blood.

"She does love you." Wade's voice was rough with emotion. "A lot of people do. Come on. We have to call the police; it's the right thing to do." With infinite tenderness, he gathered her into his arms. Meghan crumpled against him, sobbing. "I'm so sorry," he murmured into her hair. "He had no right. No right at all."

Wade carried her to Sister Apgood's. She looked small in his arms, and heartbroken. But I knew that this was a necessary step toward her recovery.

"Thank you, Wade," I whispered. He didn't hear me. Raising my face to the stars in the sky, I sent up another, more personal thanks to my Father in Heaven.

Chapter Nineteen

Angie spent the evening with the children, wondering when Meghan would be home, and if it was too soon to call the Burke's to see if she was all right. When the phone rang, she hoped the call was from Meghan. Or maybe from Gary.

The man on the other end of the phone identified himself as being an employee of the company who made the GPS locators Angie had bought for the children. "Ma'am, are you there?" came the man's voice when she didn't immediately reply.

Angie struggled to talk past the dread. "What is it?"

"It's your daughter Meghan's locator. Apparently, it's been removed."

"When."

"Just this minute. Our last records show her in the vicinity of your neighborhood so—"

"I have to find her!" Angie hung up as the employee was still talking. The panic of the night Kristin had disappeared returned in that instant. There was little room for coherent thought. Only snatches of conversation coming from the police officers: missing . . . no leads . . . any relatives who might have taken her . . . first twenty-four hours the most crucial . . .

No! She couldn't go through that again!

Trembling, she dialed the police department. "Please, my daughter, she was wearing a GPS locator. It's stopped working . . ." On she went, explaining everything first to one person and then to another. "Please help me," she begged.

Agonizing minutes passed. Finally the officer said more cheerfully, "Okay, Mrs. Marshall, I do have some information for you. About ten minutes ago there was a call about a disturbance. First let me tell you, your daughter is all right. There are policemen with her now and a friend—a Wade Burke. They're bringing her home."

Angie sagged with relief. She started to sob silently, holding her hand over the receiver.

"Apparently, there was some trouble, and your daughter's a bit beaten up, but she's okay. We have an APB out on the boy who attacked her. She was wearing the tracking device the whole time. The officers at the scene said she must have found some wire cutters and a hammer. When they arrived, she was destroying it. Her friend tried to stop her, but the lady whose home they were in made him leave her alone. A wise decision, in the officer's opinion. She was pretty upset, and destroying the device helped her calm down. Anyway, they should be to your house any minute. We'll need to have her checked out by a doctor, and then we'll need you to come down to the station and file charges."

"Thank you." Angie hung up the phone, and it was only then she noticed her younger children staring at her with scared faces, their playing cards forgotten.

"Is Meghan okay?" Benjamin asked.

Angie nodded. "Yes." She started to cry again and the kids came to hug her. She clung tightly to them.

The doorbell rang. "Hurry, it's Meghan." Angie wiped her tears as they raced to the door.

Outside on the porch were two police officers, and behind them Wade stood with Meghan, supporting much of her weight. Angie's breath caught in her throat. Both were covered with scrapes, cuts, and bruises. Meghan had a square bandage on the left side of her forehead and her blonde hair was streaked with blood. She looked very vulnerable.

Angie crossed the few steps between them and gathered Meghan in her arms. "Oh baby, come here. Thank the Lord you're all right! I couldn't bear to—oh, Meghan." Meghan cried and clung to her. "It's going to be all right," Angie said, stroking her hair. "I promise, honey."

"I broke the watch," Meghan sobbed. "It made me so mad. It didn't help. I didn't even think to push the buttons. I—I just wanted to get away. And by the time I remembered it, I couldn't reach it. He had my arm."

"Don't worry about it," Angie told her. "What's important is that you're okay."

More words tumbled from Meghan's lips—a jumble of incoherent statements. Finally, she was silent, resting in Angie's arms as they sat on the couch in the living room. Angie felt blessed to be holding her daughter. "I love you, Meghan," she whispered over and over. "I love you so much!"

The rest of the story came out slowly. When Meghan faltered, Wade took over detailing the fight with Jay, and how in the end, Meghan had refused to leave him, but had jumped on Jay's back instead.

"You did right," Angie told her, though in her heart she wished it hadn't been necessary. "But it looks like you got a pretty good conk on the head. Wade, too." She glanced toward Wade, who had a white bandage looping all the way around the top of his dark head.

"Just a cut in the back," he said modestly.

The policemen exchanged amused looks. "I have no doubt we'll catch him," one told Angie, "but we'll want Meghan to see a doctor. Her head is going to need stitches tonight. Wade's too. And we'll need to document the wounds for the court."

The policemen volunteered to accompany them as far as the hospital, and Angie accepted. Wade first placed a call to his parents, who had grown worried at his disappearance. "No, you don't have to come to the hospital. I'm fine. Just a few stitches probably." He was silent a minute. "Okay, then. I'll meet you there." He hung up looking a little sheepish. "Parents," he said with a shrug.

Meghan received four stitches on her forehead and Wade three staples in the back of his head. Afterward, they went to the police station to give their statements. At last they told the Burkes goodbye and returned to their house.

"Children," Angie told Benjamin and Jacky, "I want you to go get ready for bed. We'll meet in Meghan's room for prayer." That they went without protest showed how exhausted they were.

Angie walked with Meghan up to her bedroom and pulled back the covers. "Don't leave me, Mom," Meghan pleaded.

"I won't. Don't worry." Angie helped her daughter into the twin bed and then climbed in after her. Tucking the blankets around them, she held her daughter.

After prayer, Benjamin went to his bedroom, while Jacky dragged in a blanket and pillow so she could sleep on Meghan's floor. Silence fell over the house. Only Angie was sleepless as she held her oldest daughter and listened to her regular breathing.

After a half hour, the sound of the garage opening reverberated through the house. *Gary?* thought Angie. *But he's not supposed to be home.*

She eased out from under Meghan and met him at the back door.

"Is she okay?" His face was white and his eyes frightened.

"Yes, she's upstairs asleep. How did you know?"

"Ben called me earlier. Said the police had brought Meghan home and that she'd been attacked. He didn't know anymore. I took the first flight home."

He held out his hands and Angie gripped them, grateful for his presence. "It was that boy, Jay. He tried to rape her."

Gary's face hardened and tears glistened in his eyes. "Did he . . .?"

Angie shook her head. "She's just beat up a little. Wade caught up to them in time—thank heaven."

Gary briefly closed his eyes, temporarily masking his enormous relief. "Thank heaven," he repeated. When he drew her to him, Angie didn't resist, but instead clung to her husband, offering and receiving comfort. Not for the first time that evening, gratitude for Meghan's life filled her heart.

★ ★ ★

Meghan stirred as her mother left the room. The doctor had given her pain pills that seemed to make her drowsy, but she was afraid to be alone. She hoped Angie would return soon. The strength her mother had shown that evening had amazed Meghan. Her love was even more of a revelation. She really cared.

There were things Meghan knew she had done wrong—dreadfully wrong. The first was going out with Jay, especially behind her parents' backs. The second thing was that she had not given her parents enough credit for their feelings toward her . . . or given them enough of her heart.

And Wade. Just thinking of him made her feel warm. She was so grateful to him for saving her from Jay.

What's more, for the first time in a very long time, Meghan felt the love of her Heavenly Father coming to her from those around her. He had saved her from her own folly when she had not been sure she was even worth saving. Now she vowed to somehow get back on the right path and stay there.

In the distance, she heard a telephone ring. The sound of her father's voice came to her, but not his words. Meghan forced her sagging eyes open again. Her father was home? What would he say about all this?

She didn't have long to wait. Her parents came into her room together, and her father immediately fell to his knees by her bed. "Are you okay, sweetheart?" he asked.

A lump rose in Meghan's throat. She nodded. "I'm sorry, Daddy."

"Hush, it's not your fault."

"I shouldn't have been with him."

He glanced behind him at Meghan's mother. "There's a lot of things we all have done that we shouldn't have. But together, we can make it through. We can." One of his hands gripped Meghan's and the other smoothed her hair. "I love you, sweetie. And don't worry, everything's going to be all right. The police called just now; they picked up Jay."

"Good," Meghan said fiercely. "I'm glad."

Her father gathered her into his arm and held her for a long time without speaking. Meghan cherished every second of his touch.

★ ★ ★

After their embrace in the kitchen, I expected my parents would talk and finally work things out. I thought they might be able to say goodbye to me. But I guess it takes some people more nudges than others. Instead, they went their separate ways again: Father to my room, while Mother stayed with Meghan just in case she was needed in the night.

"Don't you see how good you are together?" I pleaded with them. "Don't you see how you came together tonight and were stronger? That's how it should have happened when I left. You should lean on each other. Dad, Mom doesn't want to leave you. She doesn't give a hoot about Brother Loveridge. She loves you! And Mom, Dad needs you—can't you see?"

Neither listened. I watched Father check his e-mail messages to see if there were any from the parents of other missing girls in Florida or the surrounding states. I watched Mom lie down next to Meghan, stroking her hair until long after my sister returned to sleep. My only comfort was observing how much more relaxed Meghan appeared—even under all her scrapes and bruises—and how she clung to our mother.

I floated on the ceiling in Meghan's room, debating whether I should return to Paradise or stay there. Time passed as I contemplated my future. Had I tried my best? Did I need to ask for help? What more could I do? *Oh, Father,* I prayed. *I don't seem to be doing very well here. I'm so grateful You allowed me to talk to Wade, that he could save Meghan. But I think I need Your help again. Will You tell me what to do?*

The answer came much more forcefully than the answers to my prayers when I had been a spirit; having seen my Father and felt His arms around me, there was no room for doubt.

Stay there, child. The time is at hand.

I didn't know what that meant, but I knew I'd soon find out. I wondered if the police would call to tell my parents that my kidnapper had confessed. Or maybe my body had been found. I was tempted to zip over and see, but I had been told to stay. You couldn't have dragged me out of Meghan's room with a hundred new nebulae to explore.

My mother was dozing. Her breath came regularly but her fingers still moved in Meghan's hair. I remembered vividly when it had been my hair she'd stroked. I remembered the soft sound of her breath, her smell. When she arrived in Heaven, I'd tell her how much it had meant for me to feel her touch, to know she was my mother and that she loved me more than life itself. I hadn't fully understood that love—until my experience as an angel. And it was that same experience that allowed me to not mourn the time we'd lost, but to look forward to the glorious future together in God's Kingdom.

There was a movement in the hallway, and a shadow crept into Meghan's darkened room. Muffled steps led to the bed. Mother sensed a movement, and her eyes flew open. "Aaaaahhh!" she screamed, holding her hands against her chest. I rushed over, practically squishing myself into her. Her heart pounded. I could feel her fear.

The dark figure jerked back, startled at my mother's reaction. "It's just me."

My mother gave a little sob of relief at hearing my dad's voice. "Oh, I thought . . . I didn't know you'd come to check on . . . I thought you were . . . Oh, dear Lord."

She was trembling and the beating of her heart was still erratic. Her fingers went to Meghan, who still slept soundly under the influence of the painkillers.

Dad's hand had also gone out to Meghan and their hands accidentally touched. I know he could feel Mom's trembling. He grabbed her hand. She didn't resist as he pulled her from the bed and into his arms. "It's okay," he murmured. "You're okay. Everything's okay."

From my spot by Meghan's sleeping form, I watched in amazement and secret joy.

"I've been so alone," my mother whispered. There was more she should say—I knew it. Remembering the idea I'd had with Randy in Heaven, I glided toward them, pressing myself between them.

"Communicate through me," I told them. "Spirit to spirit. I know that you can feel each other if you try."

"I've missed you," my dad said. "Oh, Angie, I've missed you so much!"

Mom buried her head in his shoulder and cried. Emotions seemed to flow between them. Not as it did in Heaven between spirits, but there was at least a touching of their spirits. I withdrew from them to see what would happen next. That's when I realized that I wasn't the only spirit there. The Holy Ghost was with them, and the communication and understanding He gave them far exceeded any brief connection I had been allowed to open for them.

"I love you," my mom said, raising her head at last.

"I know." His voice was almost wondering. He placed his hand over her heart. "I can feel you. I thought I'd lost you . . . I love you, Angie. I'll love you forever."

She hiccuped softly. "I want to go on. I want to be there for the kids, but I don't know how to let Kristin go. I'm afraid I'll never be able to let her go. I ache so badly inside. I just want my baby back!"

Dad's forehead met hers. "I know. But I think it's time we did let her go. We both love Kristin very much, but we have three other children who need us. We can't sacrifice them for our guilt over what happened. We must let her go to save the others."

"I know." Mom's eyes raised to the ceiling. "Dear God . . . dearest Father. How can we do such a thing? How did You let Your Son go?"

Dad held more tightly to Mom. "We'll pray," he said. "We'll talk. We'll be there for each other. Kristin will be always in our hearts."

"But what if she's not . . . gone?" Mom asked. "I know the timing makes her seem part of those killings in Florida. But there is a very slight possibility she's in some foreign country or something. It—it would be easier if we knew."

"You're right, it would. But we may never know. Many families don't." Dad's eyes searched hers in the darkness. "The way I see it is we both have felt very strongly that she's okay. Where else would she be okay except in Heaven? Don't you see, Angie? We can't keep blaming ourselves, living in limbo. I'm not saying we give up searching to find the person responsible, or that we don't follow any leads that may come up, but we must put our trust in God. We must learn to live again as though she's never coming home. Otherwise, it's not just Kristin he's taken, but a whole family destroyed—an eternal family."

"I know," Mom whispered. "And it frightens me to think he almost did."

Holding hands, they went to their own room where they knelt down by their bed and began to pour out their hearts to God. The

Holy Ghost was so strong in the room that I wondered they couldn't see Him. After a few minutes, I returned to Meghan's room to allow them privacy. Their mourning, their healing, their communication with God and each other was too private for even me to witness.

Chapter Twenty

I had learned since leaving Earth that bad things often happened to good people, and that being a faithful member of the Church didn't guarantee a trouble-free life. My uncle had once used his agency to choose a horrible path, and because of his choice my Aunt Lesa had to bear many burdens. My parents may not have chosen as wisely as they should have in the past seventeen months, but that didn't mean they deserved the pain they had suffered. It also didn't mean they were terrible people or that the Church wasn't true. The fact that bad things happen to good people only meant that people make mistakes—some more grievous than others.

What is truly important in the end is what we do with the trials we are given. I was proud of Meghan that night for fighting Jay, of my mom for reaching out to her, of my father for being there, and of Wade for saving Meghan. And most of all, I was proud of my parents for deciding to let me go. They are heroes in the face of the unspeakable.

There was a change in the spirit of the house after that night. My parents were united in both appearances and in spirit. Looking at them, I saw such strength that I almost didn't recognize them. My siblings sensed the difference immediately, and while at first they regarded my parents with caution, they soon relaxed and began to reach out to them. Meghan in particular sought out my mother at every opportunity.

They talked about me often. Not with the raw pain of before, but with a trust in the Lord that was beautiful to see. They weren't perfect, and occasionally had bad days—very bad days—but they were finally moving in the right direction . . . and going there together.

One day, Jacky painted the family having breakfast. I was in the picture, sitting in the middle of the table reading the scriptures to them as I had become accustomed to doing since my passing. Dad looked at the painting. "I think it's time for us to start reading the scriptures again. We should never have stopped. Tomorrow, we'll need to get up twenty minutes early." No one complained, not even Benjamin who was the hardest to get out of bed.

Another miracle. I laughed softly to myself.

Though Dad spent much more time with the family, he still researched kidnappings on the Internet and was in touch with the police practically every day. He didn't forget that the days were passing quickly—which meant another innocent girl would soon fall victim to the kidnapper. With no new evidence against my uncle and his apparent reformation, the police were at a loss as to where they should focus the investigation.

Then nearly a week after Jay's attack, Detective Lowder called my dad at work with some news.

★ ★ ★

"You're saying there's a tape?" Gary asked, looking up from the reports he was entering into his computer. "A tape—really? How could the Florida police have overlooked something that obvious?" He wondered if this was the break they'd been waiting for.

"The girl had a troubled history. Apparently, she was in and out of juvenile detention. She'd been missing a year with no trace when the call came. The family was out, so the call recorded on their answering machine. Police thought it was a hoax. You know, some kids in the neighborhood or something. But the mother saved it all these years. The recording was bad—garbled—and the FBI had a time cleaning it up. They want your wife to listen to it to try and make a match. But even without that, we can at least compare the voice patterns to our suspects."

Gary knew that chiefly meant his brother. "What was her name?"

"Sandra Bringhurst. Fourteen. Only child from a good, working class family. Good grades, active in school until she fell in with some bad kids. She was brought up a few times on theft charges and for possession of drugs. A week after her last stint in detention, she ran away. The most recent information we found on her was that she'd joined some new wave spiritual group. The parents are divorced now. Too much hurt and blame. Sad situation. If we can find a match, I think it would bring them some peace."

"I understand." Gary did—all too well. He knew how painful it was not to know what had happened to Kristin, though he had resigned himself to her death. It was something he could face as long as Angie was by his side, and as long as they had the hope of eternity.

"She'd be victim four," Detective Lowder added.

Gary studied his own notes. He noticed his hand was trembling. "That would mean we've found them all—if we include Jenni Wright, the missing girl who could be number seven. I know she's older than the rest, but I think she's part of it. And that got me to thinking last night. I realized I didn't catch the name of the man who told the police about her dog being left behind when she drove off to her new job and never arrived." He didn't add that the impression had come while he had been praying. "Any chance he's connected with any of the other cases?"

"Not that I'm aware of, but I'll look in my files and make a few calls. When you come down later to hear the tape, I'll give you any information I find. Might have a picture too."

"Good. I'll call my wife and have her meet us there. I'll come right from work." Gary hung up the phone, sending a prayer of gratitude upward.

★ ★ ★

"I'm sorry, but the tumor is cancerous," the doctor said.

"Cancerous?" the patient repeated. "No, you must have me mixed up with another case."

The doctor's mustached face showed pity. "I'm really sorry. I know this is difficult to hear. And unfortunately, this particular cancer is fairly aggressive. There are treatments—none of them very fun, but you'll need to see a specialist. The good new is we have a great cancer center here in Utah."

He despised the doctor's pity. Rage burned inside, consuming him. He leapt to his feet and sneered, "Are you saying I'm going to *die*?"

The doctor stepped back. If he felt surprised, he didn't let the

emotion register where the patient could see. "I'm really not qual-
ified to give you any firm prognosis, but I believe your case is very
serious. The best thing you can do is accept my referral to the
doctors at the Huntsman Cancer Institute. They'll be able to help
you further with the very latest medicines and procedures. You
should know at the outset that studies have proven attitude greatly
affects survival. The spiritual well-being and the well-being of the
body are inextricably connected."

"So you want me to get religion, do you?"

"Not necessarily religion, but a positive attitude could help the
outcome."

"I don't believe that crap." He'd heard it before somewhere; the
body and spirit were connected and if the spirit became sick then
the body would soon follow. Oh, yes, it had been that girl, Sandra.
She had been studying spiritualism with that band of new wave
hippies when he'd found her passing out flyers in her bikini at the
lake. It had been easy to gain her trust and get her to go with him.
Her philosophy meant nothing. He was brilliant. He should not
have cancer—he was too important to have cancer. The doctor
must be lying. But he would fix that.

As he quietly accepted the address the doctor gave him, he
stared at the picture of the doctor's family. Blondes, all of them. The
youngest looked about twelve. She had huge, trusting blue eyes. Too
bad she didn't swim often anymore.

Oh, but according to her father, she dances. He smiled. *There isn't
much difference between a dance outfit and a swimming suit. And I bet she
dances with friends.*

One for Mother, one for Lilet.

There was still plenty of time. He had at least another week or
two before the leeway he allowed himself—two weeks either side
of the original altercation with Lilet—had expired.

★ ★ ★

"Okay, I'm going to play it now," Detective Lowder said. He
flipped the switch on the tape recorder.

Angie closed her eyes, shutting out the fluorescent lighting and the faces of the three officers around the table. She was trembling, and felt grateful for Gary's hand closing over hers. His grasp was so much more than a simple touch, conveying his support and love. She didn't want to listen to the voice. There were other things she'd rather do—like contemplate the recent changes in Meghan. Unbidden tears sprang to her eyes as she thought about how much she and Meghan had shared these past days. And how far she and Gary had progressed.

Along with Meghan, they had begun seeing their grief counselor again to learn strategies for coping with loss for the long term. She was beginning to see how blaming Gary was a substitute for her own feelings of guilt for Kristin's disappearance. Meanwhile, their improved relationship was rapidly filling the void in her soul. Her yearning for Kristin had dimmed, and the pain was bearable now that she was learning to share . . . and to let go, to face the fact that Kristin was gone.

The recording began. "I wanted to let you know that your daughter, Sandra, is just fine. I'm keeping her safe. Don't worry."

"Play it one more time," she requested, clinging to Gary for all she was worth.

"Do you recognize the voice?" asked Detective Lowder.

She shook her head. "I can't be sure, but that I swear the man who called me used the exact same words. Except for the name. He didn't use Kristin's name."

They played the tape again.

Ignoring the tears sliding down her face, she looking pleadingly at the officers. "It's got to be the same voice. I'm almost sure. You say Sandra had been missing a long time before this call, just like Kristin. She was probably already dead." For the first time the connection between Kristin's disappearance and the other kidnapping cases became real for Angie. Five of the girls' remains had been found. Three hadn't been, including Kristin and the girl whose family had kept this tape.

Oh Kristin, you really are in Heaven, aren't you? Instead of the old, crushing pain, Angie felt a warm reassurance. She didn't know if it was Gary's firm grip, or something divine, but her heart felt afire with comfort. She nearly wept with relief. She might never find

Kristin's earthly body, but she knew exactly where her spirit was—with her grandmother and other relatives in Paradise.

She turned to Gary, wanting to share this epiphany with him, knowing he would be grateful. But the officers had placed a photograph in front of him. The man in the photograph had a receding hairline, shaggy brown hair, and a droopy mustache. His eyes could be light brown, but it was hard to tell.

"This is the guy?" Gary asked. "You gotta be kidding. He looks like a flower child."

"Yeah, tell me about it. But that's him. The guy who reported the dog in the Jenni Wright case."

"She's the girl who disappeared before Kristin, isn't she?" Angie asked, squinting at the photo. It wasn't a clear shot and his facial hair prevented her from really seeing his features.

"That's the one. Name he gave the cops was Victor Ford, but we can't find him now. He isn't registered with social security."

"I don't recognize him," Angie said.

"Me either." Gary brought the photograph closer with his free hand. "Although there is something about those eyes."

Angie looked again but shook her head. "I don't see anything strange about the eyes."

"I mean, they look familiar."

"Could it be your brother in disguise?" asked the FBI agent whose name Angie had not caught.

"No." Gary held up the photograph. "Well, I suppose it could be if . . . no. I don't think so. The eyes aren't the same color. Phil's are hazel, not . . . whatever color this man's are."

The officer shrugged. "Could be wearing contacts."

"But he was here at the time of that disappearance, wasn't he?" Angie asked.

"He lived here," Detective Lowder said, "but he and his family were in Florida, at Disney World."

Angie met Gary's eyes and he nodded once. "Oh, I didn't realize," she said. "Gary didn't tell me that." There were many things she and Gary had not discussed in the past year and a half. "Well, I'm sure Lesa wouldn't lie about being with him."

"Lesa Marshall can't verify his whereabouts for every hour of the entire three days they were there." Detective Lowder was quiet for a moment before saying to Gary, "Could it be the neighbor you asked me to check into?"

"Loveridge? No, I don't think so."

Angie gasped and let go of Gary's hand. "What? Dale. No! Not in a million years. Gary, you asked him to check on Dale?"

"Yes. I did." Gary's eyes met hers steadily, pleading with her to understand. "Do you blame me? He's someone from your past. It could have been a revenge thing. I mean, I know he had a lot of bills from his wife dying, but I don't understand why he didn't buy a house if he is who he says he is, instead of renting with students. And why aren't his sons living with him? I didn't think it would hurt to do a background check. I didn't tell you because I didn't want to hurt you."

Angie took a deep breath and let him take her hand again. "I suppose you're right. I guess it could be anyone. I have to admit that sometimes a doubt or two about him has crossed my mind." She wiped a tear from her left eye.

"Well, he came up clean—mostly," said Detective Lowder. "Except for a couple of parking tickets. But interestingly enough, one was given to him in Florida about the time of the sixth kidnapping. It seems he was also visiting Disney World with his family during that time."

Angie clutched her head, feeling a headache coming on. "Is that all today?" she asked.

"Yes." Detective Lowder tapped the photo in Gary's hand. "You can keep this copy, Mr. Marshall. Let us know if you think of anything else."

"We will, thanks."

Angie and Gary were silent as they walked out of the police station to Gary's car and the van, parked side by side in the parking lot. "See you at home in a few minutes," Gary said, leaning over to kiss her briefly.

"Oh, I'll be a bit longer. I have to get Sister Lottie's little girl from her dance class. Meghan had to stay after school so I asked Sister Lottie to watch Ben and Jacky while I came here. She agreed, but asked if I'd pick up Hailey for her on the way home."

He laughed. "You know, Ben's twelve now. He's probably ready to baby-sit."

She gave him a wry smile. "I'll think about it. Anyway, it'll only take me a few extra minutes."

"Take all the time you need. I'm not going anywhere." He kissed her again, more lingeringly. "And don't worry, I'll go next door and get the kids."

Angie felt happy. Her relationship with Gary wasn't perfect yet, but it was exactly what she needed. "I love you, Gary," she said softly.

He smiled. "I love you too, Angie."

Angie arrived at the dance class just before it ended. She parked the van outside and was about to go in when she caught sight of Dale Loveridge a few car lengths ahead. The hood was up on his car and he was by the curb, hands in the pocket of his suit, looking very irritated and cold.

"Dale," she called, walking toward him. Immediately, the irritation smoothed away. "What happened?"

His chin motioned toward a small store behind him that sold educational supplies. "Stopped to get some things and when I came out, car wouldn't start. Darn thing."

"Oh, I'm sorry. What are you going to do?"

"Well, lucky for me someone who knows something about cars stopped to give me a hand. I hope he'll get it going enough so that I can take it to his uncle's shop."

Angie hadn't realized someone was looking at the car. Sure enough, when she stepped around Dale, she could see a man in cords and a heavy shirt with sleeves rolled up to the elbows. There was something familiar about him, but she couldn't tell if it was his stance or his tousled brown hair.

Just then he looked up and smiled. "Hi," he said, flashing her a grin. "You're Mrs. Marshall, right? You take your car to my uncle's shop."

"Oh yes, I remember you. You helped my daughter with her math once." What Angie remembered most, though, was the poor job he had done on the sensors in her van—or rather the lack of his work on them.

"Lucas Lyman's my name, in case you don't remember." He started to offer his hand, but glanced at the grease and changed his mind. "I don't work for my uncle anymore, but I still know my way around a car." His gaze switched to Dale's face. "I'm just about done here, but this battery needs replacing."

"I appreciate your stopping," Dale said. "Not everyone would."

Lucas shrugged as he wiped his hands on a rag Dale had produced from the car. "Well, it's a dangerous world we live in. People are afraid of being attacked when they stop to help."

"And you're not?" Angie asked.

He shook his head, meeting her eyes with his pale brown ones, and making Angie feel uncomfortable. "Nope. It's a pretty public place. Besides, I know a good man when I see one."

"Thank you," Dale said. "And I also know a good man when I see one. I'll be sure to tell your uncle how helpful you've been. Thank you."

"You're welcome." Lucas' gaze went beyond them. "Looks like a class just got out or something."

Angie turned around to see little girls in dance leotards spilling onto the sidewalk, some carrying their coats, and others pulling them on. Most climbed into waiting cars, but a few stood on the sidewalk talking to their friends.

"Sister Marshall!" Hailey came running up to her, dark hair trailing behind.

"Hi, honey." Angie greeted the little girl.

"Did you come to pick me up? My teacher said Mom called and that you'd be here." She looked around. "Where's Jacky? I wanted her to see me dance. I think she'd like doing it with me." Her eyes flickered past Angie, and immediately she fell silent as she noticed the two men. "Hi, Brother Loveridge," Hailey said, recognizing him.

"Hi, Hailey. How're you doing?"

"Good. I was dancing."

"I can see that. Did you have a good time?"

"Yep, a really good time. I love dancing." She looked at Lucas Lyman. "Who are you?"

"He's a man who stopped to help him Brother Loveridge with his car—Mr. Lyman."

Hailey nodded at Big Ned's nephew. "I hope you can fix it. Brother Loveridge is my brother's teacher at church, you know."

Lucas smiled. "Well, then I'll certainly do my best."

"I'd better get home," Angie said to the men. "If you're sure you're not going to need help, Dale, I'll be on my way."

"I'll be fine. Thanks."

Angie was walking back to her van when Hailey stopped. "I want to say goodbye to Courtney," she said. "Can I?"

"Sure." Angie watched as she dashed to a girl with long blonde hair, who was standing by the door to the dance studio. She was talking to another blonde girl, but smiled radiantly at the dark-haired Hailey as if she genuinely liked her. The girls chatted together for few seconds before Hailey waved goodbye and ran to the van.

"Courtney is the best dancer in our class," Hailey confided on the way home. "She's been dancing for two years instead of one like me, but she's older."

"She seems really nice."

"She is. Some of the girls say she's stuck up, 'cause her dad's a doctor and he makes a lot of money, but she's always nice to me. She says I have real talent."

"Your mother says so too."

"Is Jacky going to take dance with me?"

"Well, if she wants to maybe she could try it out, but she's really into painting right now."

"She's good at painting," Hailey said generously. "But I hope she takes dance because I've really missed her this year. I don't get to see her much anymore."

Blinking away sudden tears, Angie smiled at Hailey. "I'll see what I can do. Every girl should take at least one dance class, right?"

Chapter Twenty-One

"I used to wonder why God sent us down here if He already knows what we're going to do," Meghan said. She and Wade were sitting outside her house in his parents' Camry, since he had sold his car to help pay for his mission. "I mean, on the surface it seems much more simple for Him to give us what He knows we would deserve, doesn't it?"

"Yes, but we need to prove it to ourselves," Wade said. "For instance, if they told me I was going to choose to follow Satan, I wouldn't believe it—no way."

Meghan's lips curled in a smile. "You're going to have to do better than that, Elder Burke—if you're going to be a missionary."

"Okay, so what's your take on it?"

"Well, an idea came to me yesterday after I finished my appointment with my counselor. When my parents made me see the counselor before, I didn't listen much and basically told her what she wanted to hear so that I wouldn't have to go anymore. But this time, I'm really trying to work things out. Anyway, we'd been talking about our purpose here on Earth. She's a member of the Church, too."

"And?" Wade nodded at her encouragingly, looking a bit odd with his new extra-short haircut. His dark eyes were the same as ever—so deep she could drown in their depths.

"And I think we came to Earth partly because God knew we needed the experiences to become exactly what He knew we could become. Sure, He knows what we would choose in the end, but if we didn't actually go *through* the experiences—even the bad ones—then we wouldn't grow and become that strong person."

"That does make sense." Wade's voice was full of admiration. "I never thought about it like that. I'm impressed, Meghan. You never cease to amaze me."

She laughed softly. "I've come a long way—especially in these past two weeks. You've helped me a lot. I appreciate all the long talks we've had. And all the movies and the other stuff we've been doing."

"Dollar movies didn't exactly change your life," he said with a grin. "Seriously, though. I didn't do anything, Meghan. You've always been strong. You just got lost for a while."

She gave him another smile. "I'm still a little lost. But I know what direction I'm moving. I know there are going to be some tough times ahead, but I don't think I'll ever feel as horrible as I did before."

His hand covered hers where it lay on her thigh. "I'm so glad. I'm almost sorry to be leaving. I hope you don't outgrow me spiritually while I'm gone." He smiled as he said it, but his eyes were serious.

She laughed. "Oh, Wade, that's what I keep thinking about you! You know how it is when missionaries come back. You hardly even recognize them."

"Oh, you'll recognize me. I'll send you plenty of pictures." They both laughed, knowing she hadn't been speaking of his physical appearance.

He walked her up to her door, but didn't turn to leave immediately as he usually did. Meghan's heart started thumping in her chest. Was he going to try to kiss her? A quick glance down the street assured her they were quite alone.

"I've been wanting to tell you something," he said instead. "You know that night at the church with Jay? Well, I heard Kristin in front of my house. She told me to go after you. That's how I knew where to find you."

"You heard her?"

"Yes. I know it sounds strange, but I was praying and I heard her voice. Only a few sentences. I think she'd been looking after you for some time, and she didn't want you to be hurt again."

"I have felt her close," Meghan confessed, "but I pretty much dismissed it. I've never heard her speak, though. Then again, I haven't exactly been close to the Spirit until lately. I'm not surprised she'd come to you—she always liked you." *Or knew how much I liked you*, Meghan added silently.

"I guess she's your personal guardian angel."

Meghan frowned and stared at the ground. Against her will, a tear slipped from the corner of her eye. Seeing it, Wade cupped his hand under her chin and gently raised her face so he could gaze into her eyes.

"What is it, Meg? Tell me."

She blinked and another tear squeezed out and ran down her cheek. "It's just the thought of Kristin watching me this past year and a half—if she has been—it must have been hard for her. And then I start to wonder—where was her angel when she was being abducted? Why didn't God interfere for her like she did for me?"

Still cupping her chin, Wade wiped at the tears on her cheek. The tenderness in his touch matched the expression in his eyes. "I don't know, Meghan. Perhaps it's something we won't ever understand completely down here. But it seems to have something to do with what you said before in the car. We have to go through these trials to grow—to become who we were meant to become. We can't pick and choose our experiences, but the Lord can. He knows what we need, what we can endure."

"That's right," she said with a wan smile. "Use my own words against me." After a pause, she continued, "You're right. Still, I wish I could have learned about missing Kristin some other way."

"For what it's worth, I do know the Lord loves us and that He wants us to be happy. Wherever Kristin is, she's happy, too—I'm sure of it."

When he said it like that, happiness suddenly didn't seem like such an unlikely possibility. "I believe that, too," Meghan said. "And I think, Elder Burke, that you're going to be a wonderful missionary." Then she added more softly, "I do wish I could see Kristin just one more time." Her voice was slightly unsteady, but she didn't let herself cry again.

"I will pray for just that," Wade promised. She smiled and he released her chin. As she reached for the doorknob, his tone became light, almost teasing. "But there is just one more thing."

"What?"

"Tomorrow I'm going to be set apart as a missionary. You know what that means—two years with no dates. So I'm wondering—can I uh . . ."

To Meghan's delight he blushed a bright shade of red. "Can you what?"

"Can I have a kiss?" He held up his hands and hastened to add, "Doesn't have to be a real big one, or anything. Just enough so that when I'm on my mission and showing your picture around, I can tell them you're my girlfriend."

She laughed, feeling euphoric. He wanted her as a girlfriend! During the past two weeks dating him, she had begun to want nothing more than to be in his arms. "Okay," she said, infusing her voice with amusement, "but just a little one. I wouldn't want you to not focus on your work or anything, *Elder* Burke."

He grinned. "Deal, *Sister* Marshall."

Their lips met, tentatively at first. She could tell he felt as awkward and inexperienced as she did. With growing assurance, Meghan's arms crept up around his neck and his went around her waist. The pressure of his lips on hers left her breathless. She loved being so near him, from the woodsy scent of his aftershave, to his strong arms wrapping around her. Oh, that this moment could last forever! All too soon the moment was over. Meghan was pleased that Wade looked as stunned as she felt.

"Wow," he murmured. "I'm walking on air, see?" He jumped off the porch, missing the stairs altogether. "See you tomorrow, Meghan."

"See you." She waited until he had driven off before going inside.

Jacky and Benjamin were sitting on the couch with false expressions of innocence. Then Jacky burst out in song: "Two little lovers sitting in a tree, K-I-S-S-I-N-G."

Meghan just gave her a smile and practically floated upstairs to her room.

★ ★ ★

Meghan drove to the Mission Training Center with the Burke family. She felt honored to be the only one outside their immediate family invited to see Wade off. After a short meeting, the missionaries bid farewell to their parents. Sister Burke began crying and dabbing her nose with a tissue. She clung to Wade for a long time. Brother Burke's expression was steady, though the occasional glimmer in his eyes and the way he hugged his son belied the outer composure. Tamara also blinked back tears as she kissed her brother's cheek, and the family's two young boys hugged Wade tightly through their sobs.

Last of all, Wade turned to Meghan, drawing her aside. She felt odd that he would leave her for last when his family was more important. Yet in his eyes she saw an unspoken promise—one that went beyond the duty of a child to a parent or sibling.

"Hey, don't cry," he said softly. His expression was tender.

"I'm not crying."

"Then your eyes are leaking. You should really get that fixed."

She laughed through the tears. "I'm going to miss you, Elder Burke."

"Me too—you."

She smiled, then sobered. "Look, there is one thing I want you to do for me."

"Anything." He said it with a trust she wasn't sure she deserved.

She plunged ahead. "In Florida there are some other families who have missing daughters. My dad and the police think the cases could be linked to Kristin's. And ever since I heard you were going to Florida, I've been thinking . . . well, I have this feeling . . . uh, maybe that's part of your call. To at least try to give them something. A gift from Kristin. The gift of the gospel. I have here all the information I could find about them. I know they might not accept, but we have to try. I've written my testimony in these books. " She bent down to retrieve a package under her chair. "Do you think you could take them to the families?"

"Sure." He accepted the books. "I'll do it. Even if I can't get to them myself, I'll send other missionaries who are in the area. They deserve a chance to hear the gospel."

"Thank you." Her tears started to fall. "Just knowing Kristin is alive somewhere, and that she's happy in Paradise—some days that's all that holds our family together. I want them to have the chance to know their daughters are okay."

Wade was now the last missionary in the room and was being

motioned toward the far door by a man in a suit. "Goodbye, Meghan," he said urgently. "Write me. Whatever you want, but write. I may be on the other side of America, but I'll always be here for you."

"I will," she whispered. More tears came then, so quickly she didn't actually see him leave. But she wore a smile so he would remember her that way.

Chapter Twenty-Two

After I watched Meghan say goodbye to Wade, I left the MTC, giving a smile of encouragement to the hosts of angels guarding the place. I even recognized a man who often sang in the Heavenly Choir and had helped me perfect one of my hymns on the piano. It had been a good week—a very good week. Mom and Dad were spending time together; Benjamin had advanced to the high yellow belt in his Taekwondo class; Jacky was taking dance with Hailey from next door—not yet in the same class, but at the same time and place where they could see each other often; and Meghan and Wade were falling in love—or beginning to. Whether or not they ended up together, I knew their relationship would help Meghan recover.

There was one nagging worry. Meghan had refocused on school but was still studying subjects I had enjoyed. Even after receiving an excellent score on a short story in English, she didn't return to her love of writing. I didn't understand why. If she believed I was all right and continuing my life in Paradise, then why did she still feel obligated to take the spot I would have filled on Earth? It seemed a contradiction of beliefs. I didn't think she had come to love science—her longing glances at her English texts and rows of unread novels clearly showed me that.

"Give her more time," Grandma counseled.

"Hey, what choice do I have?" I was lying on a hammock in Grandma's backyard, while she sat on a blanket with a book of poetry.

"Oh, look who's here," she said, raising her eyes.

I sat up, tumbling myself to the soft grass.

Randy chuckled. "Good morning, Miss Graceful. I have come to take you star-hopping, if you're able."

"Well, I don't know," I said as he helped me up. "Some of us have been working, you know."

"I do know. You've been gone for some time." With a smile for my grandmother, he drew me away. The sky overhead was a bright blue and everywhere around us radiated the light of Christ.

"Miss me?" I asked softly.

His eyes met mine. "Yes. It's lucky we have eternity to be together, or I might be jealous of the time you spend on Earth."

I opened my eyes wide. "Eternity?"

He nodded. "Eternity."

"But—" I began.

"I love you. I think I loved you from the first moment I saw you again in the Music Center." He smiled. "I mean, I know I had a crush on you back on Earth, but you were older than me—never once looked my way."

"You were ten!" I protested, buying myself time.

He laughed. "Hey, I was a mature ten." He took my hand and suddenly we were speeding through space and time. Stars and planets flashed by. At last we landed far away on a brand new world, whose sun shone brilliantly in the sky. "I helped organize this," he told me. "Call it a lab experience, if you will. And this spot . . . well—" He knelt down in the tall, soft grass, the greenest I had ever seen outside of Paradise. He took my hand. I felt ridiculous and wonderful all at once.

"Kristin." Randy gazed up earnestly into my eyes. "Will you marry me and be my partner forever?"

I could see the sun reflected in his eyes. I could also see the love he had for me. In my heart I knew I loved him, too. How simple it was to love him!

"Yes," I whispered. "Oh, yes!"

He hugged me tightly, and our lips met. Then our thoughts merged as well.

Our temple work will need to be done, I told him. *And I don't know when we can be sealed.*

He gave me a brilliant smile. *It doesn't matter when it happens, as long as we're together in the end.*

I had to agree. My soul sang with happiness. My family was on track, and I was in Paradise with the man I loved. What more could I ask for?

There was only one thing that worried me—that is, beside Meghan's persistence with her science classes. Time on Earth *was* important for someone. I knew only too well that the seventeen months of my kidnapper's cycle had ended, and he would be looking for another victim.

I extracted myself from Randy. "I wish I could stay, but there's something more I have to do."

★ ★ ★

Who did they think they were, kicking him out of his room? Yes, he'd been late on a few payments, but that didn't mean he'd stiff the landlord. He'd find another job somehow—it was always easy to convince people to hire him. That restaurant job was a dead end anyway. He didn't need it; he should have quit before they fired him.

First his boss and now his housemates had turned on him. More than likely they were trying to clear him out because they didn't like him. He bet they would rent out his room to that girl Barry was seeing. Stupid kids. What right did they have to even be in the house? They should be in jail for all the drugs they sold. He shouldn't have stooped to living with them anyway. He had pride, not to mention responsibilities.

But where to go now? Pondering the options over and over, he knew he had no choice but to turn to family. *Ha!—some family*, he thought bitterly. *Mother's gone now, not that she ever cared about me.*

How deeply embarrassing it was that he who had once been so great was now brought to an all-time low. He'd lost Lilet, his mother, every job he'd ever enjoyed, even his new car had been repossessed, forcing him to drive that broken down piece of charity garbage. And now there was cancer, eating away at his brain like a persistent insect on a decayed carcass. Oh yes, he had begun to believe in the cancer. He could barely think past the pain, and his hands wouldn't work as they once had.

Oh, how low ye have sunken!

The thought brought an acid taste to his mouth, caustic and painful. Well, he may have lost much, but he was still the best. The darkness in his soul didn't mind the changes, whispering how nothing mattered but the fact that he would soon prove he was better than any cop in Utah—or in the whole country.

One for Lilet, one for Mother. It would be easy. The mothers were often late, and darkness came early. Especially on a stormy day like today. It would take only a minute and a little help from the green substance Barry had gotten for him last week. A whiff and they would sleep like babies.

He drove to the place where he would have to stay, trying not to stumble in the freshly fallen snow when he exited the car. He smiled at his benefactor when he directed him to a small, dusty room with a cot. The door had a lock—that was all he would need. Pulling on gloves, he drew the pictures from the metal box, but agony waved through his head, blurring his vision. He shoved them back inside, clutching the box to his chest until the torment passed. Then he fumbled in his suitcase and found the pills, gulping them down without water.

Stretching out on the cot, he waited for them to take effect. He didn't need food. He didn't need medicine. He didn't need anything but the little white pills. They would make him strong. They would help him keep face. They would give back what the world seemed determined to rip away from him. Yet at the same time he detested the weakness the pill represented. He had always depended on himself, on his own great mind.

Well, they won't know, the darkness whispered. *You can succeed better than before.*

He closed his eyes, relieving them of the twisting shadows on the ceiling that almost seemed to be alive. The whispering continued—black and insidious. For a moment, he was afraid—and hated that weakness too—but then the pills began to take effect.

Soon . . . maybe tomorrow when I wake.

Chapter Twenty-Three

The feeling wouldn't leave. Gary recognized it for the Spirit, or at least he was pretty sure it was inspiration. He picked up the phone on his desk and called Angie.

"Is everything okay?" he asked.

"Yeah. Meghan's doing homework, and I'm about to take Jacky to dance class."

"Hmm, it's just . . ." He trailed off. "Are you sure they're okay?"

"Yes, I can see everyone now."

"Well, I just had this odd feeling that I needed to check on you. I know it's strange." Gary laughed at himself. "It seems I'm getting a little paranoid."

"You're entitled," Angie said. "Is there any news?"

"No, but for some reason I keep seeing those eyes in that picture they showed me at the police station."

"You still don't know who they remind you of?"

"No."

Angie was quiet a moment. "Gary, you can call to check on us anytime. I don't mind."

"Has it stopped snowing?" he asked. His office didn't have a window to the outside.

"Yes, and the streets are pretty clear. We'll be fine. I'll take Meghan and Ben with me, though, if it'll make you feel better."

"You don't have to." Gary could have kicked himself. His wife was careful enough with them as it was, and now he had added to her fears.

"I don't mind, neither will they. Or at least not too much."

"Okay. Call me if you need me."

"I will."

* * *

Angie hung up the phone, feeling goose bumps forming on her

neck and arms. She was accustomed to worrying about the children, but it wasn't like Gary to call her with a concern. "Jacky, are you almost ready?" she asked. "Meghan, Ben, you have to come too. Don't ask me why, I'll explain on the way, okay? Please. And don't give me any trouble."

Meghan shrugged. "I guess I can work on my math just as well in the car. Mom, do doctors have to take a lot of math in college?"

"I don't know," Angie murmured. "We can ask Wade's mom. Her brother's a doctor, isn't he?"

"I guess. I don't remember." Meghan's face turned dreamy, and Angie knew she was thinking of Wade. A rush of gratitude filled her heart. Only a few weeks ago Meghan had seemed like a child without hope, but now everything was different.

Angie slipped into the living room unseen. She fell to her knees. "Dear Father. Please bless us with Thy Spirit. Please protect us—especially our children. Open our eyes so that we may see the obstacles in our paths. But . . ." Here she hesitated because this next step was a very large one for her. "But let it be done to us according to Thy will."

The drive to the dance studio went without incident. Angie breathed a sigh of relief as they drew up to the curb. "Go on in," she told Jacky. "Hailey will be there already. She had an eye appointment and her mother brought her directly here afterward. I'll pick you both up."

"My teacher says if I practice hard, I might get to move up to Hailey's class."

"That's great, honey! Look, I'll be right out here when you get done. If I'm late at all that's because I got held up at Ben's Taekwondo. Just stay inside with Hailey. Inside, hear? I'll be right back."

"Okay." Jacky pushed open the door and jumped out. They watched her enter through the glass door, greeted by her instructor. *Okay*, Angie thought. *Jacky's fine.*

"Mom, look," Meghan pointed at an old blue wreck two cars in front of them. "Is that who I think it is? That mechanic guy's nephew? Do you mind if I ask him for help with my math? He was really good at explaining. You could wait right here. It'll only take a second."

"No," Angie said, "there's no time. I need to get Ben home so he can change before I drop him off at Taekwondo. Then I'll have to come back to pick up Jacky. I'm sorry, but Dad'll have to help you with your math later."

As she pulled into the street, Angie wondered what Big Ned's nephew was doing again by the dance studio. *Lucas*, she reminded herself. *His name is Lucas*. He was parked far enough up to be waiting for someone who was inside one of the nearby shops. But was he? The uncomfortable feeling she had experienced with him the other day when he had been fixing Dale's car returned with force. Pushing it aside, she drove toward home.

★ ★ ★

The feeling of unease stayed with Gary. When the phone on his desk rang, he grabbed it, half expecting Angie. "Hello?"

"Mr. Marshall? It's Detective Lowder. I've got some news."

"What?"

"I've been over the case again. Something's been bothering me about the first killing in Florida. There was an ex-boyfriend they interviewed. The guys out in Florida tried to question him again, but he seems to have disappeared. His name's Lucas Lyman. Does that ring any bells?"

Lucas Lyman. A vision of the brown-haired nephew of Big Ned came to Gary's mind. His heart lurched, and a sick feeling grew in his gut. "It's him, the guy in the picture! The one who told the police about the missing girl's dog. Oh, why didn't I see it? I knew I didn't like that guy!"

"This Lucas Lyman is the same guy as in the picture? The guy we knew as Victor Ford? Are you sure?"

"Yes. His uncle's my mechanic. He must have been using an assumed name when he went to the police about that dog. And I'll bet he was hoping the police wouldn't connect him or the missing girl to the other kidnappings." Then Gary gasped as a new idea came to him. "We dropped our van off at that shop on the day Kristin came up missing—just before we took them to the pool. Lucas Lyman was there. I bet he found out where we were headed."

"This puts an entirely new light on things." Detective Lowder's voice was grim. "Do you know where we might find him?"

"I have his uncle's shop address," Gary said. "He can probably tell you more. But let me know the minute you know anything. Please."

"Of course."

★ ★ ★

Heat rushed out at them as they entered the garage. Big Ned Lyman came toward them smiling, a cigarette dangling from his mouth. His smile faded as he took in their blue uniforms.

"I'm Detective Lowder from the Orem Police Department," Lowder flashed his badge. "We're looking for your nephew. Do you know where we can find him?"

Big Ned shook his grizzled head. "He's not here. Was, though. Left about an hour ago. What's this about?"

Detective Lowder countered with a question of his own. "Do you know where he's staying?"

"Yes," said the old man, "but I ain't sayin' one more word until you boys tell me why you're here."

Detective Lowder was becoming impatient. "Look, Mr. Lyman, Gary Marshall has positively identified your nephew in a photograph that is linked to a possible murder in Florida. Another victim was his former girlfriend, who was found dead after a pool party. The Marshalls dropped off their van here on the day their daughter disappeared from the Recreational Center. Your nephew was here that day. We think he had something to do with Kristin's disappearance. Time is very important now. We would really appreciate your cooperation. Another girl's life could be at risk even as we waste time talking."

Big Ned pulled at his gray-streaked beard with one hand, simultaneously grinding out his cigarette with the other. "Come on," he said. "Follow me."

He led them to the back of the shop and opened a room with a key from his pocket. "He came here yesterday—out of money as usual. I refused to give him any, because I think he's been spendin' it on drugs. Eyes look funny, if you know what I mean. But I told him he could crash here. Gave him a key, but I kept the other. You have my permission to search it if you want, or wait for him. He should come back. Though if he's really in trouble, he might not come in with the cop cars outside."

Detective Lowder sent two officers to move the cars. He and the fourth officer, Darren Womack, pulled on gloves and began searching. He was glad the old mechanic owned the place and had given them permission to search. It would save time getting a search warrant. Meticulously, they went through two suitcases, a box, and a duffle bag that were strewn haphazardly on the dusty floor. Big Ned watched, hairy arms folded against his stained T-shirt.

On his knees, Lowder drew back from the suitcase, feeling an urgency he couldn't contain. "Any luck?" he asked Officer Womack.

"Not much out of the ordinary except rubber gloves and dozen of candles."

"Those could be important. Bag them." Lowder looked at Big Ned. "What about those filing cabinets?"

"Mine. And I keep 'em locked. You can search 'em if you want."

Big Ned was handing over the keys, when Officer Womack called out. "Here's something. Medical papers. You're not going to believe this—this guy has cancer." He handed a folder to Lowder.

He scanned the papers. Words jump out at him: aggressive, fast-growing, inoperable. This was not good news. Almost all serial killers eventually escalated their killing patterns, whether it was upping the body count, increasing the gruesomeness of the endings, or carrying out bolder attacks. But a desperate serial killer could make this terrible situation even worse. He might change his MO altogether. He could do anything. Lowder bagged the papers before resuming his search.

Under the bed he found a metal container the size of a small suitcase. "Look at this." A feeling of dread hit him in the chest. *This is it,* he thought. *I think we're close.*

There was a lock, but it wasn't a good one, and in a few minutes, he had jimmied it with a tool from his pocket. He lifted the lid. Sitting atop a pile of multi-colored swimming suits was a small stack of instant photographs of young girls. Each was dressed in a white nightgown, their blue eyes large with fear and their blonde hair disheveled. Lowder's gut wrenched and a profound sadness filled his heart.

Big Ned gave a grunt and fell to his knees, reaching out to touch Kristin's photo. Detective Lowder grabbed his hand. "This is evidence." He recognized sorrow in the old man's face—a deep, lasting grief that would not soon heal.

"I—I didn't know," Big Ned muttered. "I swear I didn't know."

There was a pain in Lowder's chest, a feeling of great loss and terrible anger he didn't want to control. *It's not fair! It's not right! How can these things happen?* He pictured the Marshall's faces when they learned the news. And what about the families of the other victims? *So much pain! So much suffering!* His fury almost consumed him. If Lucas Lyman had been in that room, he might have strangled the man out of pure rage.

Then for an instant, Lowder could almost feel a small hand stroking his cheek. A calm settled over him. *She's all right*, he reminded himself. *No matter what happened, she's fine now. She's with God.* The assurance gave him the courage to say, "Of course, you didn't know, Mr. Lyman."

"But we have to find him *now*," Womack added. "It might already be too late. Any ideas where your nephew might have gone?"

The old man seemed to pull himself together. He rose, shaking his head. "No. But he was drivin' an old blue four-door I gave him a few weeks back when his new one was repossessed. It's a Ford. Got the license plate number if you want it."

"I'll call it in." Lowder reached for his cell phone. After talking to the police station, he called Mr. Marshall at work and let him know what they'd found.

There was a long silence as he absorbed the information. "So, it's finally over," Gary said softly.

"Yes, or almost." Lowder glanced at the date feature on his watch. "Except that we need to find him. With this cancer hanging over him, he could do anything. ' can't guarantee that he'll stick to his old MO."

"I know where he might be." The words sounded strained.

"Where?"

"Last week, when my wife went to pick up a neighbor girl from her dance class—he was there helping someone we know with a car. I remember thinking it was odd for two people we knew but who didn't know each other to meet like that. It was just too coincidental. Then again, I never really liked either of them. But now you say he might be desperate enough to change his pattern. So what if he has? What if he couldn't find anyone to take at a pool? Detective Lowder, my daughter's at that dance class—along with a bunch of other little blonde girls. You've got to get there fast! Just in case." He paused, then added, "Never mind, I'll go myself."

Lowder was moving well before Gary had finished speaking. "No! You stay put. Tell me where it is. I'll get right there and call you back."

Lowder left Womack to await the officers from the crime lab and took the others with him, calling for backup even as he drove. He didn't know much about profiling, but he suspected that kidnapping another Marshall child might fit the killer's desire to prove himself in the face of his medical death sentence. If he was dying, there would be no reason to hide his identity from the police or the public. There would be no reason not to kill as many innocents as he could.

Chapter Twenty-Four

Benjamin took his sweet time changing, and Angie knew she would be late dropping him off. That would make her late to get Jacky—a thing that she made sure never happened. She felt irritated and out of control. The vision of Big Ned's nephew outside the dance studio seemed to haunt her. What was he doing there?

It's nothing, she thought. *You just don't like him.*

"Uh, Mom," Meghan said, "you're going the wrong way."

"I'm already late," Benjamin complained.

"I have to get Kristin first," Angie said. "I want to be there when she gets out. You'll just have to be late today, Ben."

"Kristin?" Meghan looked at her worriedly. "Don't you mean Jacky?"

Angie nodded. "Yes, I do. Sorry. Sometimes . . . they look so much alike."

"I know, Mom. It's okay." Meghan gave her a smile. "I see it, too."

"All I see is that I'm going to be late," muttered Benjamin.

Angie shrugged and pushed on the gas.

★ ★ ★

I watched it all from the snowy roof of the dance studio. I saw Mom arrive and pick up Jacky and our neighbor Hailey, relieved when she didn't see Lucas' car. She didn't notice that he had moved and was several cars behind her position. She sped off to Taekwondo.

I saw Dad at his desk, calling Mom at home when she arrived. I saw Mom and Meghan's horror when Dad told them about Lucas Lyman. I saw their mutual relief at Jacky's safety.

And of course I saw the police cars as they sped through the town, sirens screaming. Cars moved quickly out of their way, but not fast enough for Detective Lowder, who wore a determined expression on his face. They pulled up at the dance studio as only two little blonde girls remained outside in the cold, zipping coats over their skimpy leotards.

The police cars cornered Lucas Lyman's car, but he didn't even try to get away. The officers were not gentle as they shoved him against the hood of his car and checked for weapons before cuffing him and reading his rights. To everyone's surprise, the top part of his tousled hair fell onto the hood of his car. I couldn't help but smile at the sudden exposure. He had even less hair than my dad and my uncle!

He was already cuffed and in the police car when the doctor's wife arrived to pick up her daughter, Courtney, and her blonde-haired cousin. Both would forever remain unaware that they had been Lucas' intended victims.

Grandmother came to sit beside me. "So, it's over. Or almost."

"Unless he gets off on a technicality," I said, more sourly than I should have, given that Lucas Lyman was in custody.

"Not this time. That detective is one of the best. I know his grandfather. Tells me stories about him all the time."

I nodded to let her know I was listening. "You know, I expected to feel happier when he was finally caught—and I am happy for my family because I think it'll be good for them to have closure. But I also feel sad. Lucas is going to face an awful lot of consequences both on Earth and in Heaven. I feel really sorry for him—even after all the horrible things he's done. Not enough to free him or anything—I'm not crazy. But it's just so sad when I think about the potential he had and all he gave up because of his twisted heart."

Grandmother nodded. "It is indeed an awful thing to see any being so destroyed. Given the right support and discipline, he might not have turned into the monster he is; but ultimately, he made his choices, and he will pay dearly for them."

They took Lucas down to the station and booked him. At first he denied everything, and he actually laughed when no fingerprints were discovered on the photographs or the metal case they were in. Somehow he'd managed to ditch the key, so they couldn't prove the case was his. Yet slowly the pieces came together—bits of my hair were found in his repossessed car, a rope in Big Ned's shop was found stained with my blood, and a rental locker filled with all kinds of child pornography had been rented in Lucas' name. The biggest discovery was a partial print taken from one of the swimming suit tags.

Then Lucas began to toy with the police, dropping unreleased details of the case and then claiming he'd made a lucky guess. After several weeks, the collective proof was all laid out before him, and he admitted to everything. At last he could brag about what he had done. He gave details to the investigators, including how he had slipped my CTR ring into our van when my mother and Brother Loveridge had taken it to the shop. He also told them where he'd hidden my body.

Things in Florida were moving even faster than in Utah. In record time, Lucas was brought up on charges in Florida for six of the seven murders he had committed there. Additional charges were pending in Florida and Utah. Prosecutors were demanding the death penalty, and the media carried news of the story every day.

My parents were finally able to hold a funeral for me. It was a day of tears, of prayers, of family togetherness, of closure. But most of all it was a day of gratitude for the eternal Plan of Happiness devised by a loving Heavenly Father. The knowledge that families could be together forever made all the difference.

Uncle Phil and Aunt Lesa came to the funeral, and for the first time since Uncle Phil's past had been made known, they talked from their hearts. My parents had long ago assured themselves that Phil had never been inappropriate with Jacky or Meghan, but only now that they knew about me could they honestly put his past behind them. Of course, there would need to be forgiveness from both sides, and a certain reserve would always remain, an unspoken line that would not be crossed. I knew there would be no more sleep-overs or unescorted visits to the amusement park with Uncle Phil. I agreed with that decision because my parents had every right to protect their children, while at the same time forgiving Uncle Phil. It was a beginning everyone was willing to accept. Mom and Aunt Lesa were so happy to be reunited that they clung to each other for a good portion of my funeral.

At the grave, my father held my mother close. "I love you," he whispered in her ear.

"Do you feel her near?" she asked.

"Yes. I do. I really do."

They did because I was close to them for much of the day. But Randy was waiting for me, so when they went back to the church to eat, I left with him. He took me on a romantic trip to see a new star being born far out in the Universe.

"How long is this going to take?" I asked. "I have to get back for choir practice, you know. We're doing a new piece, and I'm going to play the organ—or at least I'm going to try."

"Only a few billion years," he said. "Don't worry, it'll still be here when we come back." Laughing, we returned to Paradise.

Chapter Twenty-Five

Dear Meghan,

The weirdest thing happened two days ago in my new area. I was tracting and giving my typical spiel. I was having no luck at all, to tell the truth—unless you count getting the door slammed in my face without busting my nose as luck—when a door was opened by a woman with brown hair. There was nothing extraordinary about her, except that her eyes . . . well, I know this will sound strange. They weren't blue, or as beautiful as yours, but somehow they reminded me of you. I felt prompted to give the door approach about how families can be together forever. To my surprise, she started to cry. She invited us in, and I thought we were going to give her the first discussion, but instead she told us about her daughter, Rosemary, who had been kidnapped and killed about seven years ago.

I was stunned. I mean, I'd sent most of the books you'd given me out to the victims' families by way of missionaries I knew were in the area. Only one did I get to deliver myself, and that was to the first girl's father (Lilet was her name). He didn't want to hear our message. I found out only last week that he's since had a heart attack and died. Weird. I hope missionaries in Heaven have better luck with him.

Anyway, I only had two books left and didn't realize that either of them might be in my new area since I don't know it that well. But sure enough, I looked in my planner and this was one of the addresses. I'm floored. I mean, I could have already given this to another missionary, but here I still had their book, and I had found them without using the address! I tell you, I've never prayed harder than I did that day as I told her about you and Kristin and about how you wanted me to give her a book (which was at our apartment). She knew about your parents and the rest of the case, of course, and invited us back the next day. That was yesterday.

When we got there, she and her husband weren't the only ones there. With them were the remaining couple I was supposed to give one of your books to! (And no, I didn't bring the other book because I didn't know they were going to be there—seems my inspiration is working, but it's still very rusty.) Apparently, they work together in a group that educates people about kidnappings.

We talked a lot about you and your family, but then I took a deep breath and launched into the first discussion. I tell you, I've never been so intent on teaching before. I felt as though my heart—even my very soul—would break apart if they didn't listen and accept the love our Father in Heaven offered. The discussion lasted four hours! It took so many side turns and twists that we got in most of several other discussions as well, including the one about the Plan of Salvation. It was incredible—I just followed the promptings in my heart. My companion was great. His experience in the field helped us answer the questions they had. I have never felt the Spirit so strongly.

Oh, Meghan, I wish you could have been there! I wish you could have felt that Spirit—it was almost something I could touch—that's how strong it was. My companion and I were the only missionaries in that room, but our weak efforts were aided by those beyond the veil— they had to be to have such a Spirit there. Kristin perhaps? Or maybe their daughters, Rosemary and Patricia? I think so.

Then this morning, Rosemary's mother called me and said that after we left she went to bed and had a dream. She saw Rosemary and Patricia (who she's never met in person) sitting by a large basin filled with water. They were dressed in white. Rosemary pointed to the water, and as she did, her mother noticed that there were oxen supporting the basin on their backs. She wanted to know if I knew what the dream meant. I had to sit down before I could explain about how the baptismal fonts in the temple have oxen supporting them. Then she said, "I think Rosemary wants to be baptized into your church. Can you get that done for us?" I told her yes, but added that she could do it herself if she became a member. She said that was exactly what she would do.

I feel so blessed, so fortunate to have met these people. Thank you for the part you played. They have your Book of Mormon, and I know they will treasure it always.

Thank you for your letters. They are priceless to me.

Yours always,
Wade

★ ★ ★

Dear Wade,

I cried and cried when I got your last letter. I was so glad you found those couples in the way that you did. I could almost imagine how happy Rosemary and Patricia must be—and Kristin along with them. I sometimes think how all of this would make a great novel—one that might just change lives for the better, but that thought is fleeting. After all, I want to save lives, not write about them. (Or do I?)

I think I have fully accepted Kristin's death. Having her body buried in a place I can visit has helped. I still halfway expect to see her there. I pray to see her because . . . I don't know why. I just have this yearning. I owe her so much.

I shared parts of your letter with my family. They are so grateful to the Lord for His help to you that day. I hope those couples will soon be baptized. I'm proud of you, and I pray that the Lord will continue to give you what you need to help these families.

Oh, you'll be glad to hear that two of the other families have written to me. I am keeping in contact with them, sharing my thoughts on the gospel. So far, they have been very accepting. Brother Jackman, my seminary teacher, has been helping me know what to write and what to say because I just want to tell them everything and I didn't know where to start. He gave me a copy of the discussions, so I guess I'm a missionary too, in a way. Brother Jackman has been very kind. I'll miss him when I graduate next month. I guess I'll have nearly a year done in college before you return. (Hey, I'll be caught up with you!)

I'm sure you've heard by now that Lucas Lyman died yesterday. His cancer killed him before his appeal could be heard. I still can't believe he was even granted an appeal after being convicted to die for all those murders! I have to admit that I'm glad he's dead. Not only will the taxpayers save money, but there's no chance he will ever hurt anyone again. I suspect the Lord is much better equipped than we are to deal with people like him.

I wonder if Kristin will say something to him in Heaven or if she'll just stay away. That's what I would do. Last night after hearing the news about his death, I had a dream about him. He was met in the

Afterlife by beings much like himself and escorted to Spirit Prison. It was a horrible place. Just like it says in Alma 40:13-14. I have written some of it here so you kind of get the sort of dream it was:

> *And these shall be cast out into outer darkness; there shall be weeping, and wailing, and gnashing of teeth, and this because of their own iniquity, being led captive by the will of the devil.*
>
> *Now this is the state of the souls of the wicked, yea, in darkness, and a state of awful, fearful looking for the fiery indignation of the wrath of God upon them.*

In the dream, I knew his sentence was just, that he deserved his torture, but I was amazed to find I actually pitied him just a little. Imagine having to pay the price of so cruelly murdering innocent children! It is not something I want to think about. I hope I do not dream of him again.

Speaking of prison, Jay was let out early for good behavior—can you believe it? Apparently, he's been a model prisoner. But at least he's moved out of Utah so I won't accidentally run into him, thank goodness. I've stopped hating him as much as before. I feel good about that because I can let it go now and look to the future. There was a time I wasn't sure that would ever happen.

I only see my counselor once a month now, and I do that basically to please my parents. They still worry way too much. But then maybe that's what parents are for. As I've told you before, mine are very cute together. They are constantly going out, joking around, and hugging. I can tell they're really in love.

Oh, I almost forgot, Brother Loveridge has finally started dating someone! She's a single mother with a little girl, and we all really liked her when he introduced us at church. He finally bought a house in the ward and his boys are back with him. I think we'll hear wedding bells soon.

Keep up the good work! My prayers are with you.

> *Love,*
> *Meghan*

★ ★ ★

I didn't visit Lucas Lyman when he arrived in Spirit Prison. I had no desire to do so. He was a part of my life that no longer mattered. Whatever plans the Lord had for him, they did not include me. Lilet did try to visit; however, he could not endure the brightness of her appearance, nor would he accept any learning materials from the missionaries. I'm afraid the same spirit that possessed his soul on earth possesses it now. He lives in constant fear and pain. As it is written, it is truly better for a person to have a millstone tied around his neck and be drowned than to have offended one of God's innocent children. Soon judgment will be meted out and justice will be done.

I'm glad so many others do listen and accept the Lord because the alternative is just too horrible to contemplate. Experiencing the joy when a lost son or daughter of God does return to the fold has made me so much more aware of the importance of mercy. The entire heavenly host sings songs of jubilation; it is beautiful to hear and behold. For Lucas, there will be no such songs. His own mother does not weep for him, but only our Brother, who has experienced the sorrow of all mankind.

★ ★ ★

Another Earth year passed, and it was time for another visit to the mortal world—this time to the temple. Randy and I had never seen Rosemary and Patricia so excited as they were today. We stood next to the officiator at the baptismal font as Rosemary's mother slowly descended into the water.

Happy tears escaped Rosemary's eyes. "Oh thank you, Mother. Thank you, Father," she murmured. Then she raised her eyes and gave thanks to our Heavenly Father.

The angel officiator touched her gently on her shoulder. "Do you accept?" he asked.

She gave him a radiant smile. "Yes, I accept this baptism, done in my behalf by my wonderful, beautiful mother. I accept with my whole heart!"

Then it was Patricia's turn. Her sister waded into the water as her parents watched eagerly from the other side of the glass in the observation room. Patricia clung to my hand so tightly it would have hurt if we had been able to feel that sort of pain.

"Yes, I accept!" Patricia glided down into the water and hugged her sister, who had a look of pure joy on her face. "Finally," Patricia whispered, "we are on our way to being an eternal family." Then she gave a low laugh. "This is the happiest day of my life!"

I held Randy's hand, and together we passed through the glass where my parents and Meghan stood next to Wade and his parents. Wade had been released from his mission all of two days, and his parents had come to pick him up so he could share this day with the families of Rosemary and Patricia, whom he had baptized a year earlier. My parents and Meghan had also been invited since the families had become close through letters, e-mails, and phone calls over the past year.

Patricia's parents hugged Wade and then Meghan. "Thank you both so much. All these years we've been searching and didn't know what it was we were looking for. But today we know where our daughter is—in Paradise with Jesus. All the pain we once held in our hearts is gone, simply gone. The Lord has taken our burden and changed it into something else entirely. We will never forget that."

★ ★ ★

Meghan was tingling all over. Wade had asked her to meet him in the science building at UVSC. He had come to register for summer classes, and she had just finished her last final. What could he want? There had been a somber tone to his voice, one that evoked this shivery feeling in her heart. She wasn't sure at all if it was enjoyable.

After class, she'd had just enough time to stop by the bookstore and get a medical book she would need for a summer class. The concepts were so difficult for her that she would need all her extra time for studying

Not that there'd been much time for studying since Wade had come home nearly two months ago—the best two months of her life. If she'd harbored any doubts about her feelings for him while he was on his mission they were gone now. She wanted only to be with him.

Unable to concentrate, she looked up from her open book to stare at the Foucault Pendulum that continued its steady path—up and back, up and back—as the world turned around it. If there was one thing she had learned thus far in school, it was how ordered the Universe was and how only an omniscient God could have been its Creator.

"What's so interesting?"

Meghan jerked. "Hi, Wade." She leaned over to accept a kiss on her cheek. As usual, his very nearness made her heart race. "I was just watching the pendulum go up and back. It's really incredible."

"So are you."

Meghan blushed and stared down at her book.

He shut it. "Come with me." Taking her hand he led her up the stairs to the second floor.

"What's this room?"

"It's the planetarium. Come on. You'll like it."

A man stood at the controls behind a podium. Wade grinned and gave him a thumbs up sign. The overhead lights began to fade and the ceiling became a dark blue with scattered pinpoints of light. Meghan was barely aware of the other man leaving.

"This is what the sky looked like on the night I first knew that I loved you," Wade said over the romantic music that began to play. "That was the night we talked outside my house at the Valentine's party. This was the sky I prayed under when I needed to find you."

Tenderness rose in Meghan's heart. Yes, that had been a terrible night in many ways, but for her and Wade it had also been a beginning.

Wade suddenly slipped to his knees. "Meghan, will you marry me?"

A tear slid slowly down her cheek as she whispered, "Yes, Wade."

Wade stood, and their lips met in a brief, promising kiss. When they drew apart, Wade laughed and hugged her until she gasped for breath. With a loud thump, her medical book hit the floor. Meghan bent to retrieve the heavy tome, but Wade beat her to it, bringing the textbook close to his face to read the title in the dim light. His eyes went slowly from the book to Meghan.

"There is one condition to our marriage." His tone was teasing, but his eyes were serious.

"A condition?" Meghan didn't know if she should laugh or feel offended. "What do you mean?"

"I mean this." He held out the book. "Meghan, I know you, and I love you more than I've ever loved anyone in my entire life. You are one of the most talented people I've ever known. When you talk about people, about stories, or about your English classes, I see a light in your face. You light up. But when you study this, there's a heaviness in you—I don't know how to say it any better than that. You say you've come to terms with Kristin's death, and yet you still study something you don't love. Why? Meghan, honey, if you really want to be a doctor, then I'll stand behind you one hundred percent, but I want it to be for you, not for Kristin. We must live our dreams now—as I believe she's living hers."

Meghan blinked back tears. How many nights had she gone through this dilemma in her mind? To be a doctor and fill Kristin's place in the world, or to follow her own heart? On the surface the answer seemed clear. But could she give it up? Her medical and science courses seemed her last tangible link with her beloved little sister.

"Are you saying you won't marry me if I become a doctor because of Kristin?"

Wade looked suddenly unsure. "Is that what you want me to say?" he asked, flashing her a crooked half-smile. "Would you still marry me if I said it? Tell me, Meghan, is this"—he tapped the book—"what you really want?"

"No," she whispered. The word came without her permission. "No."

He nodded. "Okay then, I definitely won't marry you unless you give it up."

Relief flooded Meghan's heart. For the first time in years she felt completely unburdened. She laughed softly. "I love you, Wade Burke. I think I've always loved you."

Her heavy textbook fell to the ground again, and this time they were both too busy to notice.

★ ★ ★

Meghan was alone. In a few minutes she would go into the sealing room and kneel across the altar from Wade. There they would pledge their eternal love. Her heart was so full of gratitude that she asked everyone to leave her alone for a moment to pray. Since there were no other weddings that morning, she stayed in the brides' room, seated gingerly so as not to wrinkle her dress.

"You look beautiful, Meghan," came a voice. It was familiar, and yet it was not.

Meghan looked toward the voice, which came from behind her where there was no door. "Kristin!" she gasped, coming unsteadily to her feet. Though it had been four years since Meghan had seen her, and she looked very different, there was no doubt it was her sister. "You're here."

Kristin's face was bright and glowing. She wore only a simple white dress, but the brightness of her countenance made it the most beautiful gown Meghan had ever seen. "Of course I would be here," Kristin said. "You're getting married aren't you? I wouldn't have missed this for anything. And luckily, I have permission for you to see me here."

"For years I've been praying to talk to you! I've missed you so!" She took a step toward Kristin, her arms outstretched.

Kristin shook her head with obvious regret. "You can't feel me. I am a spirit now."

Meghan checked her forward movement, contenting herself to gaze at her sister. "You look so beautiful," she murmured, "and older than me."

"I'm an adult in spirit."

"Are you happy?"

Kristin smiled and the radiance was so bright that Meghan had to blink. "Oh, yes, Meghan. It's all true—what they teach in church. Only so much better! I wish I could tell you everything. I wish you could see . . ." She gave an impatient shake of her head. "But I can't.

It is impossible for you to understand it yet. You'll just have to take my word for it." She laughed. "Oh, Meghan! I never saw anything before I arrived here. I never heard sounds properly. I never knew the full depth of feelings. And that's only the beginning."

A tear slid down Meghan's cheek. "You don't know what it means for me to hear you say that." Though she suspected that Kristin *did* know. Why else had she found it necessary to come?

"And you don't know what it means for me to see you here, getting married. You kept our promise. There were times when I didn't think you would."

Meghan smiled ruefully. "Yeah, I know. Those were hard times, but it's all in the past."

"The past built the future," Kristin countered. "You're stronger now."

"I know." They stood facing each other in silence. Meghan's heart was even fuller than before. She would remember every detail of this moment for the rest of her life.

"Oh Meghan, I'm so proud of my big sister!" Kristin said at last. "I want you to know that. Tell Mom and Dad how much I love them. And Ben and Jacky."

"Will I see you again?" Meghan asked.

Kristin shook her head. "I don't think so. A visit like this is rare. But I'll check in on you from time to time, when I can. I'll try to be there if you need me."

Meghan wanted to say she would need Kristin every day, but she knew that wasn't true.

Kristin cocked her head as though listening to something Meghan couldn't hear. Then she looked again at Meghan. "Mom and Aunt Lesa and Sister Burke are coming. They'll be here in a moment. But even though you won't see me, I'll be staying for your wedding." Kristin's expression brightened even more. "And I won't be alone. Grandmother will be there, and other relatives. And a friend of mine."

"A friend?" Meghan was happy to know Kristin had friends in Heaven.

Kristin laughed, her eyes dancing. "Yes, his name is Randy. You know, Randy Williams. And we're actually a lot more than just friends. But that's another story—one of your love stories. Maybe one you'll write someday. I have to go now. Goodbye, dear sister! I love you!"

Kristin took a step until barely a half inch separated them. Meghan's heart seemed to reach toward her sister. All at once, she felt Kristin's thoughts, her spirit, her very essence. Then the brief moment of sharing was over and Kristin was gone.

Meghan put her hands into the air where her sister had been, cupping them and bringing the air to her face and then to her heart. Joy flooded her entire being. "Goodbye, Kristin," she whispered. Her eyes went heavenward. "And thank you, Father. Thank you so much!"

★ ★ ★

"Kristin," a voice came to me. It wasn't my grandmother or Randy as I expected, but my older Brother.

"Yes?" I asked, already knowing what He wanted.

"It's time. Say goodbye."

I hugged each member of my family as they stood around the altar where Meghan and Wade had been sealed for time and all eternity in the temple of God. They couldn't feel me any more than they could see me, and I couldn't feel them, but I hugged them anyway. Not with sadness, but with joy. This parting was but a moment in the eternity of time when we would all be reunited in Paradise. "I love you," I whispered. "I'll be watching from up there."

That is, when I had the time. I wouldn't be visiting anymore, unless they needed me in the future, and then I would have to obtain permission. I didn't mind. I knew the Lord's will was for the best. My family was on the right track now, and I didn't think anything would ever again make their faith waver as it had with my passing. They had become strong through their trials.

As for me, there are no regrets. I can be so much more than a heart surgeon where I am now. I've already helped repair the spiritual hearts of my family—the most important gift I could give them. Because of my passing others have been led to the gospel, and through my teaching efforts here to those who have never heard of the gospel, I expect many more souls to come unto Christ. I'm part of the Lord's Kingdom, and I will build it up to the best of my ability.

Of course, it is not all work here. There are many moments to rest and enjoy ourselves. Smiling, I put my hand in Randy's and together we went to visit a new star.

Epilogue

From the Diary of Meghan Marshall Burke

Strange how one minute can change your entire life. If only life were like a computer that permits you to highlight and delete at will. But life can never be like that, nor should we wish such a thing. You see, we must experience the lows to appreciate the highs. We must continue on, trusting the Lord to get us through the double-edged sword of heartache and growth. It won't be easy—it never is—but He is always there.

Always.

I have learned that to find true happiness, I must put my entire trust in the Lord and allow Him to be my Savior. Allow Him to take away the pain and bring the joy. Dear God, I do that now—with my whole heart. I place myself before Thee; I am yours.

Some time ago I decided to write this book about what happened to Kristin and everything that came after. This is my way of using the talent my Father gave me to celebrate the experiences that made me who I am today—a strong, faithful woman who is not afraid of the past or of the future. A woman who trusts in God and not in the arm of my own understanding.

The writing has gone better than I'd ever hoped, even for me, though I entertain the dream of becoming a brilliant author one day. At times I feel I am but a typist for the feelings, the heart of this book—especially as I imagine Kristin's life in the Hereafter. It is as if I can feel her next to me and can hear her words in my head. I know how much she worked to help my family heal. Though most of my portrayal of Paradise has come from my own imagination, and thus is very limited and likely full of human error, I do know that my sister is happy there.

Not everyone is permitted a glimpse beyond the veil as I was the day of my marriage in the holy temple of God. My parents longed to see Kristin, but they never have. Nor did she appear to Benjamin. Jacky seemed to "see" her occasionally, though not with her physical eyes, but rather with her innocent child spirit. This inspiration continues to come out in her very talented paintings of Kristin and our family. Randy's parents have also never seen their son, though they have taken great comfort at hearing that he and Kristin are "friends."

I really don't yet know why I was chosen to see Kristin, but I suspect it was because the Lord felt I needed the experience. Perhaps I needed to say goodbye.

Goodbye.

No, it really wasn't that. I will see my sister again. There is no doubt in my heart. And when I do see her, I'll put my arms around her and thank her for not giving up, for helping me to survive her passing. I'll thank her for my goal of marrying in the temple because I owe much of my present happiness to the promise we made to each other so long ago. I'll thank her for her love.

Until we meet again—goodbye, Kristin, my dear sister. Remember me. Know that you will be in my heart each day as I look down upon the cherished face of my newborn daughter, Kristin—named, of course, for you. I'm sure she knew you before she came to me here; she will know you again.

I love you, Kristin. I will always love you.

As for a final note to those who may read my story someday: if you ever feel someone close—someone you can't see—accept the comfort offered. You never know who may be just a heartbeat away.

ABOUT THE AUTHOR

Rachel Ann Nunes (pronounced *noon-esh*) learned to read when she was four, and by age twelve, she knew she was going to be a writer. Now as a stay-at-home mother of five, it isn't easy to find time to write, but she will trade washing dishes or weeding the garden for an hour at the computer any day! Her only rule about writing is to never eat chocolate at the computer. "Since I love chocolate and writing," she jokes, "my family might never see me again."

Rachel enjoys camping, spending time with her family, reading, and visiting far off places. She stayed in France for six months when her father was teaching French at BYU, and later served an LDS mission to Portugal.

This is Rachel's sixteenth published novel. She also has a picture book entitled *Daughter of a King*. All of her books have been best-sellers in the LDS market.

Rachel lives with her husband, TJ, and their children in Utah. She enjoys hearing from her readers.

You can write to her at P.O. Box 353, American Fork, UT 84003-0353 or rachel@rachelannnunes.com. Also, feel free to visit her website at www.rachelannnunes.com.

Books by Rachel Ann Nunes

Ariana: The Making of a Queen

Ariana: A Gift Most Precious

Ariana: A New Beginning

Ariana: A Glimpse of Eternity

Love to the Highest Bidder

Framed for Love

Love on the Run

A Greater Love

To Love and to Promise

Tomorrow and Always

This Time Forever

Bridge to Forever

This Very Moment

Daughter of a King (picture book)

Ties That Bind

Twice in a Lifetime

A Heartbeat Away